LIGHT THROUGH A RUSTY ROOF

A Novel by

ROY TERRY

*Isaiah 61:1-4
**Luke 4:17-21
***Galatians 5:4-6

Print ISBN: 978-1-66782-230-3
eBook ISBN: 978-1-66782-231-0

Printed in the United States of America
First Edition 14 13 12 11 10 / 10 9 8 7 6 5 4 3 2 1

CONTENTS

LIGHT

THROUGH

A

RUSTY

ROOF

CHAPTER 1

REV. PETERS

Within his mind, the battle for meaning raged incessantly. *What is life all about, and is all this effort worth it? Do I contribute anything, and is life significant at all? Do the actions and things I have contributed make for any lasting change or difference?* These questions and more swirled constantly in the mind of Rev. Michael Peters. As he sat in his office awaiting a family interested in joining the church, he pondered. Pondering might be too gentle a term. He used to ponder, but now it seems to have grown into something else. He wrote it off as a mid-life crisis: boredom, being stuck in a rut, the daunting awareness that the world was leaving him behind. At the age of fifty-three years old, Rev. Peters was feeling spent.

He looked at his watch. "Damn it! They're late. They are always late!"

"They" being everyone. His thoughts came back around to church work and people. *Oh, God! People! Everyone is only thinking of themselves and their schedules. They use the church; after all, it's free. I hate it when people show up late, and they always show up late. They want to join because they like social connections, business relationships, and they need help raising their kids. But the gospel? Oh, Jesus is "cool" and everything, but only as long as he's contributing toward their comfort. You know, Jesus is our long-range retirement plan, and boy do we love him for that.*

"Where could they be?" He questioned. "I'll give them ten more minutes!"

As the ten minutes passed, adding to the twenty minutes he'd been waiting, he found himself wringing his hands. He used to love meeting with people, especially those joining the church. They are the heart of why he entered into this service. But these days, church work is all about the numbers. After all, numbers are an indication of success. Numbers equate to funding, and funding equates to ministries and missions. Ministry and missions bring you popularity and power. He knew that most people would never be able to relate to the trappings of pastoral success, for they never equate pastoral ministry with worldly ambitions. But, pastors like to be noticed, to feel important, and to be acknowledged for their extraordinary ability to change the world. Pastors point to a Savior; but, deep inside, they want to be the "savior" themselves . . . without the self-sacrifice and death stuff. For Rev. Peters, leading a church had become routine, somewhat like running a machine; the longer you're in, the more irrelevant you become. You go through the motions, say the right things, make people happy, comfort them and convince them everything will be OK. You administrate, calm hurt feelings, apologize for stepping on toes, and repeat. But for Rev. Peters, this race had run its course, and the anxiety and frustration with it had brought him to a breaking point.

Why the hell am I still sitting here? he thought, when a tap at the door garnered his attention. "Finally!" he whispered. As Rev. Peters turned the doorknob, his whole demeanor shifted and he put on the cloak of his profession.

"Rob and Margie! How are you doing? I'm so happy you were able to join me today. And, I'm even more excited about you becoming a member of the church."

The young couple played their role as well, explaining,

"So sorry we're late, pastor. We had to wait for the babysitter. We didn't want the kids to be a disturbance for this important meeting. We love being a part of First United and can't wait to get involved."

Rev. Peters knew this was all a bunch of fluff, but he always goes with it. Occasionally, someone does take the church and its work seriously. Those folks are usually run off within a year as the ancient "gate keepers" stifle any effort at real progress. "We can't have those 'rabble-rousers' around here trying to change things!" the gate keepers proclaim, and continue, "I mean, God only knows what kind of riff-raff we might bring through the doors by reaching out to our neighborhood. We are, after all, in a dangerous area!"

While this kind of thinking always caused Rev. Peters to question the church's work, it also brought with it a certain amount of comfort. He might preach a ton of sermons about love and radical hospitality, but deep down inside, he liked the church the way it was, just as with his congregants who've settled for comfort. Surrounding yourself with people like you is a hell of a lot easier than having to get to know those different from yourself. Real ministry takes work, effort, vulnerability, and risk. The good Reverend didn't have that much adventure left in him. He told himself he just needed to keep it going, bring them in, maintain the buildings, be a presence in the community, and for God's sake, don't mess it up with any radical shit!

"Rev. Peters?" the couple asked, interrupting his reverie.

"Oh yes. I'm sorry, it's been a long day and I've been finding myself drifting a bit. Let's get you plugged in!"

He began the conversation with the history of the church and its mission to the community. A task of self-preservation and hip programing. He explained how the church moved from being "uptown" to "downtown." He spoke of the excellent security systems they had in place and the armed guards protecting worshipers every Sunday from "potential hazards." He walked them through the historic vows of membership and their responses they would recite as he brought them before the church that Sunday. He shared the background check and financial disclosure sheets required for liability reasons through the denomination. He discussed the new protective measures for coming to public worship due to a few years of pandemic pandemonium. Last, he set up on the "automatic tithe transfer system," which immediately withdraws funds from one's account and deposits them directly into the church system. He loved ATTS!

Rev. Peters smiled, "Do you have any further questions?"

The young couple shifted in their seats a bit but responded, "Nope, we're ready to go!"

"That's great," Peters replied. "After we finish up, you're practically in. Just need you to show up one Sunday morning to go through all the I do's and I will's."

He always loved saying that. As if the process of joining the church didn't require anything more, which was at the root of his dilemma— the church he had been a part of didn't require anything more. He had liked to think of himself as a progressive social justice advocate and had even marched in a few protests. His involvement in such things gave him some self-worth to keep him connected to something changing the world. He would often tell people. "If you want to know what it feels like to be alive, march in a protest." People would laugh and respond, "We love that you are so involved in helping all people!" That always made him feel better about himself. Rev. Peters was just involved enough to say he was "involved," but distant enough that there was no risk. If you can move gracefully into these positions, all would like you, and it wouldn't require much of anything.

Margie and Rob had left the office when he came back to his senses. He had found himself so deep in thought throughout their discussion that he couldn't even remember what day they had said they'd like to join the church. *Oh well*, he thought, *That's why you have an admin!* As he got up out of his chair, he looked around at his office. The walls were covered with shelves of books, crosses, religious trinkets, photos of trips worldwide, an old dusty bottle of holy water he scooped from the Jordan River along with hundreds of other tourists in the Holy Land, and pictures of his family. Rev. Peters had a spouse, and together they had a son. He felt the need to get back home, so he straightened his desk, turned off his office light, and closed the door.

As he walked down the hall and entered the front office, he could see through the windows that it was a relatively beautiful evening. There was a breeze and a warm orange glow in the sky. It was one of those afternoons where the day's dust and haze had caught the fading sunlight just right. It seemed that everything was good in the world, and that's when Rev. Peters saw him. He was standing at the corner of the parking lot, walking in tiny circles as if he had something to do but couldn't figure out the way to make it happen. His anxious movements made Rev. Peters feel uncomfortable.

Maybe if I pretend I have something to do in here, this man might go away. He had seen this man before, and even gave him a name: "the Grey Man." The Grey Man was tall, about six foot six, and wore dark slacks, beat-up sneakers, an old "Goonies" T-shirt, and a full-length trench coat. His hair was short and cut close to his head; his skin was, well, grey. Several times over the past year, Rev. Peters had seen the Grey Man walking around the church and community. It appeared as if he always had someplace urgent to go. Lately, though, Rev. Peters had seen him hanging around the church, and sometimes it seemed as if the man was staring at him. That cold stare with grey steel eyes and the grey-toned skin gave Peters the chills. *What's this guy up to? Is he unbalanced? Should I be concerned? Is it time to call the police?*

In an effort to avoid the man outside, Rev. Peters returned to his office to wait him out. He walked around his desk and plopped down in his chair. In the darkened room with only the warm light of the sunset flooding through his office window, he studied the photos of his family—images captured in a moment when life seemed more straightforward. He had a purpose, he was still sexy, and ministry was fun. Such thoughts brought him back for a moment to his earlier ponderings before the new members' arrival.

Meaning? Contribution? Effort? Does any of this shit matter? What the hell am I doing sitting in my office afraid of a man I don't even frickin' know. Afraid, because I am whooped, tired, and don't really want to do any of the things I am asking myself? I want to fade away.

As he ruminated, he realized the photos sitting on his desk hadn't changed in over ten years. Not that he was particularly conscious of such details, but what does that say about a person? He remembered a theology professor who once said, "I can tell you the seminary, and the year the person graduated simply by looking at the books on their shelf."

Locked in! We are locked in! Stuck in the past, supported by romantic notions of youth, but growing forward—it's all bull shit! Why do I even have photos of my family? I don't even know who they are anymore?

The family photo was a version of a much younger, braver, and creative self. Those were times when his wife was still interested in him and his son thought he was superman. Now, his wife tells him he's boring and his son considers him a goof.

"OK! Time to go!" Rev. Peters announced to no one, and as he stood up from his chair, he turned to his window to open the blinds. Standing at the window was the Grey Man! Rev. Peters screamed and reeled backward. As he caught himself on his desk, he yelled at the top of his lungs,

> "You get out of here you son of a bitch! How dare you stand there and scare the living shit out of me! Who the hell do you think you are? You need some serious help!"

Then, with the Grey Man standing and staring at the Reverend, he picked up the phone and dialed 9-1-1.

> "Julian County 9-1-1, what is your emergency?" a monotone voice responded.

> "A man is standing outside of my office window staring at me!"

As soon as his statement left his lips, he realized how foolish he sounded.

> "Sir, who am I speaking with, and do you have anyone there with you?"

> "No, I don't have anyone here. Well, there is someone here, but I think he's unbalanced! I'm Rev. Peters of First United, and this man is stalking me. I want a police officer to come and get this man off our church property."

> "Rev. Peters, is the man doing anything that is causing harm to himself or anyone else?" the monotone voice calmly questioned.

> "No, he's just acting unusual!" Rev. Peters replied sternly.

There was a brief pause, "Sir, can you explain what you mean by acting unusual?"

"Well," the Reverend explained, "he's been hanging out in our church parking lot and walking around. He appears to be anxious, and he's a dark man! I think he is probably black, but his skin looks grey."

Once again, as the words slid off his tongue, he wondered who he was anymore. What the hell was he saying? He was not only profiling a human being, characterizing and dehumanizing him; he was letting fear get to him. He thought, *This woman must think I'm a racist!* The more he spoke, the more he felt the bottomless pit he was digging!

"Hello, sir?" the voice calmly responded.

"Yes, I'm still here. I'm sorry for wasting your time. I am going out of my mind!"

"If you would like for me to send a police officer to help you out, I can," the voice offered compassionately.

"No . . . ," Rev. Peters responded. As he looked back up at the window, the Grey Man was gone.

"Sir?" she called out in concern.

"I'm sorry for wasting your time," the Reverend offered to reconcile the time spent by the dispatcher.

"That's alright," the voice said graciously. "I hope you are safe, and I'd encourage you to get some rest. It sounds like you've got a lot on your plate right now. Good night."

Rev. Peters hung up the phone and picked up his things. This time he was leaving, and he didn't care anymore if the man was outside or not. Once again, he shut the door and walked into the admin offices. He glanced through the window to see if anyone was around, and seeing no one; he pressed on toward the door. He unlocked the deadbolt and pushed it open. After locking the door, he looked toward the setting sun, took a deep breath, and then pivoted right into the Grey Man. That's when things started to go black. His body was heading with incredible velocity toward the ground. The weight of a thousand elephants pressed on his chest. As he fell, he watched as the Grey Man caught his limp body, and then there was nothing at all.

CHAPTER 2

ROOM 423

The beeping woke him. He could hear all the noises of the hospital room. Slowly Rev. Peters began to open his eyes. The room was dark, clinical, and crammed with several machines. An IV line ran out of his arm up to a bag suspended next to his head. A nasal cannula was bringing him oxygen, and a blood pressure cuff squeezed his left arm. He was groggy and knew he had been given some medication because the room and sounds were not as clear as they should be. He felt some pain rising from just inside his right thigh, and when he tried to feel around, he discovered a bandage. Something happened, and it wasn't good.

As he looked around the room, he noticed he wasn't alone. Sitting in a chair in the corner of the room, someone was curled up and sleeping. Rev. Peters couldn't tell who it was, so he tried to say something. "Hey!" was all he could muster.

"Michael, are you awake?" It was his wife.

"Yeah, I'm awake. What happened?"

"Well, Michael, they're checking your heart."

"What? My heart? How is that possible? I just had a physical a few months ago?" he pressed with as much energy as he had.

"I know Michael, but the doctors said these things are hard to identify, and something might have slipped past them in the physical you had."

"I don't recall having a problem with my heart! Maybe stress! All I remember was leaving the office and seeing the . . .," he stopped himself, not wanting to say anything about his encounter. "How'd I get here? Who found me?"

"Luckily, someone called 9-1-1. Nobody knows who, but the dispatcher sent a police officer because she said you had made a call to her just moments before all this happened. Why were you calling 9-1-1?"

Rev. Peters thought for a moment, "I saw a few homeless people hanging out at the church and wanted the police to get them off our property. Nothing major. What day is it?"

"Maybe the homeless people saved your life? And, today is Friday."

"What?" He exclaimed in a panic. "Friday! Oh my God, I've got work to do and what about the church? I've gotta preach on Sunday!"

"Slow down, mister! You aren't doing anything Sunday, and your associates have everything covered. You need to rest, and we need to figure this thing out! You've only been here for a day."

Rev. Peters was not happy. He hated laying around and doing nothing and awaiting tests. He considered himself the last person who should have heart problems! He ate relatively well, only occasionally drank, smoked cigars once or twice a month, and exercised regularly. At least that's what he told himself. Heart problems were for people who are weak, undisciplined, stressed out, or just old, and he didn't fit any of those categories. He didn't deserve this! Maybe something else happened. Perhaps it wasn't a heart problem. Perhaps it was that Grey Man.

Beginning to regain his wits and senses, Rev. Peters sat thinking while his wife rambled on and on about what sounded like nonsense to him, nodding his head occasionally to indicate he was listening. He tried to stir up images of that evening.

I was walking out of the office. I locked the door. I remember staring at the beautiful sunset. I remember running into the Grey Man. Falling. Nothing!

He turned back toward his wife, interrupting her codswallop.

"Did they say anyone was there when they found me?" The Reverend asked.

Jenny looked gently at him, "No, why?"

"I need to know who called, and if there was anyone else around. You know how dangerous the neighborhood around the church is. It's getting worse and worse. And, they don't know what actually caused this? Maybe I was knocked out? Where is my wallet, cell phone, iPad?"

"Michael, you had better calm down. You're in a state of denial, and you kind of sound like a crazy person. You had an incident and they need to check you out. All your stuff is still at the office."

Rev. Peters looked down at his feet, upset by the conversation, "Don't call me crazy! I know there is something else going on here. Someone hit me, knocked me out . . . something."

"Nope." Jenny gently replied to disarm his frustration. "The doctor said it could be a wide variety of things, and they want to check all the options out. Heck, Michael, they stuck that camera up the veins in your leg."

The Reverend had a moment of inspiration, "That's why my leg hurts? Was the procedure conclusive?"

Jenny leaned in, trying to get through to him, "You're going to have to make some changes, buddy. You're a stress ball and not like your usual self lately—hell, not for the past year!"

Rev. Peters reiterated himself, "Was it conclusive?"

At that moment, her phone rang. She gave him the "I need to take this" look and walked out into the hall. He looked around the room again and couldn't believe this was happening. He had no idea what time it was and he was starving. Rev. Peters tried to sit up, but his head started spinning, so he laid back down. *My God! What the hell!*

As he laid there, he was thankful that Jenny was there with him. That was the most attention she had given him in a long time. Maybe this will help them. She never talked with him anymore just as he ignored her just moments before, and they didn't have that much to share. They had more in common when they were younger—their son, cooking together, and sex. Now, their son was uninteresting and uninterested, they ate out or picked up something to go, and sex wasn't happening.

He wanted to blame yoga for the beginning of their disconnect even though he knew that was silly. Jenny loved yoga and went all the time. Then she would hang out with her yoga buddies and didn't invite him to come along. At home, he asked her about her yoga classes, but she never really shared much. Jenny would give him the old high school kid answer, "Good." He even offered to go with her one time, but she laughed and said he wouldn't look good in spandex. But now, maybe she would care about him again. Perhaps, this would help them reconnect.

Jenny walked back into the room, put her phone back into her pocket, and turned her attention back to the bed.

"Michael, it's late, and I'm going to head home. Mickey is there, and while he never really leaves his game set, I need not leave him alone all night. Hopefully, that kid fed himself. He's the worst! The end of the world could be coming and he would be stuck in his virtual reality,"

"OK," Rev. Peters responded, "thank you for being here for me."

"Of course I'd be here for you! I hope you can get your shit together and start a new chapter. I do want you around a bit longer!"

"Well, that's good to hear!" the Reverend offered in a tone of hope.

Jenny headed for the door and turned, "I will swing back by tomorrow afternoon. The doctor said you might be able to go home tomorrow night. I have yoga in the morning, so I'll see you after lunch. My yoga class is all going out for lunch afterward."

"Yoga! Ugh!" he muttered to himself. "Great. Have fun. I'll see you later. Before you leave, can you get my cell phone?"

"You didn't come with your cell phone, and I went by the church to see if it was on the ground where they found you, but it wasn't there. They found your iPad and wallet but no phone."

"Shit! Shit! Shit! How and the hell am I going to get anything done while I'm rotting in this hospital room? I need to call my staff and the church leaders!"

"Michael! You need to cool off, buddy. Everything is under control. They don't need you right now. You need to rest! Now get some sleep, and I'll see you tomorrow. I love you."

He could barely let the words out of his mouth, but he muttered them, "I love you too." He was pissed, and what bothered him the most was when Jenny said, "They don't need you!" Rev. Peters had always wrestled with the need to be needed. The church and his role as a pastor filled that for him. Pastors are some of the neediest people around. Having the title "pastor" puts you in a place of power, and you have a small kingdom to rule. Rev. Peters would never say that out loud. If he were addressing future pastoral candidates, he would handle it as the importance of leadership. But, deep down inside his being, he liked the control, the authority, the buildings, the captive audience, the ballyhoos, and the feeling like he was in charge. He liked being in charge, but now he wasn't, and that was driving him crazy! As he was wallowing in his frustrations, he drifted off to sleep. He was awakened by a knock at the door.

"Mr. Peters?" a soft voice came through the door.

"Yes, can I help you?" the Reverend responded.

"Room 432, time for some medicine."

Rev. Peters straightened himself up in the bed, "Come in. What time is it?"

"Well, Mr. Peters, it's 2:00 a.m., and you have been here for a while. I am your evening nurse, Margret, and it is good to see you finally up."

"Well, thank you, Margret, and thanks for taking such good care of me."

For the moment, the "pissed-off-ness" seemed to fade as Rev. Peters was able to connect with another human being. He was good at the schmooze—funny, delightful, and full of personality. Rev. Peters could put on the charm and flirt with the best of them.

"Margret?" Rev. Peters asked humbly.

"Yes?" Margret graciously replied.

The Reverend looked at her, "Anything going on in the world?"

"Well, Mr. Peters, a whole lot is going on in the world, but whether it's worth any attention or not might be another question."

Rev. Peters clarified himself, "I mean, anything significant I've missed over the past day?"

Margret smiled, "If you mean world-changing, no. But I'm not a good person to ask. I don't watch the news, and I work the night shift. My family gets the rest of my attention when I'm home. I know it's a mess out there, and I hope it gets sorted out soon, but I'm just keepin' my head down and takin' care of my own business."

The Reverend liked Margret, "Thanks for the honest answer, and I pray that someday you might have a schedule that will allow all of you to be together."

"Thank you, Mr. Peters. I sure hope so too. I see all kinds here in the hospital and everybody's got struggles. Some just have a little more help than others."

"I hear ya, Margret. Maybe your kids will have a different experience."

Margret just turned away at the comment and folded some towels on the chair. Rev. Peters had no real connection with where she found herself, and he had already allowed his mind to wander back to an earlier question on his mind. How did this happen? How did he get here? With that thought in his mind, he turned to Margret one last time.

"Margret, has anyone been to see me other than my wife?"

"Well, yes, Mr. Peters. I saw your son leaving with your wife when I was coming in to work. Must have been around 8:00 p.m."

"Anyone else?"

"I'm not sure about the early shift. Anyone here during my shift technically wouldn't be allowed to be here."

The Reverend looked at her with concern, "Are you sure there was no one else?"

"Well, there was...." She paused to redirect herself, "But, they were probably walking from another part of the hospital."

"What did they look like?"

"It was a man. Just a man."

Rev. Peters' paranoia got the better of him and he grew pale with worry. As he leaned his head back, Margret noticed something was wrong, and she asked him if he was alright. He nodded and said he was fine, but he wasn't. *It had to be the Grey Man! The Grey Man was following him! How could he get in, and why was he walking down the hall? If Margret saw him, did anyone else? What the hell is going on?* Margret came back to his bedside and tucked in his sheets.

"You aren't looking good, Mr. Peters. You look like you saw a ghost. Want me to call the doctor."

"No! I'm fine. I just need a little sleep. I'm fine. Will you be close by if I need you?"

"Sure will, Mr. Peters. I'm just a button push away."

With some reassurance that Margret would be close, Rev. Peters calmed down. It was 2:30 by the time Margret left. Rev. Peters thought, Most folks aren't out and about during the wee hours of the morning. He looked for the location of his call button and thanked Margret for spending some time with him. They offered their evening salutations, and Margret walked out, closing the door behind her.

Rev. Peters was still deep in thought about the Grey Man. He had seen him over the past month at different places throughout the town. He saw him at the grocery store, the community park, walking down the side of the road, and at the church. He remembered that whenever he saw him, the Grey Man saw him back, and that's when it hit him; seeing the Grey Man wasn't coincidental. The Grey Man was looking for Rev. Peters. Once again, a chill ran down his whole body. He wondered if he was going nuts. Or, perhaps he was reading way too much into things. Margret never really described the man, and he was making wild assumptions. After all, he was stressed enough to be kept in the hospital. He fluffed his pillow, took a deep breath, and rolled over on his side to get some sleep. And that's when he saw them, the toes of a beat-up pair of sneakers barely sticking out from under the pulled-back exam curtain.

CHAPTER 3

DOUGH

T he urge was to scream, but something held him back. Rev. Peters simply laid still and stared at the shoes to see if there was any movement. As he watched, the sneakers were utterly motionless. He tried to look more intently at the curtain itself to assess whether anyone was actually behind it. The more he looked, the more he thought it was only a pair of empty shoes, but why would there be an old pair of shoes in the room positioned behind the curtain? Lying on his side with his head facing the curtain, he tried to blow the curtain to see if it would press up against someone. The curtain was too heavy, and he was too far away for his breath to reach. He did notice his heart was racing, and the thought came, if my heart is bad, I am certainly going to find out now! Then he remembered the nurse call button on the table directly behind him. He slowly reached back to see if he could find the flicker without actually making too much of a commotion. If someone was behind the curtain, he didn't want to startle them into some kind of action. As he reached back, he couldn't find the call button.

After slowly moving his hand across the top of the table, he decided to take bolder action. He decided to say something. Let them know that you know they are there. Rev. Peters braced himself and then let out a timid, "Hey . . . you behind the curtain . . . ." He paused and listened, not taking his eyes off the curtain or the shoes. Again he spoke, "Hey . . . you behind the curtain."

Nothing! He sat up in the bed facing the curtain and said even more vigorously, "I know you're behind there. Come on out." But still, the curtain didn't offer any response. The sneakers were in the same place, and there wasn't even a ripple in the fabric, so Rev. Peters stood up and walked toward it, tiptoeing the few feet across the floor as if he were a little kid playing hide-and-seek, quieting every aspect of himself. Sneaking over to the curtain, in one motion he grabbed the curtain and pulled it out. As the curtain flew, making a metallic sound from the friction of the casters, all he found behind it was the wall and those empty old shoes. Relieved and yet confused, Rev. Peters stared at the sneakers for a moment, and then turned to go back to bed. As he pivoted, he saw him. Sitting in the corner of the room was the Grey Man. Holding the call button in his hand, he offered his greeting,

"It's a good morning, Rev. Peters!"

Rev. Peters screamed, "What do you want with me? I don't have any money! I'm a pastor. Don't hurt me!"

Rev. Peters was a flurry, and he screamed for Margret.

"Help! Margret! Help! There's someone in my room! Help!"

Again, he turned to the man and pleaded once more as he moved toward the door. The Grey Man did nothing but stare at the frantic pastor as though he were trying to figure him out.

Then he spoke, "Stop it!" he said forcefully. "You're acting like a fool. I'm not here to hurt you or steal from you, so chill out, dude!"

By this time, Rev. Peters had reached the door and had turned the handle just enough to be able to open it.

Again, the Grey Man spoke, "What are you doing? Trying to get away? I've been trying to get ahold of you forever! Don't you want to know why I'm here?"

This comment caught Rev. Peters off guard. He wasn't expecting the man to have come with a purpose other than hurting or stealing from him. He pushed the door open and was about to run out when the Grey Man spoke again,

"OK, take off. I'll just wait for another opportunity to speak with you, but I felt like this might be the best opportunity we have had yet. So go ahead, I'll come back another time."

Peters stopped and bowed his head.

He turned to face the Grey Man, "So, all of this is just because you wanted to talk? And, you thought the best time would be early in the morning while I'm recovering in the hospital from an event you caused me to have? Are you flippin' kidding me! Who the hell do you think you are, and why would you think you have the right to invade my space and scare me to death once again?"

The Grey Man stood, looked at Rev. Peters, and said, "Well, you aren't dead, yet."

It was probably a momentary lapse of sanity that led Rev. Peters to confront this issue rather than run down the hall like a rabbit running from a fox. But he did. He stepped away from the door, but left it open behind him. He looked at the Grey Man and told him that if he made any sudden moves, he would be on him like a fly on shit! He proceeded to walk over to the edge of the bed and sat down, looking for the first time with greater detail at this man he had seen but had avoided for several months now. The Grey Man looked to be in his 50s, and he clearly hadn't taken a shower in a while. Full-blown BO radiated off of his body. His skin was extremely dark with a blueish-grey cast to it. His fingers and fingernails were long. His black hair was tight to his head and neatly cut. Along his jawline, dawned the shadow of stubble. His eyes were a penetrating dark grey with hints of green. Weird, Rev. Peters thought like nothing I have ever seen. He was confident too, and even though Rev. Peters had sounded the alarm, the man was unvexed. Oh, and he was wearing shoes.

Once he was seated, Rev. Peters asked, "So what's this all about? And what's with those shoes over there?"

The Grey Man shifted in his seat and crossed his legs.

"I know everything about you, Reverend, and I am here to ask you to come with me. There is important work you need to do, for the time has come for everything to be made right."

Rev. Peters shifted in his seat. It was evident to him now that he was dealing with an unstable person. After all, as a pastor, he had been around plenty of deranged people.

Rev. Peters responded, "Oh, really? So I'm supposed to go with you because I have work to do? Just get up after being hospitalized with potential heart problems and go with you? Are you flippin' nuts? I'm not going anywhere!"

The Grey Man sat back more deeply in his chair, "Let's start over. I am not here for any other reason but to invite you to come with me and meet *the Others*. I know this will sound wacky and extreme, but this is something I have been called to do. You don't have to come, but I will continue to offer until you do. I know it sounds strange, but, well, OK, it is strange! But that's what makes this journey so interesting! Everything I have ever been involved with that merits anything worth all life has to offer is strange!"

For some reason, this explanation brought Rev. Peters a little more comfort. He was still on his guard, but at least he didn't believe this guy was dangerous—unusual and weird looking—but not dangerous. If anything, the man's version of strange sounded more rational and composed than most of the conversations The Reverend had ever had at the church. He was even beginning to like the guy a little.

The Reverend turned to him and said, "OK, you have my attention; tell me more."

The Grey Man straightened up in his chair as if his purpose was making progress. He sat up with an excitement and energy that Rev. Peters had never observed in him before. The Reverend had always experienced him at a distance, but now he could see him, animated, as a human being. This "Grey Man" had personality, passion, and a spark for life. Unusual, but a spark.

The man looked more intently at Rev. Peters, "I guess proper introductions might be of the first order. My name is John Dough, and I am with a collection of people we call 'The Others.' Some jokingly refer to us as Misfits."

Rev. Peters caught himself laughing when he mentioned his name.

"So, let me get this straight," the Reverend shot back. "Your name is John Doe? What the hell? Am I on some kind of TV show or something? Really, your name is John Doe?"

As Rev. Peters continued to chuckle, John Dough responded, "Yes, my name is John Dough. That's spelled D-O-U-G-H. When I was born, my parents dropped me off at a fire station for someone to take care of me. Not having any good name for me, the

Fire Chief named me 'John Dough,' at least that's what's on my birth certificate.

Rev. Peters interrupted, "Don't you mean Doe like a deer and not like a loaf of bread?"

"Nope!" John Dough responded. "It's spelled like the loaf of bread. I know it sounds wacky, and I don't pretend anyone could ever relate to my upbringing. Still, it's obvious that when the Fire Chief told the attending nurse my name, they didn't know how to spell it."

"Holy shit!" Rev. Peters shouted, "That's bizarre!"

They actually laughed at this together, and Rev. Peters was surprised by what a good sport John Dough was being.

"Yep!" John Dough stated, "I am a complete screw-up from birth! Makes me kind of unique and special, doesn't it! I also don't even know if the Fire Chief gave me the name or just the common name they give every anonymous child left at the station? I like to believe the Chief gave me the name, and that's what I'm going to go with."

Rev. Peters was floored! He had never heard anything like this before. It was both hilarious and sad all at the same time. He was also starting to feel deep compassion growing within him for John Dough. This was the most authentic anyone had been with him in years. John was purely who he was with no strings attached. A product of society without any real story driving him other than what he picked up along the way. Hell, his name is even nameless. The Reverend turned to him once again and gave him a slight smile,

"Nice to meet you, John Dough! I'm interested in hearing more and especially this important message you have to share."

The Grey Man sitting in the chair looked back at him and said, "Thanks. Just call me 'Dough.'"

Dough uncrossed his legs and leaned forward to settle in for a conversation. He looked at Rev. Peters who had grown more comfortable with the situation and was looking forward to hearing what other lunacy was about to be shared.

> Dough continued, "As I mentioned before, I am not alone in this effort of reaching out to you; there are others. I'm here to ask you to come with me to meet them and get a better understanding of everything. You are an important part of all that is happening, and you have work to do. My role is simply to get you and bring you to the Gathering."

Rev. Peters got up from the bed and started to pace the floor slowly.

> "So, what I hear you saying is that I need to go with you to meet these people called the Others to get my marching orders for exactly what I am supposed to do."

> "Yes!" Dough replied, "But they're not orders; they're the things you already know need to be done."

> The Reverend continued, "In following you to this place, everything will then be made perfectly clear, and I will know the truth, and it will set me free?"

> "Yes!" Dough replied.

> Rev. Peters pushed it further. "Upon arrival, and meeting the Others, a golden angel will descend from the heavens, bringing with her some special tool for interpretation. That tool will help me interpret all that God has planned for the end of the world!"

> "No! That'd be silly," Dough replied. "Rev. Peters, this ain't no joke. We're not playing with you. While you are assuming that

I'm giving you a whacked-out vision of some violent apocalypse, you've got another thing coming. This is real; the people are real, as is the fullness that is to be arriving soon. So, are you ready to go?"

"Go?" Rev. Peters shouted. "No! I'm not ready to go."

Dough now stood up from his seat and looked Rev. Peters right in the eye, "Now is the time!"

This is nuts, Peters told himself. *Nuts!* But deep down inside, something was telling him to go. He sat back down on the bed and asked Dough to give him a moment. As he thought, he wondered where these feelings were coming from. He hadn't felt this way in years. The moments he remembered this type of stirring were significant. The birth of his son, his wedding day, that summer with his first girlfriend, and the moment he knew God was calling him to be a pastor. All significant life moments and all requiring some level of risk, courage, and change. Just the other day, he was contemplating the meaning of life and asking if this was all worth it.

His life was full of plastic and stagnant people, and the adventure and joy in life were being sucked right out of him. What he longed for was this sense of adventure, spontaneity, and purpose. What would it hurt to go with Dough? But then he caught himself, *What would it hurt? I don't even know the guy, and he is stalking me! What would it hurt? I just wound up in the hospital, and this guy wants me to leave. What would it hurt? My wife would be worried sick, and pissed all at the same time! What would it hurt? I don't know.*

Maybe in the worst-case scenario, they'd kidnap him and ask his family for ransom, but that'd be a disappointment. Dough came to him, inviting him to simply go and meet his friends, that's all; so why not live a little bit and see where this goes? The stirring grew within him, and it felt similar to those moments when he and his best friends used to jump in the car to head out on a spontaneous road trip. He thought about the consequences one more time—his wife, the doctors, his health, and then back to Dough.

"Now is the time!" Dough said, and Rev. Peters responded, "Let's go!"

By the time their conversation had come to its conclusion, it was 4:00 a.m. The sun had yet to rise, and it was still dark outside. Rev. Peters had decided to go but needed to swing by his house to pick up clothes, shoes, wallet, and cell phone. He turned to Dough to ask, but Dough simply responded, "No!"

"No, what?" Peters asked.

"No! We don't have time for you to go home. We don't need any of that stuff anyway. We have everything we need for this journey."

Rev. Peters had no real clothes to change into but happened upon some hospital scrubs that were at least a little more decent than the gown he was wearing. The Reverend slipped on the pants and then looked for something to put on his feet.

"I don't have any shoes," the Reverend stated.

Dough looked at him and said, "Why don't you use those over there?"

Rev. Peters was disgusted by the suggestion.

"I'm not wearing those shoes! I don't even know where they came from?" He paused for a moment and then turned to Dough, "I'm all right, I'll just go barefoot."

Getting back up from his chair, Dough walked over to the shoes and handed them to Rev. Peters.

"They're the best thing you've got at the moment, and I can't have you slowing us down with your tender feet."

Peters took the shoes and tried to assess how much effort it would actually take to put the sneakers on. He sat down on the chair where Dough was seated and slipped one of the shoes on his barefoot. It actually fit and was relatively comfortable. As beat up as the shoes looked, they were a pair of high-end basketball shoes. He had always wondered what those shoes felt like, so he tried the other one on as well. When he stood up, they were soft and cushy, and he wondered again why they were sitting in his room. As Rev. Peters and Dough were ready to go, Margret, his nurse, stepped into the room.

"What ya doing?" Margret asked.

Caught off guard with no good answer for Margret, Dough offered a quick proclamation, "Ms. Margret, we are going to meet the Others!"

"You know each other?" Peters questioned.

Dough looked at Rev. Peters, "Well, yes! Margret knows the others, and she actually just lives around the block from where we meet. I've known Margret for a long time. I was also a good friend of her son."

"Well, OK!" Rev. Peters proclaimed, "I feel like I'm the only stooge that doesn't know the script of this play! Margret, why didn't you tell me the man you saw earlier was someone you knew?" Margret pretended she didn't hear his question.

"No need to worry," Dough offered.

Margret looked at the two of them with concerned eyes, and then noticed Rev. Peters feet.

"Reverend, those shoes you're wearing came from a young man who died here just the other night? We had to bring him up to this private room because we were out of space in the ER."

"What?" the Reverend stated, "These shoes were worn by a dead man?"

"Yep," replied Ms. Margret, "It happens a lot more than you know. Young men die in shoes like those all the time. My son was wearing his when they brought him in as well."

Rev. Peters once again was caught entirely off guard, "I'm so sorry!"

Margret looked back into his eyes, "No need Reverend. Now get out of here!"

She cut herself off, turned around, and walked out of the room.

CHAPTER 4

DIVISION

Dough was moving fast, trying to get them out of the hospital before something else might happen. The last thing he needed was another intrusion into the progress he had made. Rev. Peters had accepted his invitation, and he was thrilled. He actually didn't think it would be this easy. Still, there was a way to go before being able to rest in his purpose. They proceeded down the last hall, twisting and turning through the maze common to hospital corridors when he could finally see the double glass doors leading out. When he reached them, they were locked, and he knew there was probably some kind of alarm, but at this point, he didn't care. Being quick and intentional in their progress was essential for getting them to the Gathering with the Others on time. Dough looked back to make sure Peters was keeping up. Rev. Peters was slow, and Dough could feel he was still pondering whether this was really a good idea. Just a few more feet! Dough told himself.

"Come on, Reverend! You can do it! You can do it!"

As they reached the door Dough pushed the handle, and as he anticipated, an alarm went off. The alarm was loud, and Dough knew security would be coming to investigate the door alarm. If the guards reached them, Dough would have to bolt, and they would usher Rev. Peters back to his room. Dough breached the gap between the hospital threshold and the open world. A rush of air came through the doorway, and the smell of fast food, gasoline, and mold filled his nostrils. Dough hurried a few steps forward and then looked back. Rev. Peters had stopped and was standing in the doorway.

"What in the hell are you doing? Come on! The Others are waiting for you!" Dough shouted.

"I don't think I can do it. I thought I could, but I can't! I'm no man of adventure! Shit, I'm only a pastor."

Dough walked briskly back up toward Rev. Peters and planted himself directly in front of him, pointing his finger and staring into his eyes.

"What are you talking about, 'Only a pastor?' I don't care if you're a pastor or not, and I couldn't care less if you think you are 'only!' You're definitely a whole lot more than 'only.' What the hell is that supposed to mean anyway? 'I'm so weak! I'm only a pastor.' You, my friend, are spoiled, entitled, and privileged, but you are not weak and definitely not 'only!' I have come to invite you to meet the Others. Reverend, you have work to do. It's work only you can do. This is no spooky hocus-pocus shit I'm asking you to do! So get over yourself. I am here to bring you there. That's it! And, if you don't come, I'll keep trying until you do. So, what's it gonna be, Pete? You don't mind me calling you Pete, do you?"

Rev. Peters, now Pete for short, looked Dough in the eyes. He wanted to go, but this felt crazy to him. He also never had anyone call him Pete. His name was Michael. As the alarm was sounding, he could hear footsteps coming down the hall behind him, and as he looked back to see who was coming, Dough grabbed his arm and pulled him through the doorway. It was with a good amount of force that Dough tugged on his arm. As he came through the entry, the pressure caused him to stumble several feet past Dough. Dough then quickly turned to the doors and made sure they were closed. Then he looked at Pete and shouted, "Let's go!"

The two men walked quickly for a few hundred feet, crossing the paved service area at the hospital's back and jumping up on the lawn that extended itself into a commercial space. Rev. Peters knew precisely where they were as he was familiar with the hospital area. This hospital was newer than the other hospital across town that was closer to the church. The older hospital was now considered to be in a "bad" area. Rumors were spreading that the doctors at that hospital could barely speak English, so Rev. Peters was happy they brought him across town to the "nice" hospital. The Reverend was getting winded and finally yelled as best he could to Dough, "Can we please stop for a minute?" Dough stopped his jog and turned around to meet Pete, bent over and catching his breath. "Don't forget, I'm out of shape and was lying around in a hospital!" Pete mumbled out of breath.

Dough stood up straight and grabbed his hips, "I think we might be OK, and don't think anyone would call the sheriff!"

Pete looked up sideways at Dough, "What do you mean call the sheriff? I left the hospital on my own; they can't do anything to us."

Dough rolled his eyes back and adjusted his stance, "Oh, they might not do much to you, but they'll pick me up in a heartbeat. You're a notable person from around town. Sure, you're running down the streets in used basketball shoes, hospital pants, and a gown, so you do look a little odd. If you ask me, it kind of looks like you've just busted out of the insane asylum. Hell, they might actually shoot both of us."

Rev. Peters pondered for a moment and then realized Dough might be right. This story was way too wacky for any police officer or sheriff to believe. The least that might happen was that they would run them down to the station for questioning. Rev. Peters checked his pants for his cell phone.

"Shit! Shit! Shit! Shit! Shit!" he proclaimed, coming to the aware-ness that he had nothing on him. No cell phone, ID, wallet, money, nothing!

Before he could get a word out to express his frustration, Dough said, "It's time to go!"

Both Dough and Pete continued walking at a relatively brisk pace. As they walked, Rev. Peters began to think of all the repercussions that were about to come due to this spontaneous journey. He thought about his wife Jenny, not necessarily how concerned she might be, but rather how pissed off she would be. His thoughts turned to his son, who probably wouldn't even care if he was missing. The Reverend thought about the church leadership and all the trouble that would be coming his way after running off with a homeless black dude named John Dough.

While each of these thoughts brought a certain level of concern, he came to awareness. While other people might be angry with him, the only person who laid this burden upon himself was him. The more he thought about those who would be upset, the more he realized that they weren't concerned about him but only how his actions would tarnish their own image. His life work had been serving as a puppet to maintain the appearance of success. Maintaining the image and, in turn, the institution would continue to support the systems which preserved power and control. Nobody really cared about him or any-one else for that matter; they only cared about what it could get them or even protect them from. That's why the church members always loved the "warm, fuzzy" sermons. He was expected to make them feel comfortable and feel good about themselves, to maintain the image that kept them from actually seeing the truth. "As long as I have a personal relationship with Jesus, everything will be OK!" roughly translated means: "As long as I have faith, I really don't have to care about anyone else because I'm in!" Rev. Peters continued reflecting for a moment longer and wondered if maybe he was actually too harsh. After all, there were plenty of good Christian people doing some amazing things for others in the world. He continued this thought, *Maybe, I'm just tired and angry with life. Maybe, these critical judgments about others, the image, are just transference and an excuse to not have to deal with my own shit. Or, maybe, the church, and me, and the world are just that screwed up!* Peters broke from his thoughts for a moment as they crossed a busy road and headed toward a large grass embankment.

"Do we really have to walk the whole way?" Rev. Peters shouted at Dough. "Why can't we just call a rideshare and get them to drive us to the Others?"

Dough stopped on the other side of the road and waited for Pete to make it all the way across before answering. As Rev. Peters walked in front of cars wearing his hospital outfit, he could see the eyes of passengers staring him down. They were judging him! Just as he was about to reach the other side with Dough, someone rolled down their window and threw a water bottle at him and screamed, "Loser!" The Reverend was pissed and turned around to face the assailant, but the car had already sped away.

Pete turned to Dough, "You get this treatment a lot?"

"Nope!" Dough responded. "The only reason you're getting shit thrown at you is that you look like a loser."

Rev. Peters bristled a bit, "Well, I only look like a loser because I'm following you!"

In that moment on the side of the road, with the sunlight breaking and the traffic increasing, Dough looked at Rev. Peters and said,

"I don't want to get a cab to speed you across town. You need to make this journey and see the places and people we pass along the way. They're real people here who care about each other. They all love, laugh, struggle, suffer, and live life to the fullest. These people also care about you! When I first started hanging out with the Others, that was one of the hardest teachings I had to deal with! I was pissed off at those who lived on the 'other' side. I didn't want a revolution of love and restoration; I wanted a revolution of arms and violence. But those damn people kept talking about love as if it could actually heal the world! Talking about love as if it was active and alive! Talking about love as if it was the only way. And, double damn it, talking about love as if it desired the best for those you hated the most!"

Rev. Peters was not expecting that from him.

"Are you talking about Jesus, Dough?" Pete responded.

Dough just let the last comment pass as he refocused on the journey.

"We are not heading back into your comfortable world of lonely, self-loathing people, Pete. We are heading into the real world with people who work hard just to eat once a day and keep a roof over their heads. Real people who care a whole hell of a lot more about life than many of your navel-gazing church members who vote for politicians that continue to maintain the inequities you're about to experience." Dough paused and checked himself. "Sorry, I shouldn't have let politics slip in there. These aren't people dealing with their spoiled kids, but just trying everything they can to avoid the impoverished hand they have been dealt.

You need to walk with me from this place to that. I'll bet you don't even know what the name of that street is we just crossed."

Rev. Peters was embarrassed because he didn't know. They had traveled outside of his world, and amid his deep thoughts about consequences, family, church members, and image, he wasn't paying too much attention. And then a vague recollection creeped up on him.

"Isn't this the street that runs through the middle of town? Its name is . . ."

"Division!" Dough blurted out.

"Divison . . .," Rev. Peters mumbled under his breath.

Dough pointed to the street. "We have just crossed Division Street, and now you're on the other side."

Rev. Peters thought for a moment and realized that he had visited many different towns with "Division" Streets. And, while the history behind it was not always about racial segregation and Jim Crow Laws, Division Street did mark a boundary between one thing and another. If it wasn't the ethnic and cultural divides, it was the class and wealth divides. Division Street represented that place where the wealthy could push the less fortunate out and not deal with them. In this case, Division Street divided the rich, predominately white community from the low income community.

Rev. Peters turned to Dough, "So, now that we've crossed Division, how much longer until we get there?"

Dough looked up, "Are you hungry, Pete? I think it's time we got a bite to eat at one of my favorite places here on the 'other side.'"

Rev. Peters was hungry, and so he simply nodded to affirm his desire to get something to eat. The sun was making its way overhead rapidly, and it was getting a little hot. Once again, Rev. Peters was wondering about time.

"Dough, how long until we get there? And, would it be OK if I at least called my wife from the restaurant you're taking me to?"

Dough laughed, "This ain't no restaurant. I'm taking you to the Lil' Piggy Mart."

Just then, rising up over the hill they had just climbed, stood a large pink pig holding a gas pump and a burger.

"Are you serious?" the Reverend shouted.

"Yep! The best burgers around. You're in for a treat."

As they walked through the gas station area, people were pumping gas and looking with concern at the two men now making their way toward the doors.

Dough turned to Rev. Peters, "Don't stress, Pete. Not many folks around here seen a white dude walking into Lil' Piggy."

As The Reverend looked around, Dough opened the door. The first thing Rev. Peters noticed was the smell of grease. The second thing he noticed was the sound of old-school soul music playing on the stereo. Looking around the store, the Reverend saw a line of people waiting for their orders. As he moved down the aisles, following behind Dough, people would step out of his way. They all were casting their judgments like everyone else on this walk. The difference Rev. Peters noticed was that nobody felt like they had to leave. And, a few people even began asking Dough what the problem was with that guy following him.

As they both approached the deli counter, the cooks behind the counter all shouted, "Dough!" This was a familiar place for Dough. He was with his people, and everyone who worked at the store knew his name. They all hugged, shook hands, and occasionally participated in some formal handshake that was more complicated than anything Rev. Peters learned at Camp. What was clear was that these people cared about each other and wanted to hear how life was going. Following pleasantries and greetings, Dough turned to the crowd and made a proclamation.

"I know you haven't seen me in a while, and I'm sorry for not swinging by sooner, but this man who is with me is my honored guest. He looks like a real loser, but the truth is, I took him from the hospital to come and meet 'The Others.' This, my family, is Rev. Peters of First United Church. I hope you'll welcome him like you welcome me!"

Everyone erupted in applause and welcomed him.

"So good to see you, Reverend!"

"Thanks for coming by!"

"Please make yourself comfortable."

In a big, bold voice, the head chef named Stevie shouted,

"What will it be, my brother? It's on the house."

Rev. Peters was aghast. He wasn't expecting a greeting like this, and especially not at Lil' Piggy Mart! While at first a little skeptical at this warm welcome, he realized it was authentic, and that felt good. Several people got up from the only little table next to the food counter and let Rev. Peters sit down. They brought him a drink and the most enormous, greasiest burger he had ever seen. Rev. Peters took the burger in his hands, smashing the buns to make a little more room for it to fit into his mouth, and then bit into the thing. Grease ran down his chin and onto the burger wrapper he had placed on the table. People around the room just stared at him, awaiting his response. The meat was cooked to perfection, and the toppings were just right. As he chewed, all he could do was let out a giant "mmm." Once again, the whole store erupted in applause and shouts of joy.

"Another convert!" said Stevie, the cook.

Dough simply smiled at The Reverend. This might not have been the best option for a first meal out of the hospital, but it was worth it.

CHAPTER 5

POP-POP

Rev. Peters had barely swallowed the last bite of his early-morning hamburger when he saw a young boy scurry into the Piggy Mart. The Reverend watched as the boy entered quickly and moved stealthily through the people standing in the aisle and then duck into a corner between the shelves of candy and car products. It was evident that the boy didn't want to be seen; he was scared. Rev. Peters turned to ask Dough what precisely the young boy might be scared of in such a friendly place when a resounding POP-POP . . . POP . . . POP-POP echoed through the room. Everyone in the store immediately dropped to the ground. Caught off guard, Rev. Peters did more than drop; he threw himself off the chair and landed utterly flat on the hard tile floor.

"What is it?" Peters asked.

"Shh!" said a voice next to him.

"What is it?" the Reverend exclaimed again more urgently with his heart racing and the taste of hamburger coming up into his mouth.

"It's a shooting!" whispered Stevie. "When you hear the 'pop,' you drop like a rock," Stevie explained.

The only one not down on the ground was Dough who was looking out the front door window. Dough turned to the young boy who ran into the store just a few minutes earlier,

"Where?"

The boy looked at Dough and simply replied, "Hoops."

Dough pushed the door open and looked back at Rev. Peters, "Come on! Let's go!"

"Me?" the Reverend asked, astonished.

"Yes, you! We've got work to do."

"Come on, Pete!" Dough spoke firmly, "This is our work. Light in darkness."

Rev. Peters pulled himself up onto his knees and, turning to Dough, exclaimed, "There is no way in hell I am going out those doors when there are a bunch of thugs shooting people on the streets!"

"Oh, you've found hell all right!" Dough shouted.

Dough let the door shut behind him and marched over to the Reverend, grabbed him by the "Lil' Piggy Mart" shirt, and picked him up off the ground. Rev. Peters thought with astonishment, *Wow! Dough is strong!*

"Listen, Pete; I don't have time to play around with you right now. We will see who needs us out there and, holy shit, do they need us now! We can't wait for a flippin' committee to decide if we need to act on this, and we surely don't need to wait for the authorities! By the time they get here it will be too late. And, I'm not game for your cowardly shit. Courage!"

Now on his feet, Rev. Peters didn't even know how to respond. Everyone in the store was looking at the two of them as they remained close to the floor.

"You're a pastor, right?" Dough asked, and with that, he moved toward the front door.

There was no time to think, so Rev. Peters bolted for the door too.

"Wait!" he cried out, but Dough just kept marching.

"It isn't far, Pete. Only a block away."

In the distance, they could hear screaming. It was a sorrowful wailing. Rev. Peters had been through many terrible situations in ministry, with death not something new to him, but this sound was like nothing he'd ever heard before; it was beyond agony. The screams were long and deep and bigger than one person. It was like an accusation—an attack on the whole of the universe.

Dough broke into a jog. Ahead of Dough was a park. There was a playground, picnic tables, and a basketball court. It was still early, and the sun was offering plenty of light. In front of them, in the middle of the basketball court, a small group of people had collected. Those around the perimeter were anxiously moving about as if they didn't know what to do or how to respond, talking to themselves, asking questions that had no answer. At the center was a young woman holding the limp body of a little boy. Her arms, chest, and face were bloody as she clutched the child close to her breast and continued to wail.

Dough marched straight to the center of the crisis. He knelt, bowed his head, and reached out and touched the boy. Rev. Peters stood at a distance, unsure of his place in all of this and not knowing what to offer. He was shocked that Dough was able to enter and be that close.

It was apparent to him that Dough knew everyone in the community, and there was tremendous respect. He admired that about Dough and began to think about how his life and ministry would have changed if he had simply taken the time to get to know the people who lived and worked around his church. *Heck*, he thought, *I don't even know my next-door neighbors.*

Dough was fearless, honest, and present. Dough was grieving right there with this young woman. The loss was so painful that it affected everyone witnessing it. Through his confident presence, those on the perimeter started toward the woman and the young boy. Everyone stood in silence, not offering a word, as there were none to counteract the horror before them. The community had been violated and the bystanders, more than observers, bent a knee, pulled in tightly, embraced each other, and shared their grief. It was so moving, tragic, painful, terrible, and beautiful all at the same time. No one cared about anything else going on, and no one focused on pursuing the perpetrator of this horrible act.

"Is he dead?" Rev. Peters quietly asked, but nobody paid attention to him.

He realized that he was now the only one standing on the outer edge, and people were coming from the apartments, shops, and side streets to all place their hands on each other.

At First Church, the community used to hug each other, Rev. Peters recalled. After several rounds of battling deadly viruses over the years, very few people did that anymore. The intimacy of these people left him in awe. These people, whom he never knew existed, were wrapped up in each other. They clung to each other in this shared pain. They had a common bond in being oppressed by principalities and powers that generated such fear that the result was desperation that provoked violence among themselves, taking their innocence. Rev.

Peters stepped in closer and felt a hand reach up through the crowd and pull him to the center.

Dough had pulled Rev. Peters so hard that he stumbled and fell into the center of the gathering. His hands hit the ground, catching his fall. The surface was warm and wet. As the Reverend got up to his knees, he noticed his hands were covered in blood. He was about to shriek in disgust, but realized where he was. He simply wiped his hands on his hospital pants. Red streaks of the child's blood added a new color to his wardrobe. Dough looked him in the eyes and exclaimed,

"She needs you right now, Pete! Pray!"

In the background, one could finally hear the sounds of sirens growing closer to the scene. You could tell that the sirens were not a welcomed sound in this community.

"Hurry!" Dough shouted.

Rev. Peters reached out his bloody hand and placed it on the boy. He was personally amazed that he found the strength to touch the child. The mother looked up at him, wondering who this man was and why he touched her child. Dough looked at her and nodded gently letting her know she could trust this stranger. She knew and trusted Dough and she extended her trust to the Reverend. Rev. Peters prayed,

> Lord! This is terrible, and I don't even have the words to say. This is terrible, and I can't even imagine the pain this mother is going through. The child, Lord!

He paused for a moment and turned to Dough and asked, "What was his name?"

Dough softly responded, "His name is Isaiah."

Peters continued,

"Isaiah is a gift, and this community has lost one of the innocent among them. Please, Lord, bring your comfort? Please Lord, bring your peace? Please, Lord, receive Isaiah into the fullness of light that is in Jesus Christ our Lord! And, Lord, please let all the violence stop. In the name of the Creator, Redeemer, and Sustainer. Amen!"

Everyone joined, "Amen," and Dough helped the mother get to her feet to prepare for the arrival of the authorities. The sirens grew, and the people began to disperse until it was just Dough, Rev. Peters, the mother, and the child.

Dough whispered something in the mother's ear, and then he turned to Pete and stated, "It's time for us to go!" Blue lights were reflecting off the building all around them, and the symphony of sirens was almost deafening. The two walked quickly away from the scene and down a side alley. Rev. Peters wondered what would happen if they took samples from around the child's body? They were all over that kid. He turned to Dough to ask, but Dough cut him off, responding,

"Stop worrying about it! We have to move on. You still need to meet with The Others. We have important work. We needed to be present there as a witness to the light, but now we gotta hustle!"

They came to the end of the alleyway and turned to the right. A loudspeaker boomed in the distance, "Please clear the area. Any witnesses to this crime, please come forward."

As they turned down a series of alleys, the sounds in the distance began to fade. Now, the two of them were walking alone again and each quietly pondered the events. Dough turned the Reverend,

"That was nice prayer, Pete."

A little put off by his comment Rev. Peters simply offered, "Thanks, I guess."

"No, really, Pete. That was a wonderfully heartfelt prayer. I was worried that you would try some high church shenanigans talk about how God was there to make everything better and that shit!"

"Well, I appreciate that Dough, but I do have some experience with this type of stuff."

"You do? You've had to bring comfort to a mother whose child was just shot in the streets?"

"No, not exactly," Rev. Peters replied. "But I have been with a lot for dying folks in my day. The more you're around it, the more you realize that the greatest comfort isn't paving it over but confronting the reality of what's going on. Death sucks!"

"Yeah, I guess you're right, Pete. People are always trying to fill the hole in their lives with all kinds of shit—hell, even with God! But it isn't theirs to fill, actually it's more important to acknowledge it's there and do the hard work of rising above it."

"Well, I don't know about that, Dough. I still think God can fill the holes."

"Can you share with me how you've experienced that in your ministry, Pete?"

"I've seen people who have been totally out of sorts and fractured in so many ways. My experience with these people is that as they came to faith, their eyes were opened to a greater truth, and I've seen their lives completely turned around."

"I hear ya, Pete, but was that because they filled the fracture in their lives, or they found the strength to move beyond it? I don't think you can fill the voids, and I don't think God intended to take care of that for us. I do think one of the greatest gifts the Creative gives us is to see the void, the gap, the fracture, and name it, point to it, call it out, and know that, while it never goes away, life will go on! Heck, even after the resurrection, the Human One still bore his scars!"

"I get where you're coming from, Dough. I'm just going to need to process all of this a bit. Holy shit, what a day!"

It was getting close to lunchtime when Rev. Peters hamburger began to wear off. It seemed like a week had passed since they were eating at the Lil' Piggy Mart. They had moved out of the maze of alleys. Old warehouses with broken windows, graffiti, and rusty metal dotted the sprawl around them.

"I'm sure you're getting pretty hungry again." Dough asked.

"Yep! Got any ideas of a place to eat around here?" Pete shot back.

The two of them looked pathetic—Dough in his long trench coat and dark jeans and Rev. Peters with his Lil' Piggy Mart T-shirt, blood-stained hospital pants, and borrowed basketball shoes were quite the pair. *Homeless* was the word that came to the Reverend's mind.

"Hey, Dough, I've been meaning to ask . . . why the trench coat? It's hot out here."

Dough stopped and looked Pete in the eyes before saying, "It's my house."

"Your house? Don't you have a place to live?"

"Nope, I don't have a place, Pete. It's just me, and the road, and the people who let me in. When I don't have a place to rest my head, I ball up in my trench coat. This sucker is Australian Outback shit. It keeps me dry and warm. So, I hang on to it all the time. Have you ever been homeless, Pete?"

"Nope. I've never even slept outside on my own before."

Dough turned back around and started walking again. Rev. Peters wondered if he had said something wrong.

"Dough, I'm sorry if I said something that offended you."

Dough turned to the Reverend and shook his head "no."

"Listen, Pete, we all come from a broad tapestry of places and situations. Some have more than others, some have certain privileges, others don't, and some never even really know the difference. I'm not one to cast judgment or intend to bring shame; I want to point in the direction that all might come to know, love, and desire the best for one another. I long for a day all will be respected, find equity, and abundant life. But, to get there, well . . ."

At that moment, someone cried out from what sounded like the top of one of the warehouses.

"Dough!" the voice shouted.

Dough shouted back, "Ma Green!"

Rev. Peters looked at Dough, "You know this person?"

"Yep!" Dough offered, "She's my street momma."

As the two motley gents continued down the street, Dough pointed up to a window at the top of what appeared to be an abandoned warehouse. Hanging out of that window was a woman waving and motioning for him to come on up. The side of the old building had a large sliding door that looked like no one had used it in a very long time. Industry in this part of town had moved out years earlier when textiles and other domestically manufactured products made their way overseas. For a while, in the '60s and '70s, a few companies tried to modify these buildings from their original use for various other industrial purposes. By the late '80s they were completely abandoned and left for the rats.

Dough pushed the door a bit and slid inside. Rev. Peters followed him, and found himself in a vast room. The air grew heavy of mildew and oil residue. It wasn't as offensive as the Reverend would have thought it would be, for the most part. Dough walked to the opposite side of the room where rickety metal stairs ascended to parts unknown.

"Come on!" Dough shouted excitedly.

Rev. Peters got to the stairs and began to climb behind Dough. The structure actually was in reasonably good shape. The railing was smoothed from the many hands drawn across it. They climbed up two, three, four flights until it opened onto a large landing that overlooked the warehouse space below. At the far side was an old office, which seemed to have been converted into a home. Standing in the doorway was Ma Green. Dough ran to her, and she opened her arms wide to receive him. They held each other for what felt to be at least five minutes. They kissed each other's cheeks, and then she turned toward Pete.

"Welcome, Reverend Peters. What an honor to have you visit my home! You can call me Ma. Everyone does."

She knew of him and that he would be visiting her.

"It is nice to meet you too." Rev. Peters offered, "And, it is an honor to join you in your home."

The pleasantries were exchanged, and wafting through the air was the smell of something delicious cooking.

"Are you hungry, Reverend?" Ma asked inquisitively.

"I sure am, Ma. I haven't eaten since early this morning, and we have had quite a morning!"

They all walked into the office house together and there, Rev. Peters saw all the comforts of home. It was a beautifully quaint little place. Rev. Peters was drawn in by the bubbling pot with aromatic steam swirling out from the top. Greens—collards, to be exact—and they were making his mouth water. Ma Green invited the two men to grab a seat in the living room as she took care of a few final preparations.

Dough and Pete sat on a couple of soft chairs in the central area of the space. A variety of photos—some old, probably distant relatives who now were just a memory, others more recent, including a few pictures of Dough—covered the table between them. One of the photos was of Dough when he was younger. He was wearing a football uniform and was a part of some local youth team. Another picture was of him in a cap and gown, graduating from high school. The last picture was of Dough and Ma standing in the Quad at Harvard. Rev. Peters couldn't believe his eyes. He picked up the photo and asked with astonishment, "Is this you?"

"Yeah. I don't know why she keeps all those pictures."

"You went to Harvard?"

"I did."

"What happened?" Rev. Peters inquired.

Just then, Ma Green shouted, "Dinner's Ready!" and Dough got up and went to help Ma Green set the table.

CHAPTER 6

BREAKING BREAD

*H*arvard! Rev. Peters kept saying to himself to the point he wasn't thinking about anything else when Ma Green started serving each of them mismatched plates crackled with age that she'd mounded with collards.

"Ma Green," Rev. Peters addressed, "these sure do look delicious."

"Well, you haven't even tried them yet. But, thank you anyway," she replied humbly.

After seeing to it that everyone was served, Ma Green sat down at the table and looked at Dough as if he was supposed to offer grace or some liturgy.

"Me?" Dough asked.

"Yes, you!" Ma Green retorted.

"OK, then. I would like everyone to grab a piece of bread from the center of the table."

Ma Green grabbed the loaf and tore off big chunks that she handed to each of the men. Both thanked her, and then Dough continued,

"I would like everyone to share something they're grateful for."

Rev. Peters thought before speaking, *I'm not sure grateful is the word I would use at the moment, but I'll give it a shot.*

"You first, Pete," Dough nudged, "you're our guest."

Rev. Peters shifted in his chair and blurted out, "I am grateful for my wife and son."

Both Ma and Dough just stared at the Reverend.

"We know that, Pete." Dough replied.

"You asked, and I gave it to you! I'm thankful for my wife and son."

Ma Green interrupted, "Thank you, Reverend. I'm sorry for Dough's rudeness in not accepting your earnest response. Dough, what are you grateful for?"

Dough thought for a second and shared, "I am grateful for this place and the amazing hospitality you are offering us. How about you, Ma?"

Ma Green looked into their eyes and offered her gratitude.

"I am grateful that the old is passing and the new beginning is coming. I am grateful that the lies of the past will not be able to hide from the truth that lights our path. I am grateful that some people still respond to the tug of the *Breath*. I am grateful that we still recognize the Human One in the breaking of bread."

Both Dough and Rev. Peters sat reflecting on her words.

She continued, "So, let's eat, gentlemen; you've still got a journey ahead of you, and you'll need to be at the Gathering before the light passes."

The collards were delicious and cooked magnificently. The hot juice ran down their mouths as they savored each bite. It wasn't a lot, but it was sustenance.

As they ate, questions began to flood Rev. Peters mind and began tumbling out of his mouth faster than he could process them.

"I wish I could continue to pretend that I am not in shock, being swept away from the hospital and experiencing the most bizarre journey I have ever taken in my life. But I can't! Who are you, people? Are both of you a part of The Others? What the hell is this place, and how long have you all lived here? Where are you getting this food, electricity, and water? Why am I here? Is this some crazy-ass cult, and am I ever going to see my family again? How do you exist without any cell phones, radios, televisions, or even a dial phone? Am I being videotaped? Harvard? What's with all the heady 'spiritual' language? Are you all talking about Jesus? Holy Spirit? God? Help me, people! And, what the hell was that we experienced back there in the park with the dead kid?"

It was a rant, but it felt good, and as he ranted, Ma and Dough just kept eating.

Dough looked at Ma, "You have any hot sauce?"

Rev. Peters head about popped off his shoulders.

"Is anyone listening to me? WHAT THE HELL IS GOING ON?"

Ma Green finished chewing her food and then looked at Rev. Peters

"If we gave you all the answers to your questions, would you feel better?"

"Yes!" Rev. Peters exclaimed.

"I'm not sure you would," she replied, "but, I'll give you what I can. Reverend, we are both a part of the community you've heard us call The Others. We are a collection of misfits who have gathered over the centuries to fight for justice and demand equity for all people. In return for our faithfulness, the gods have granted us superpowers. Some of us can hear things from far away. Some of us can run faster than a speeding car. And, some of us can leap tall buildings."

"That's bullshit!" The Reverend shouted and stomped his fist on the table. "I'm serious. I appreciate your hospitality, but I'm out of here if you don't give me some answers."

Dough and Ma Green laughed at his outburst, and then seeing he was not responding well to their amusement, she continued,

"OK, we will address some of your confusion, but I was serious about not giving it all to you. You see, life is a lived journey, and you must experience it for yourself. If I *tell* you the answers to the questions you're asking, then it's just knowledge. But, if we invite you to the journey, take the time, let you experience it for yourself, then it becomes something altogether different. It becomes something alive, experienced, and connected too. It contributes to your growth in wisdom."

"Oh, that makes perfect sense." Rev. Peters snarked, "Thank you for clearing all that up for me!"

"Now, Reverend. Do you think Dough would have risked all he has to get you and bring you to this point if there wasn't something to this? And, if it's nothing, then you had one heck of a ride and some damn good collards."

Rev. Peters got quiet, and it was evident he was growing frustrated.

Feeling the tension, Dough chimed in, "Pete, this shit is real, and the call that you felt—what moved you forward to follow me out of the hospital—is all a part of it. We are all caught up in this new beginning that is happening whether we like it or not. And we're not alone; it's happening all over the world. We're no better than anyone else and are simply honored to have fine-tuned our hearts and lives so we were able to catch a glimpse of it . . . just like you leaving the hospital. Those who hear the call early are burdened with moving the reality of this incredible good and challenging news out into the greater world. The invitation and welcome is for all. There is no 'in or out,' 'saved or damned,' 'right or wrong,' 'us and them'—it is all 'us' because we are all One. The Breath has filled the lungs of those who are humble of heart. And cleansed the burden of consumption. The Breath moves all things toward the fullness. The 'Human One' prefers the poor, the meek, the oppressed, those who long for right."

Rev. Peters looked even more confused than before. He wondered what the hell any of this had to do with him. He paused to calm himself a bit. Poised, he turned to both Dough and Ma Green and politely asked,

"Can you at least tell me how this all got started? The short version?"

"Sure," responded Ma. "Shortly after the election of 2016, a group of us all started wondering if the stories we had been told about ourselves were true or a lie. Sure, we had thought most of our experience in life screamed 'Lie!' but the fruits that feed the hope of prosperity, well they're delicious.

"Conversations began on the streets, in the barbershops, in the workplaces, and even in the churches. White men with power and their divine institutions set the narrative and led us to believe that we were a part of it. But, we began to realize we were never actually included. Sure, we could have come alongside their worldview by being accommodating, but that meant denying our own culture, giftedness, diversity, and identity. As the division in this country grew over issues related to the equity of all people, those of us on 'the other side' reached a breaking point. Yes, the promise of economic prosperity is appealing, and being fed the line that everyone has an equal chance of attaining that is a tempting dream, but it's a lie. And, it's a lie for everyone, not just those of us who were never invited to the table."

Rev. Peters looked on with a bit more intrigue. He resonated with the truths Ma Green espoused, even though he had never experienced them lived or expressed that way. The Reverend understood how the narrative told makes all the difference. He looked back at Ma, and just when he was about to open his mouth, she held up her hand to stop him.

"Hold on, Reverend; I'm not done yet," Ma proclaimed. "As the dialogue continued, we became aware that we weren't living the lives we were intended to live, but only those which we had been told we should live. The lies we had been told battled against the meaning of life, relationship, and put us at odds with our neighbors, ourselves, the creation, and our creator. If all you have been told your whole life is that the meaning of life is success through consumption, then eventually, you'll be consumed yourself. Everything was coopted by this dark story to the point that economics, education, science, art, recreation, agriculture, work, and even theology was fabricated to keep us dependent. So, we decided to change that!"

"Damn straight!" Dough emphasized.

By this time, Ma Green's collards were cold, but they were still sweet. The Reverend sat there contemplating what he had just heard. While Ma's philosophical ruminations were deep and well thought out, they were still just words. He wondered about the many other questions that remained unanswered, from the complex to the practical. Still, he decided that he shouldn't worry about too many minor things for the time being. After taking a sip of his water to cleanse his palate, he sat back in the chair, crossed his leg, and ordered his final questions in his mind before speaking.

"OK, so, if I'm understanding what you're saying, you all got together a decade or more ago, realizing the system was against you, and you were no longer going to live that way. In the process of letting go of as many worldly attachments and temptations, your hearts and minds were fine-tuned to hear the voice of God more clearly. This gave you a greater insight into the truths of God as revealed through Jesus Christ. That work has brought you to where you are today and the mission to make the world right again. How was that?"

Dough straightened up in his chair, and Ma Green just kept eating.

"Pretty good, Pete! Being a pastor, I think you have an advantage over most, for you've already been formed in a lot of the language of faith, hope, and life."

Ma Green nodded, not wanting to break away from her lunch.

"So, Dough? Are you all Christians? New Age? Conservative? Liberal? Biblical? Whacky? What?"

Dough rubbed his chin for a moment, and then responded, "Yes!"

"Come on, dude, you have to give me more than that," Rev. Peters blurted out.

Dough nodded, "We come from all those backgrounds and more. Our goal is to deconstruct all those images, metaphors, and language that have been so damaging to people, the world, and the church itself for ages—to stop playing the game as if somehow Jesus made us Lord while he's been away. Language and images have been used to manipulate and coerce. Language has been used as a weapon. Language has been used to convince people that there is only one way, one experience, one road, one way to look and be. First, we don't use the name of Jesus a lot because it comes with so much baggage. I know that's going to be hard for you to hear, Pete, but it's true. Most of the time, people are simply name-dropping Jesus anyway as if that somehow proves they know Jesus. Or, better yet, to convince themselves they might be 'in.' They think, *If I say Jesus enough, and with passion, just maybe this salvation stuff is true.* Maybe true faith means less name-dropping and more living into the great equity and relationality the One desires for all creation and people.

The church throughout the centuries has turned Jesus into just another consumer commodity to be bought and sold. In commodifying Jesus, they can control the narrative, which ultimately means they form God in their own image. Suppose Jesus is a product with the ultimate sale value of an eternal reward. All you need to do then is take him for yourself and screw everyone else. It's a toxic theology that has continued to oppress and enslave people and communities for ages. Jesus doesn't need us throwing his name around anymore, Pete. Jesus, the one we call 'The Human One,' needs us to live and conform our lives with his. That, in turn, affects the way we treat others. Jesus isn't our token to maintain our own personal comfort.

"OK, so you are Christians." the Reverend offered in a semi-relieved tone.

"Dude! Stop it!" Dough exclaimed, "Let's just get moving so we don't miss the light and The Gathering."

So much deep thought and conversation left everyone at the table a little fuzzy-headed. The food was excellent, and the conversation was somewhat helpful. Still, now the priority was leaving Ma Green's place and heading down the road a few more miles for the Gathering. Rev. Peters got up and took his plate and cup to a makeshift sink. As he stood there, he could see outside through a window.

"Solar!" he exclaimed. "I knew you were getting your power from somewhere. How did you all get solar?"

Ma Green turned, "You might think we are homeless vagrants, Reverend, but we have chosen this life. We aren't homeless, and we are definitely not inept. The community has disconnected from possessions and learned to share gifts. We also share products around the community to help people. Fresh vegetables from our gardens, which you ate for lunch, for example. We operate on a barter system. We have plumbers, electricians, and construction folks who exchange their services for goods they need. Artists and singers who perform and share their gifts around town and with our community. It is quite the collective. By acknowledging each other's unique giftedness and sharing what we have, there is enough. Occasionally, the local authorities get a whiff that we are settling in properties that we don't own. Still, for the most part, they leave us alone. After all, we are good citizens and contribute to the well-being of everyone's lives that are in our community. Even those who have lost their way. Now, don't get me wrong. We are an imperfect and messy bunch, and we screw things up all the time. But, we keep striving to live into the imagination of a better future, and with that, the Breath guides, equips, and leads us to the next place we should be. OK, enough sermonizing for one day. You two have got to go!"

With that Dough and Rev. Peters offered their thanks and headed out the door. As they crossed the landing, the smell of collards still filled the air. They descended the stairs and walked through the massive warehouse. As they squeezed through the sliding door, they found themselves once again on the beat-up street.

"Let's make a right here, Pete."

Rev. Peters followed Dough. The sun was out, and the warmth of its afternoon rays was resting on their shoulders.

"Shoot!" Dough exclaimed. "I totally forgot to get you a fresh pair of pants!"

Rev. Peters looked down and looked up at Dough, "Nope. Let's keep moving; it's time to meet 'The Others.'"

CHAPTER 7

WARM SENSATIONS

The day grew warmer as the two walked through the miles of empty and newly populated warehouses. Rev. Peters was getting pretty damp as the sun was shining directly down on them and the sweat rolled down his neck and into his hospital smock. Dough just kept moving forward, and the urgency was evident in his pace. Dough couldn't wait to get the Reverend to the Others. They passed stray animals, huge dumpsters, chickens, and the occasional person walking briskly or riding an old bike. To each person they passed, Dough would offer, "Peace!," and those walking by would respond in kind. It was clear that everyone knew everyone in this part of town and that Dough was well-liked and respected by all. Rev. Peters was in awe of the size of the warehouse district. The area was not just a mile, but many miles.

"Man, this place is big," Rev. Peters exclaimed, trying to make for some conversation amidst the intensity of the journey.

"Yep!" Dough replied, "Well over fifteen by fifteen miles."

As Rev. Peters looked up at the enormous steel buildings, he asked, "What did they do down here again? I don't ever remember this place being in business."

Dough ignored him for a moment as if he was tired of talking about the place in the past tense.

"The District was used for just about everything you could imagine—textiles, machinery, markets, bodies, but that was years ago. Now, it's home to thousands."

"Thousands?" Rev. Peters questioned.

Dough turned to look at him, "Maybe more."

"How much longer until we get there?" the Reverend asked, sounding like a kid in the back seat of a car on an extended summer trip.

"We are not too far. Maybe a couple of hours. We need to be there before the sun starts going down. So, we need to boogie!"

After a long, straight march through many rows of buildings, Dough finally made a sharp left. Rev. Peters was exhausted after an already long walk from the hospital. As they turned, the roads opened up a bit more, and they encountered more people out and about, walking the streets. A dog jumped out from between two buildings, barking at the Reverend.

"You don't like dogs, Pete?" Dough asked.

"I like dogs, OK," Rev. Peters responded.

Dough looked at him with a judgmental smirk, "Dog's don't seem to like you!"

They crossed over a large railroad track that led right down to an enormous train loading and exchange station. The main track they crossed split into many more tracks, each guiding a train into a docking station. As they marched past the docking area, the warehouse buildings began to take on more life. It was a place that had a lot more activity, and the buildings looked used. Used healthily, Rev. Peters thought about how similar this was to church buildings. When no one is around, they are cold, distant, abandoned, even spooky. But, when there are people in the buildings, they come alive. Movement, laughter, tears, relationships, breath, songs, dancing, playing, fellowship all bring life. As they walked along together in silence, the Reverend began to wonder if the remainder of this trip would be in silence. Just as he was about to resign himself to that notion, Dough spoke up.

"How about you, Pete? What brought you to faith? How did this all begin for you?"

Rev. Peters hesitated, deciding where to start. "It happened when I was in youth group. Growing up, my family went to church. Every Sunday it was a battle to get us dressed, out the door, and stick around after Sunday School classes to attend worship. I never really understood why you would have Sunday School classes and worship services on the same day. It always seemed overkill to me, and during the service, you couldn't hang out with your friends. We, my sister and I, often negotiated with our mother, begging, 'Can't we skip church today and all head over to the 'Big Chef?'

"My mother was a sucker for eating out and loved Big Chef. If my father had enough money in his wallet, we would go. I'd say we didn't make it to worship but maybe once a month. Sunday School we attended every week. I liked the Sunday School class because you could see your friends and goof off. Our teachers, bless their souls, were decent but not much smarter than the kids in the classroom. Their commitment was admirable, but their Biblical knowledge and theology sucked! Once, a kid in my class asked our teacher why his puppy had to die, and the teacher told him, 'Everything dies because God wants it all back. Oh, and dogs don't get to go to Heaven.' My friend was traumatized for months. He still won't step through the doors of a church to this day. I'm not blaming the teacher completely, but holy shit! Sure, we had a curriculum, but you could tell they didn't do a lot of preparation before our class. They did bring copious amounts of snacks and crafts!"

While the Reverend rambled on, Dough kept listening intently, trying to understand this experience different from his own. Something new might help him make sense of his own experience with the churches and people who gather on every street corner. What might have come across as a boring story to many was fascinating to Dough. All of this formation, education, routine, pattern, discipline, buildings, programs, for what? Dough had been on the street his whole life and found community with the Others.

Ma Green was his street mother. They had many siblings pass through their doors as Dough grew up in a community that strived to genuinely connect through their relationships and dependence on the Breath. It was messy, and it was alive. There were no Sunday School classes or volunteer teachers. The community itself was the classroom. It was a life together, embodying hospitality, offering forgiveness, and working on reconciliation. It was in sharing all things and drawing on gifts, speaking truth because the truth is love, that formed Dough and the Others. There was simple gratitude, for all life was a gift.

Rev. Peters was on a roll by this point, and as he continued his stride alongside Dough, he continued to share.

"When I became a teenager, I was invited to join the church youth group."

Dough interrupted, "You had groups just for youth?"

"Yes, Dough! All youth need a place they can grow with each other!"

His response to Dough was abrupt, as if everyone in the Christian faith knew the importance of a great youth group. Many churches spend enormous amounts of money on hiring and equipping that specially gifted person who is charismatic and energetic enough to keep their youth engaged in the church. The last thing churches wanted to do was lose their kids to the "secular culture." Youth Group programs held a special place in the '80s and '90s throughout predominately American white Christian churches. The "entertain me generation" needed to be lured into loving Jesus, which was the church culture of the day. This movement evolved from youth groups to music worship wars, fancy backdrops, and trendy sermon series.

"Youth group!" Rev. Peters continued, "and that's when everything started to change for me."

Dough grew more interested in hearing what the Reverend had to say next.

"At first, I was reluctant about going. But then a few friends and I were sitting around the neighborhood one Sunday evening wondering if there was anything else to do, specifically anything that might involve cute girls. 'Youth Group!' I exclaimed, and we all went to my house and asked my mother if she would drive us to the church. 'Of course!' My mother was thrilled! She would do anything to keep her little heathen sinner son from turning away from God and jeopardizing his soul to hell, so she loaded us up and off we went. When we arrived, there were lots of young people and, much to our delight, they were mostly girls! Cute girls! Our plans had come together, and to be honest, we had a blast."

Dough interrupted, "Your mother didn't think you were going to hell, did she?"

Rev. Peters looked at Dough, "Yeah, she did."

"Like an actual place of fire and torment?" Dough asked in shock.

"Yep, complete with eternal suffering and asphalt skis."

"So, let me get this straight," Dough said firmly, "Your church offers a youth program to attract kids to Jesus through entertainment because they are afraid that you all might get bored? And you all went to youth group not because you cared a flip about Jesus, but wanted to meet girls. And, your mother was thrilled to bring you because this entertaining experience would ultimately save you from going to hell."

"Yes. Sort of. Well . . .," Rev. Peters knew of no other way to respond. "Dough, I know this might sound foreign to you, but it's pretty much the norm throughout the church, and it gets better."

Dough waved his hand, encouraging him to continue.

"Youth group offered us a wide variety of experiences to help us grow in faith. We had a summer camp, which was sure to bring hundreds of teens to a relationship in Christ. Most of those serving churches within my denomination had their 'Jesus moment' at camp—not the church, but camp. Camp was cool. Then we would go on bonding trips. Those adventures included white water rafting, snow skiing, camping trips, water skiing, paintball, and a whole smattering of fun, engaging experiences. Trips like these were offered to some of the poorer kids around the church. Those kids never had the money to enjoy these experiences, and offering these opportunities made folks feel good about themselves. Church members raised money to help needy kids. And then there were the concerts.

"That's right, Contemporary Christian Concerts—Rock and Roll for Jesus! We would try to go to as many Christian concerts as we could. Smoke, lights, guitars, amplifiers, leather, and power! At each concert, there was an altar call at the end. Droves of people would flood the stage, committing their lives to Jesus. Many were first-time commitments to make Jesus their 'personal savior.' Hell, I gave my life to Jesus for the first time at a concert, and at least two hundred times after that. After you'd go up to the altar, a mentor, who was usually an adult who had all the 'Christian language,' would come alongside you and applauded you into the kingdom. Those concerts made you feel special and unique, and the message was that Jesus is yours, and he loves you and forgives you. Those mentors would let you know that once you had Jesus, you could never be separated for all eternity. What masturbating, porn-viewing, school bus-mo-lesting teenage boy doesn't need that?"

Dough was floored. He was at a complete loss for words. He had heard about all of this going on at most churches but wasn't completely aware of how large and shallow and dark it was.

Rev. Peters continued, "It was there, at youth group, that I first met Jesus and made him the Lord of my life. I had the time of my life! I miss those days! After that, I went to college, became a youth director, married, and went to seminary. There ya go!"

Dough and the Reverend walked in silence for a moment. It was a lot for Dough to take in. He was trying not to be judgmental, but *Lord*! it was tough not to. He finally mustered up enough energy to graciously ask a follow-up question,

"So, is it still like that today?"

Rev. Peters could sense the critique behind Dough's voice.

"Kind of Dough. It will never be like it was in the '80s and '90s. I sense your skepticism and it is justified. There's a darkness behind it all, and it continues to kill the church today. We still have youth groups, but the numbers are smaller. Many parents who had those 'Jesus moments' back in the day don't attend church at all anymore. The entertainment value only holds up for so long before it really begins to feel hollow. The younger people today have so much accessible to them now that when the church tries to compete with the culture, it just comes across as phony or cheap.

"The church isn't Hollywood. Dough, while I know God can use everything, and I'm a product of *that* church, it isn't sustainable because it isn't real. That church is an institution that maintains the lies for prosperity and comfort. It's a church that depends on consumers feeding off Jesus as if he's some sort of self-help product. The church that sells him the best gets the most patrons. And that's why I'm tired! I can't keep up, and I feel like so much of keeping the church alive is dependent on me! Because it's not dependent on God!" Tears began to fill Rev. Peters eyes. "I'm a salesman of folk religion whose aim is self-preservation, false comfort, and prosperity."

Dough stopped his march toward the Others for a moment, stood up tall in front of the Reverend, pulled him toward himself, and gave him a big hug.

"Wow! Pete! I never knew it was that bad. It's no wonder I hear the churches are all in decline. They aren't real; there's no 'Breath' in them."

As they stood there looking at each other, Rev. Peters felt a warm sensation. It was running down the back of his leg.

"What the hell!" shouted the Reverend. Dough began to laugh and scream at the same time, "Get away, you damn dog!"

Rev. Peters turned to kick at the dog, but slipped and fell to the ground, landing hard in the puddle at his feet. He just laid there, looking up at the sky, thinking, *What else could happen next?*

Dough was laughing and offering sympathy at the same time. "I'm sorry, Pete, but that shit was way too funny!"

Dough helped the Reverend to his feet. There he stood, all dressed in the most ridiculous outfit one could imagine, full of blood, dirt, sweat, and now piss!

Dough looked at him with compassion, "Now, Pete, you're starting to look a lot more like the church!"

CHAPTER 8

APOCALYPSE

Rev. Peters was getting tired. This journey of hours was beginning to feel like weeks. The emotions, fast pace, and accumulated filth on his body had brought him to the edge.

"How much longer do we have to go? I am ready to call it quits!" The Reverend spoke in exasperated tones.

"Not too much longer, Pete. We are almost there!" Dough offered in a quick reply. "I have one more place to swing by before we get to the Others, and it will only take a few moments. I promise."

"One more place? *Really?*"

For the first time in a while, Rev. Peters was thinking about home. He thought about his warm shower, clean clothes, stocked refrigerator, and flat-screen. That brought his attention back to the fact that he had been missing from the hospital for pretty much an entire day.

Surely, there was something about all of this on the news. He wondered which of the newscasters was covering his story. He hoped it was the cute blonde on Channel 2 because she always put a lot of passion into her reporting. But he definitely didn't want the old white guy; he was always such a dud. Continuing the march forward, Rev.

Peters noticed that the number of people walking the streets in this area was growing.

"Is this the center of 'Otherdom?'" the Reverend quipped.

"Yes, it is Pete, and we are almost to the place I promised to take you. I need to turn up here and visit Pico for a couple of minutes before we make our way to the Gathering."

Rev. Peters, while exhausted, gave in a little bit, "OK, I guess one more stop. Who is Pico?"

Dough slowed his pace and looked at Rev. Peters.

"Pico is a community artist. Up ahead at her place, you'll see some of her work. She's the shit!"

Rev. Peters liked art and was looking forward to seeing what Pico could do. As they came around the corner, everything opened up into a large courtyard area. Hundreds of people were all standing around talking and enjoying each other's company. Children were playing with anything they could find—a balled-up piece of paper became a soccer ball, a stick became a wand, and there were both children and adults playing tag. It was a hangout, and upon closer inspection, the incredible diversity of people became more apparent to Rev. Peters. A large mural across the courtyard caught his attention and captivated him. He wandered away from Dough who was talking with a few other people in the courtyard, and let himself be completely drawn in by the image.

The mural consisted of three sections, each flowing into the next, and they illustrated some sort of transformation, evolution, or progress. The first section was a painting of a black woman wearing a rich magenta dress that was frayed at the ends. The woman was strong, but not overtly muscular; you could see in her expression and her posture that hers was a strength born of experience, struggle, fight, and confidence. She was moving toward the next section of the painting.

In her arms, she carried the body of a young white girl draped limply over the woman's arms. The girl's arms dangled in a way that gave testimony to the power of gravity over the lifeless. Her eyes were wide open, deep blue, beautiful, and horrifying. It seemed her state resulted from something brought to her, and it was haunting. The black woman marched forward with this white child of innocence as if to save her from something. With each step forward, the black woman's feet left a footprint of blood. She had been through the ordeal and was bringing the dead to the other side.

Blurred images indicating movement, change, transformation, new birth created the transitions between sections. Coming out the other side into the second section of the mural was again the black woman. Her dress was no longer tattered and even a little longer now. Her facial features still conveyed great confidence, but now it appeared as if her direction was clear. Her feet no longer left footprints of blood, but made their way through puddles of water pooling from the falling rain. The young girl was no longer limp but alive. Her little arms wrapped around the neck of the black woman who was her apparent savior. Droplets of rain trickled down their skin before falling to the ground. The dirt, sweat, and blood no longer clung to their skin. They were washed, and they were free.

The final transition moved into a profound truth about progress, suggesting that it doesn't come without effort, struggle, pain, and others to carry us through. The Reverend pondered, *Who is this strong woman, and where does she get her confidence? Who is the child? Where is her family? What left her limp and dead in the first section?*

As his eyes moved to the third section, Rev. Peters was enraptured by the strong black woman surrounded by brilliant light. By her side was the young girl holding her hand and walking forward with her in what appeared to be a new day. The trials of the past life were now behind them, and the new day was ahead. Rev. Peters remembered a sacred text, "Those who set their hand to the plow and look back are not fit for the kingdom of Heaven." Even more powerful was the new position of the young girl. She was now leading the black woman into what appeared to be the glorious unknown. These women, clothed in magenta, dresses flowing in the wind, walking boldly as the Breath surrounded them. Their facial features no longer burdened with the need to survive, their confidence was now an expression of joy.

"What do ya think?" Dough asked, walking up behind the Reverend.

"I'm at a loss for words." Rev. Peters replied.

"Well, that piece only took her a month to paint. It's huge, isn't it!"

The Reverend couldn't take his eyes off it.

"Come on, Pete, I need to stop by and see Pico before we join The Gathering."

Rev. Peters sauntered with Dough while continuing to stare at the mural. It was amazing.

"Dough, what is this all about? The end? The second coming? Why did you need me to come along with you?"

Dough paused for a moment before speaking again, "Yes, but not the end. Yes, there will be comings, but nothing is second. And, yes, you are an important part of how all this is going down."

With that, both men were standing at a large door. It was painted sky blue and had an assortment of stars, moons, and other astronomical figures. Dough knocked, and the door opened, revealing an extremely tall woman. She had long, black, shiny hair. She wore a lot of jewelry, including enormous hoop earrings.

"Pete, I'd like you to meet Pico."

"Good to meet you, Pico." Rev. Peters stuttered.

"Welcome to my home Rev! We, and I mean all us Others, have been awaiting your arrival for quite some time. It seems things are moving; the Breath is making it all happen! I'm so excited for all that is about to happen!"

The Reverend could not keep his eyes off Pico as he had never seen a woman that tall before. He thought, *She's surely gotta be at least 6' 6"tall.* Pico walked them into a living area and invited the two men to grab a seat. As the Reverend got settled into the chair, he asked,

"Pico, I hope you don't mind me asking but are you a basketball player?"

Pico responded quickly, "No, silly, I'm just tall and fit all the stereotypes."

"Oh," Rev. Peters blurted and blushed.

"Stop it." Pico interjected, "Rev. I know you may not have encountered anyone like me before and maybe that makes you uncomfortable, but our community does not judge anyone for how God created them to be. I'm glad to get to know you and I hope you will come to value who we are."

Dough caught Pico's eyes and asked if he might have a word with her before the Gathering. They both invited Rev. Peters to join them in the other room, but the comfort of the chair was calling his name.

"Thanks for asking, but I think I'm going to rest for a few minutes while you two catch up. Oh, and by the way, Pico, that mural you painted is spectacular!"

Across the room, on a small table, Rev. Peters saw a tiny television set. It was old.

"Pico, before you go, does that TV work?"

"Well, yes, it does, Reverend. It gets one station. Would you like me to start it up for you?"

"Yes, please. I just want to see what's going on in the world."

Both Dough and Pico looked perplexed, and both simultaneously replied, "Why would you want to do that?"

Pico got Rev. Peters settled, and then she and Dough went into the other room. The little TV picked up Channel 2. The afternoon news was on, and they were sharing stories from around the world. Rev. Peters was only interested in finding out if anyone had even noticed he had been gone. The station ran through the local updates, international news, a report on the struggling economy, and the weather. Stories came on one after the other, but nothing about the disappearance of a pastor from the hospital. As the newscasters rambled on, the Reverend found himself drifting off, and then his chin dropped heavily onto his chest.

The Reverend was startled awake as the little TV began to scream with the cries of people, ambulances, and a dramatic report of concern as something terrible was unfolding in the world. He sat up on the edge of the chair and focused on the TV watching the images of people running aimlessly through the streets, children crying and wandering around, obviously looking for their parents. The reporter commented, "We aren't sure what's happening, but it appears as if the heavens are falling from the sky and chaos is unleashing on the streets."

Rev. Peters was struggling to process all he was hearing. Another reporter jumped on the news feed. "Live from the Holy Land. A multi-head nuclear missile has hit Jerusalem, destroying most of the Holy City and killing an unimaginable amount of people. The devastation is so great . . . ssss." The news feed was interrupted, and then the little TV went entirely out.

Rev. Peters sprang from the chair and ran into the room where Pico and Dough had gone to talk, but they were not there. He ran through the warehouse that Pico called home, calling their names but received no response.

"Where in the hell could those frickin' people be?"

He ran back to the door they used to enter Pico's home, pushed it open, and peeked outside to ensure everything was safe.

"Maybe this is it: the end of the world! Maybe it started without me, and their plans were foiled?"

Outside, bomb sirens wailed, and at a distance, he could hear people yelling, screaming, and carrying on. The courtyard, bustling with people just moments before, was barren. He was alone, in the midst of a crisis, in a place he wasn't familiar with, and far from home.

The Reverend ran out of the courtyard and onto the road that brought him to this place. The air was thick, and his nostrils stung with the smell of sulfur. Fog had settled on all the streets like a tribute to something monstrous that had just taken place. Gunshots echoed in the distance as vigilante justice took over amid the fear. Rev. Peters ran toward the sounds in hopes of finding someone who could tell him what was going on. As he kept running, he began to find dead bodies littering the streets—one after the other, most shot in the head. The swarm of helicopters in the distance gave commentary on the magnitude of events in the city. Then it happened. The Reverend was flung backward by the blast of a bomb detonated from an unknown source. He clutched his head and could hear nothing, but he was still alive. He slowly opened his eyes and scrambled to his feet. Soldiers dressed in all black were marching toward him. He didn't know if he should run or ask for help. As they drew closer, he could tell they weren't there to offer their assistance, rather they seemed more like a dark ops team.

The soldiers in the front row stopped and directed their attention to Rev. Peters. They lifted their guns and trained them on his quivering body. He could tell they were shouting something at him and, mustering every ounce of courage and strength he had in him, he turned and ran away from them down a side street.

Rev. Peters was amazed that he was able to run so far so fast. He kept weaving his way in and out of the maze of buildings, hoping to avoid the dark ops and find someone who could make sense of this madness. At that moment, he noticed an older woman lying along the side of the street, crying and clutching the body of an older man.

"They shot him!" she sobbed.

"Ma'am, I'm sorry for your loss, BUT WHAT THE HELL IS HAPPENING?"

She stopped crying and looked right into the eyes of Rev. Peters. Her eyes grew intense and dark.

"It's the great tribulation! The violence of God is unleashed on all flesh! The suffering of humanity has come. All the brokenness, idolatry, and sin are its cause. Nations rising against nations and learning war. There is no peace! No peace!"

The Reverend recoiled from her comments.

"You!" the woman accused, "You are a part of this! You knew this was all coming, but you didn't warn us! You are stuck here with the rest of us! The others are all taken away. But you!"

With that, she turned back to the man she clutched in the street.

"This is nuts! What the hell! What the hell! What the hell!"

Just as he turned to slip around the corner, the dark ops were upon him again. Each of the soldiers was shooting anything that moved. All Rev.

Peters could do was run. He found another side street that appeared to lead more into the city and out of the other side. It took him back in the direction he'd come from, across the highway, the train tracks, Division Street, and over into the neighborhoods that were more familiar to him. Nobody was on the streets, and there were cars crashed and abandoned everywhere. He thought, *I was only gone for less than a day! How could all of this happen in less than a day?*

The sulfur fog in the air was growing thicker, weighing heavily on Rev. Peters' lungs. The sirens had stopped, and an eerie hush fell over the city. It was as if the majority of the damage was done, and now the forces causing this devastation were taking a break. Perhaps, it was simply the eye of the hurricane—still and beautiful for a moment, only for the backside to return and take its toll. Regardless of what was going on, Rev. Peters needed answers, so he kept moving toward the town center.

This was his town, but elements of it had changed. The lamp posts lining the streets were no longer bright but dim, pale, and blue. The sulfur was growing so thick that Rev. Peters couldn't see much in front of him, but he kept walking. All of a sudden, he found himself standing in front of a vast royal palace. It was magnificent. The steps before him were many and ascended to six great red doors. On each side of the doors, there was a guard. Rev. Peters climbed the stairs. With every step, he thought he could hear a whisper. As he tuned in, the words *fear*, *hate*, *violence*, and *power* grew from a whisper to a shriek with each step. As he reached the top of the stairs, he realized that the guards were nothing more than skeletal remains filling the armor they wore. Upon a closer look, the Reverend noticed that these Guards did not die a natural death from age, but from the sword, each having large sabers thrust through their chests where flesh once covered bone.

The doors were large and framed with thick steel. Rev. Peters reached to grab the door handle, which felt moist and warm. Rev. Peters pulled his hand back and noticed his palms covered with blood. He took off his Lil' Piggy Mart shirt and wrapped his hand with it. He grabbed the handle once again and pulled with all his might. The door swung open to a great hall bisected by an enormous banquet table. Sitting around the table were twelve robust white men, gorging themselves on an abundant spread of decadent fare covering the table. No one noticed Rev. Peters as he walked into the room and approached the table. There he saw that each man had a nameplate in front of them: Consumption, Greed, Economy, Gluttony, Self-Centeredness, Inequity, Racism, Division, Slavery, Violence, War, and Power. They all feasted on the flesh of humans being brought to the table by demonic envoys.

Hiding in the dark corners of the room, miserable shadowy figures crawled onto themselves, trying to hide from their shame. Rev. Peters walked over to see why they were cowering in the corners. He saw these were false teachers who used their religions for their gain, manipulating their subjects by generating fear or promoting violence. Rev. Peters actually recognized many of those hanging out in the shadows, and knew their history. Many of these teachers thought they were doing what was right, but only for the cause of being right and not out of concern for people. All of this was making Rev. Peters sick, and he ran to the door. He turned around to look one more time at the spectacle that was lying before him and thought, *Is this the end of the world?*

As he stood there watching, he realized that this scene was no different from the suffering many have experienced in the world. The cause was far from God, and as he watched, another figure appeared, dominating the room. At first, Rev. Peters thought it might be Satan, but then he realized it was not. The figure was a giant, undead looking man with unkempt white hair and tight grey skin wrapped around sinew and skeleton. His eyes were of fire, and in his pocket was a little toy figure that looked like the Devil. This figure stood up, full in height. Strings were jetting out of his hands and down to each of the twelve men gathered around the table. Puppets they were. Rev. Peters squinted his eyes to try to make out the shirt this undead figure was wearing. It said, "EDDIE - World Tour!"

"Pete! Pete! Wake up, Pete!"

Dough was shaking the Reverend, and Pico was standing there looking at the very sleepy pastor.

"What! Where! Go!"

Rev. Peters jolted, and spat, and jumped up so high it startled everyone in the room.

"Calm down, Pete; it's just us!"

"Oh my gosh! Where am I?"

"You are here on the other side with Pico and me."

Rev. Peters shook his head and wiggled as if to purge himself of anything unclean, "Is it happening?"

"Is what happening?" Pico asked.

"THE END!" Rev. Peters shouted.

"No!" replied Dough.

"Thank God! I had a horrible dream about the end, and it seemed so real."

Dough straightened up and began walking away, "Horrible? If it was horrible, it wasn't the end."

CHAPTER 9

THE GATHERING

Dough, Pico, and the Reverend left the house and started walking down the road directly into what was turning out to be a beautiful afternoon. The sun was perfect, bright and warm, but not too hot. There was a delicate and soothing breeze touching their bodies, reminding them that life is breath. As they walked, Rev. Peters saw more and more artwork from multiple artists. They also expressed more profound truths through people, colors, plants, animals, and composition. They were all spectacular, and Rev. Peters wished he could spend more time just taking it all in.

As they walked, more people joined them, and together they all headed to The Gathering. Their pace was not too quick, but he still felt a collective urgency to arrive at a particular time.

Rev. Peters asked, "So why is it so important that we are there at this specific time. Is it going to start without you?"

Pico looked back at the Reverend and responded, "Yes, it will!"

"*It* will?" Rev. Peters questioned, but he knew enough at this point to understand that there was no more to be said; the time had come to experience this thing—this event, movement, energy.

As they walked, Rev. Peters couldn't get the horrible images of the dream out of his head. The dream itself created stress, and it had Rev. Peters all out of sorts. He was also struggling with a "short nap hangover." The dreaded dilemma of being so tired that you drift into a deep sleep quickly, only to be rocked out of it within minutes of dozing off, was unsettling. He turned to Dough and asked how long he had been sleeping? Dough told him that he was only "out" for ten minutes at most. The dream seemed like an eternity, and it was so vivid and real. He wondered, *Where did that violent, dark, dream come from?* The realization came that it was initiated by what drives most conversations about the end of time. Being taken from the hospital and launching out on this urgent campaign, he had dredged up all those dark images. After all, while Dough, Ma Green, and Pico hadn't referenced it directly, they were talking about "The End!" Their word choice had him perplexed.

"End Time" prophets standing on the street corners proclaiming a message of certain doom have no problem letting everyone know "THE END IS NEAR!" But, these Others never speak of endings but only beginnings. Rev. Peters thought about all the contributors of fear throughout his lifetime.

He remembered all the predicted dates, calendars, books, rapture theories, and theologies of his upbringing. The Reverend recalled all the Armageddon stories, movies, TV series, podcasts, magazines, and religious tracts that he had consumed, pointing to humanity's doom. He recalled receiving little pamphlets in his younger days from people on the street who asked him if he was "saved" or not? When he answered, "I don't know," they would start preaching at him and telling him, "If you died tonight do you know where you would go to spend eternity?" Then they would hand him a little tract featuring cartoonish draw-ings with some super scary shit in it! One of the tracts was a story of Santa standing in the fire alongside Satan, revealing Christmas's secret message. "Santa and Satan are pretty much the same names, the same person!" the pamphlets proclaimed. Rev. Peters was only seven years old when he had that experience.

He thought about how the mainline Christian tradition always spoke more about "original sin" than "blessing." He thought about how scared he was as a child, a youth, and even as an adult, of getting it wrong and allowing sin to take him down. Each reflection pointed to a wrathful God who wanted nothing more than to destroy humanity and clean the slate. Jesus became the scapegoat sent to earth to take care of business for us and shield us from the wrath to come. His primary mission was to take all our shit and bring it to hell so that we "are covered by grace" and not susceptible to eternal punishment. It's kind of like a "holy cloaking devise"—we are all covered but only because Jesus can distract God's judgment from us. Oh, and we're still piles of shit, but now we're under the snow. All this coming, covering, making right, scapegoating, substitutionary blah, blah, blah was couched in the language of love. God loves us so much that he sends Jesus to be treated terribly for us. Isn't that what love is? Jesus covers us so we don't get what we deserve and can all escape to Heaven. While in Heaven, we can spend all eternity hanging out in white robes, singing to a lamb sitting on a throne, and waving victory flags. Meanwhile, those who don't receive this free "get out of jail card" get fried for eternity, in the never-ending flames, mind you. In and of itself, this treatment is harsh considering that most are going to suffer for *all eternity* for minor offenses.

Rev. Peters felt outrage brewing within him as he saw how this toxic apocalyptic view has dominated the world and humanity's fragile belief systems to the point that we have forgotten the depths of love. His heart broke as he realized we spend more time worrying about the end—our sin—and the punishment God has in store for us, and that love has become the result of our rescue rather than the driving force of our lives. This apocalyptic end times crap is a story created by people who don't have enough imaginative capacity to see "the end" any other way. Or the necessity of having an "end" at all. The world feasts on violence, and unfortunately, the paradox is that violence is the only way the world knows how to maintain peace.

Rev. Peters was becoming aware that while he could critique all this darkness, it was only because he was a participant in it. He had perpetuated these "Christian myths" just as much as anyone else. Rev. Peters remembered a time, just over a decade earlier, when they were entrenched in a scare with a worldwide virus, a psychotic presidential election, and deep divisions on just about every subject. The false prophets and political conspiracies that grew out of that trying time were abundant and still affecting relationships today. He also remembered not speaking up to advocate for the changes that needed to occur because he was afraid of losing church members and "big givers." Those years had such a significant impact on human life, the church, and the economy that things never really got back to the way they used to be. Things got worse. Divisions between rich and poor, race, education, politics, and an economy that refused to bend away from its consumption propagated a continuance of the darkness, which led to the crisis in the first place. When the priority in life is caring only for your self-interest, it's hard to move toward caring about others, communities, and the earth.

"Pete!" Dough shouted in a pleasant and joyful tone.

"I'm sorry, Dough, I've been off in my head again, and I haven't been paying much attention. Where are we exactly?"

Both Dough and Pico lifted their hands in the air as if to announce royalty. Their six-foot-six frames highlighted the building that was just ahead of them.

Together both of them declared, "We are here!"

Rev. Peters gazed at the huge warehouse in front of them. It wasn't fancy or pretentious. It did have several doors leading into the place, and people were flooding in from all directions, flocking to this place in the late-afternoon without any of the entertaining trappings most churches strive to achieve. Another mural covered the wall featuring colors, flowers, and images of people of every race, nationality, color, age, size, ethnicity, dress, and ability, with powerful words that expressed the story of the community. At the top, it read, "Love, a story bigger than yourself." In the middle of the mural was a large tree that looked ancient, strong, and wise, and the words written along its outstretched branches read, "All Belong and Are Becoming." And scrawled at the base of the trunk, where the roots began extended into the soil was, "Deep Roots, Broad Branches." Then, across the ground upon which everything in the mural rested, a final message: "Earth Care, Life Care."

As Rev. Peters took in this incredible mural and read the words, tears formed in his eyes.

Looking at the Reverend, Dough spoke softly, "Come on, Pete, The Others are here, and they want you to join them inside."

The vast warehouse was dimly lit with a soft, warm light. You could see the faces of all the people gathered. They represented as much diversity as the images of the people on the mural outside, perhaps more. They were talking and laughing, and you could tell that other new visitors had come that day. There was no place to sit down, and everyone was standing around the perimeter of the open bay. Across from Rev. Peters was a younger woman in a wheelchair. Her legs were amputated. At first, the Reverend flinched a bit, but she smiled at him and waved him over. He strolled over, and she introduced herself.

"My name is Eve, and who do I have the privilege of meeting this evening?" She chuckled.

"Eve, my name is Rev…," he stopped himself, and said, "Pete."

"Welcome, Pete! It looks like this is your first time participating in The Gathering."

"Yes it is, and it's been quite a journey getting here."

Eve chuckled, "It has been quite a journey for us all. No one here has had it easy, and if anything, everyone here arrived as damaged goods. And, that's what's so beautiful about it."

Again, the awakened Pete felt tears coming down his face, but he didn't know why he was crying.

"Where are you from, Eve?"

"I'm from right here, and that's all that matters—right here. Pete, what are you expecting this afternoon?"

Pete cast his head down to the ground, "I don't know for sure. I am here because someone invited me, and my life was so static and unfulfilling I figured why the hell not!"

"Who invited you?" Eve asked.

"Dough."

"Dough invited you!" she said with great enthusiasm.

"Yes, and we have been traveling the whole day to get here to be with you."

Eve's eyes lit up, "You've got work to do, Pete. You're here for a purpose. I'm guessing you wouldn't have come here if Dough didn't invite you?"

"Nope, and what a journey!"

Eve and Pete spoke for a bit longer, and then she politely excused herself to greet a few others. Pete continued to scan the crowd. A group of random musicians collected at the far end of the open bay—guitars, congas, fiddles, drums, and even stand-up bass—played in the background, and as Pete tuned in, the words were familiar. People were also singing, but the sound was so tight you couldn't make out who was taking the lead. There was one voice that was rising above the others. The voice was beautiful, comforting, and penetrating. The song invited the community to gather, take up the courage to be themselves, and open their lives to the Breath. The community began to sing along with the voice, and there was harmony. But, Pete heard one voice directly behind him that was majorly out of tune. He turned to see who could be that tone-deaf. It was Dough.

"You can't carry a tune in a bucket!" Pete said to Dough.

"Damn right, Pete. We all have our gifts, and music ain't mine! Don't mean I will be silent."

They both laughed and then allowed themselves to get caught up in the music. Then, on cue, the voices softened to a hum. Some lifted their hands, others bowed their heads, and some held on to each other. Again, rising out of the community gathered a voice said:

The LORD God's Breath is upon me because the LORD has anointed me. He has sent me to bring good news to the poor, to bind up the brokenhearted, to proclaim release for captives, and liberation for prisoners, to proclaim the year of the LORD's favor and the vindication for our God, to comfort all who mourn, to provide for Zion's mourners, to give them a crown in place of ashes, oil of joy in place of mourning, a mantle of praise in place of discouragement. They will be called Oaks of Righteousness, planted by the LORD to glorify himself. They will rebuild the ancient ruins; they will restore formerly deserted places; they will renew ruined cities, places deserted in generations past.*

As the reading finished, the whole place erupted in applause, shouts, and robust laughter. People were dancing, celebrating, and taking in every word they heard. They were expressing the joy found in the proclamation. It was clear that expressing oneself was utterly free, and there was no judgment. Then the music started back up again, and everyone in the room began singing. Pete didn't know a single word to the songs, but he started to catch on by the time they sang them in rounds. Pico walked up next to Pete and spoke into his ear,

"You doing OK? If you don't have the words, you learn the song in your heart."

Pete turned to Pico and smiled. He couldn't stop crying. Here before him were people from every background, all gathered because, as the mural stated outside, "Love is a story bigger than yourself." Pete knew many of the people gathered in this space never would have been accepted or included in the mainline churches he served. They would be welcomed but not included. It was apparent that everyone was encouraged to share their gifts, be honest about their talents, and use them to benefit and edify the community. Pete considered that everyone gathered there that evening had every reason to turn their backs on faith, the church, and life in . . . he paused as he chose to embrace the new term he'd learned: The Human One. But there they all were. Then it grew quiet again, and another voice filled the room without any indication of where it was coming from.

Dough turned to Pete, "Magical, isn't it?"

Pete just nodded his head.

"Actually, it isn't; it's acoustics. Bob, the plumber . . . he's sitting way over there. The room carries all our voices and makes them sound like one."

Bob read:

> The Human One unrolled this scroll and found the place where it was written:

> The Breath of the Creative is upon me because the Creative has anointed me. The Creative has sent me to preach good news to the poor, to proclaim release to the prisoners and recovery of sight to the blind, to liberate the oppressed, and to proclaim the year of the Creative's favor. The Human One rolled up the scroll, gave it back to the synagogue assistant, and sat down.

At this moment in the reading, everyone sat down on the ground. Pete slowly lowered himself as well. Then with one voice, everyone proclaimed:

> "Today, this scripture has been fulfilled just as you heard it!"**

Everyone able jumped up into the air shouting, applauding, and projecting so much energy that the whole place was rocking. It was overwhelming and the experience was speaking to the depths of Pete's heart. He had been crying so much his head hurt a little bit, and yet he felt free. And then it happened. The light that was illuminating the room began to crawl down the side of the walls in the warehouse. Points of light of various sizes were shooting through the roof and landing on everything in the bay below. The shafts of light were robust, bold with every beam visible. Those gathered ran into the center of the bay area opening their arms and allowing the light to touch every one of them. The sight was so beautiful it took Pete's breath away. Light streaming through a rusty roof. It strangely all combined for a mystical moment—light, rust, motes drifting elegantly, human shapes in the illumination.

Along with the other participants, Pete bathed in the light, and that's when he saw them. Others beyond these others were joining them, revealed in the light. Pete rubbed his eyes and refocused, trying to make sure he actually saw these new people. They were still there, made clear in the beams of light. In his best effort to make sense of what he was experiencing, he thought he might be seeing ghosts, holograms, or vapors. But, these people were animated—revealed, alive, and aware—present along with everyone else. *The veil is thin*, Rev. Peters thought, referencing an ancient Celtic understanding of God's present future. They are alive.

The light began to fade with the sun's setting, and those in the room gathered in a symbolic embrace. It was evident that they knew most of these people who appeared in the light. And, there, illuminated by three beams of light, standing in front of the Reverend was a young boy. He was smiling, happy, and held out an open hand to Rev. Peters as if welcoming him to come. The Reverend recognized the boy. It was the boy from the playground. Chills shot through his spine and tears poured down his cheeks. It was unbelievable.

People continued bathing in the light until the sunlight dimmed, and everyone returned to the edges of the room. With the departure of light, everyone applauded and shouted once more. Just before the sunlight had moved entirely out of sight, a single shaft of light remained, and a little girl wandered into the center of the room. She waved her hands, and other children came running, skipping, and joining the gathering at the center. They all grabbed hands and then ran out of the room.

With that, the gathering was over. There was no great rush to depart. Many had trekked almost an hour to get there, and so they were catching up on the day. Pete noticed a table full of vegetables harvested from the community gardens at one end of the room, and people were filling their bags with the produce. Each person was careful not to take more than one bag, and for those who had difficulty getting the produce into their bags, others helped them. One man standing by the vegetables kept touching his chest, the table, his head, and then his shoe. He was talking with someone that wasn't there.

Dough turned to Pete, interrupting his reflection, "Wow! What another great Gathering! What did you think?"

Pete was at a loss for words, and just when he was about to respond, they were interrupted.

"You two need to join us for 'Afterglow.'"

Ma Green stated, along with Maggie from the hospital, Pico, and several of the Others.

Dough told Pete, "I'm glad we made it in time!"

Rev. Peters lifted his head, "So am I!"

CHAPTER 10

THE MEETING

Walking down a side street with the group headed to this "Afterglow" meeting, Rev. Peters was excitedly curious about what it was all about. Finally, he might gain some insight as to his purpose in all this. As they walked, several others joined them. A short man of about forty came up alongside Ma Green. He belonged to this "inner group." He was handsome with dark curly hair and brown skin. His hands were calloused and his fingernails dirty and tattered. Ma Green greeted the man as he approached, and they gave each other a side hug. She called him Roo. Standing in front of the procession was another person waiting for the group to catch up. It was a lady of ample proportions and had an eclectic fashion sense. She looked like a rainbow—her face painted with layers of makeup, and her fingers and neck adorned with chunky, flashy jewelry. She stood there as if she had been waiting for hours.

Dough shouted out, "Roxie!"

She waved eagerly, and as the group caught up with her, she turned on her toes and joined the procession. Rev. Peters just kept moving along, still trying to navigate the experience he had at The Gathering. He had many questions about their community, worship service, and their work. He was overwhelmed with all he was taking in, and even though he had a short nap before the service, he was exhausted.

"So, how many people were at that service?" Pete asked Pico, who was walking closest to him.

Pico looked back at the Reverend quizzically, "I have no idea."

"There had to be several thousand people there, and you have room for a bunch more! You all are doing something right."

The Reverend was blown away by the attendance and active participation and still couldn't handle the appearances of those figures in the light.

"How did you grow the community to that size?"

Dough chimed in, "Luck, I guess. Or even better, need."

"Did you advertise, promote the Gathering; how did you get the word out?"

"People told other people, that's all." Pico responded, "We never really wanted a group that size; it just happened."

"Our denomination," the Reverend muttered, "Would crap all over itself if it had a church that size and that passionate about what they believe. And how did the 'appearance' thing start happening? That's incredible! Do they show up every time?"

Pico rolled her eyes, "When they want to, they participate."

"What's your offering?"

Dough stopped in his tracks with that last comment.

"Pete, Pete, Pete, you just experienced an incredible moment of unity and immersion in the Breath, and you are thinking about numbers and money! What the hell is wrong with you? The numbers are meaningless! WE DON'T CARE ABOUT NUMBERS!

And, we don't take an offering. The people are the offering and all the resources we need."

Rev. Peters knew he was right, but he couldn't get his mind away from thinking that way. Success in his world was rooted in numbers, finances, and facilities. Leadership was defined by how well you could create and maintain those three areas in the church's life. Sure, there was talk about transformation, service, mission, and ministry. But it was more about self-preservation than self-denial, service, and others in the local church.

"I'm just in awe of all the work you all are doing here. You have to tell someone about this! Get the word out! Share what you know about how to 'be the church!'"

Ma Green, overhearing the conversation, chimed in, "Yeah, we should write a book, set up a tour, sell curriculum! How's this: *44 Ways to be the Church.*"

"I think that would be great!" The good Reverend missed the sarcasm.

Ma Green sighed with strained patience, "That's not who we are, and we are certainly not interested in growing an institution or maintaining one. The beauty of the Others is that we don't have any strings attached. It's a messy bunch of beautifully creative and loving people that get on each other's nerves. But, there is no need for money, staff, or buildings. We use what the Creative gives and celebrate the gifts of all involved. You, Pete, are a part of that work. In a moment, we are going to share the new beginning you're about to be involved with."

"You mean you don't pay the musician and singers in that praise band?"

"No, Pete!" Dough exclaimed.

Pico also chimed in, "If the focus is on numbers, maintaining facilities, staff, and building an economy to support the endeavors, then there will always be restrictions. Restrictions on how and in what ways the community can serve, invite, and welcome. You must break all that shit down. Would I be invited to lead or share my gifts in the church you serve, Pete?"

Rev. Peters thought for a moment, "Well, we are an affirming congregation. We had that battle in our denomination many years ago. But . . ."

"Exactly!" Pico exclaimed, "Affirming means that *we* are welcoming and will *tolerate* people of difference in our community, but including them in all ways, well, that's a different story."

The Reverend was a little burned by Pico's last statement. He reflected on the great loss that occurred, how standing for what was right related to inclusion cost the denomination and his ministry. Pico could see that her last comments hurt Pete.

"Pete, I'm sure you're a good pastor and that you have made sacrifices along the way. Some have probably brought you discomfort. But you're responding not out of abandonment but privilege."

Pico reached out and pulled Pete to her and held him there for a moment. At first, Pete clenched, not expecting to be received in such an intimate way by Pico, but then he softened and received what she had to offer. He was not just welcome here but included.

"Can we keep moving? It's getting late!" Roo shouted.

Pico released the Reverend, and everyone turned their attention back to getting to where they needed to go. Roxie led the way and came to a rusty red door on the side of another warehouse only a few hundred yards from the Gathering.

"Come on, ya'll! Let's get this train moving!" Roxie urged.

The room was well lit and had a large round table set in the center. It was a conference room for the factory that existed many years ago. The chairs around the table were all old but in decent shape. They were leather, dark wood, with casters on the legs. The table had a beautiful mahogany top with inlays of other types of wood, which formed a map of the world at the center. On the map, yellow dots were sprinkled all over. They seemed to indicate locations that were relevant to those who used to gather there. Surrounding the world was a slogan: "Making Things People Want!" Apparently, nobody wanted what they were making anymore. Each of them took a seat and invited Pete to do the same.

The wood floors were scratched and worn from years of use. The walls were lined with old pictures of industry—large cranes building the warehouse district, white men smoking cigars, digging shovels into the ground together, cutting ribbons in ceremonies, and smiling at their accomplishments. Then there were images of workers operating every type of machinery possible, images of industrial success. And now, sitting in this room of past power and empire, was a collection of misfits making plans to unleash hope on the world. Not hope that was dependent on them, but the Breath. Those who had claimed the Creative's call and purpose.

Margret, who had tended to Rev. Peters at the hospital, gave the Reverend a glance and a wink.

"It's good to see you, Reverend. It's been a long time coming!"

"You knew all about this the whole time?" Rev. Peters asked.

"Sure did! How do you think Dough got in so easily and the two of you escaped without too much commotion? Oh, I'm not saying I didn't have to cover for you because your wife was *hot* when she found out that you left on your own."

"You told her I left on my own? Shit! Why would you tell her that? She is going to be all over me when I get home, and that's the last thing I need to deal with."

"No worries, Pete." Dough said, entering the conversation gracefully, "You did leave on your own—"

Ma Green interrupted the exchange with an abrupt, "Excuse me!" She garnered everyone's attention. "Now it's time to get down to work."

For a moment, Rev. Peters' mind wandered again. He was tired, spooked, and emotionally spent. This gathering also reminded him of all the meetings that dominated most of his time and energy. Meetings on finance, trustees, building, programs, mission, marketing, ordination, leadership, and the lists go on and on. Meetings about other meetings to determine if there was a need for another meeting. Most of the conversations at the meetings amounted to nothing but were just a formal way of covering one's ass. Then the church meetings would drone on and on about how we needed to grow, bring in young families, and make the church strong again. These conversations depleted Rev. Peters the most. Everyone offering suggestions on reaching out, evangelizing, seeking new people, with all the attention on how the pastor and staff should make this happen. Those conversations were an effort to make everyone involved feel like they were doing something about their decline. Their views on inviting and welcoming new people usually were exclusive to people who looked, worked, played and lived like them. Outreach was about maintaining their comfort with people of means and had nothing to do with those on the margins.

Many years ago, meetings were physical gatherings, and then after the "virus," everyone moved to digital platforms. Once the world figured out how to live with the virus, digital media stuck. The convenience and accessibility overtook the travel and time needed for physical meetings. But, it also came with its own set of challenges. Ease of accessibility meant even more meetings as everyone could zip right online with folks from all over the world. It also diminished the value found in the effort of gathering. Many people started attending meetings as if it was an obligation rather than an essential part of the work. Sitting at home through a meeting meant that you could multi-task and barely pay attention to the conversations. Some folks would log on, mute their screen, and throw up some random picture of themselves and call that "attending the meeting." At Rev. Peters church, meetings all moved to a digital format, and folks would only gather physically if the facilities had an issue that they needed to look into.

"Pete, are you still with us?" Ma Green asked from across the table.

"Yes, ma'am!" Pete replied somewhat startled. "I'm sorry, my mind slipped away for a moment, but I'm back."

Pico leaned forward with her arms resting on the table, "Let's pray. 'Oh, Creative, the giver of life, love, and peace. We are thankful that you are making all things new and that we can participate in this story bigger than ourselves. Oh, Breath, bring forth a passion in us and courage to burn with love for all people. Oh, Human One, may the fullness of the flesh you bore find its place on your people and grant us your wisdom in knowing that our lives will be incomplete without a full life with others. We offer our prayer!'"

Everyone nodded, shouted, and expressed themselves in the way they felt appropriate. As Ma Green lifted her head from the prayer, she turned and thanked Pico for the offering. She then directed her full attention to Rev. Peters.

"You are here, Pete, because you are an important part of the work needed to live into God's future together. You are a man given great power and authority."

Rev. Peters began to squirm a little in his chair and sheepishly replied, "Well, I don't know about——"

"Pete! You have authority and power, and you need not diminish that truth. You need to pay attention because the work the Breath has for you will be difficult. It's going to push you to limits you've never experienced before, and it's going to ask you to surrender everything for the work that is before you. The new beginning is not something we are waiting for but has been here from the beginning of time. The Creative is making all things new and has launched this movement through those the world considers the least.

"For many years, communities calling themselves 'faith-based,' the language of preference for the power, the least, the broken, and the lost, were believed to be an acknowledgment of the need to serve and offer mercy to these people groups. The assumption was The Creative's preference for the poor was an effort to wake up the church and redirect attention to help lift them. This, my good sibling, is not what that means. It means that only the poor can be the witness and hope for the world. Those who have nothing have everything, and in their freedom, they can embody good news, for there are absolutely no strings attached. The world's marginalized people are to be the witnesses the Human One has invited to welcome all to the great feast."

Rev. Peters' mind was whirling as he tried to take in all that Ma Green was saying. It had been a long day, and his head was confounded by the experiences and events that found him along the way. He just wanted a warm shower and a comfortable bed. He was hungry and

wanted to find something to eat. He just wanted answers to the purpose of it all. He wondered, *Is God making all things new?* The group sat
in complete silence, giving him a moment to collect his thoughts. The
aroma of something delicious began to waft into their midst.

"So, you're saying the marginalized people of the world are the
witnesses for the end of the world?"

"No" Ma Green replied, "They are the witnesses to its new
beginning."

"OK, this is all great, and I am honored to be invited, but what
in the hell does this have to do with me?"

Just then, Eve came wheeling into the room through a side door located
opposite of where Rev. Peters was sitting. A large bowl resting on her
lap steamed with freshly cooked collard greens. Everyone straightened
in their chairs, and Dough grabbed the collards from Eve and placed
them at the center of the table.

Ma Green broke the silence, "Reverend." She stated with authority, "The Others are coming to inhabit your sanctuary.'"

CHAPTER 11

THE PROPHET

"What?" Rev. Peters was dumbfounded. "What in the hell are you talking about?"

Ma Green simply reached across the table to grab the bowl of collards.

"Would you like some?" she graciously offered the Reverend.

"Sure, but what are you talking about 'inhabit'?"

"Well, Pete, the new beginning is upon us, and now is time for us to move into the world. Be the good news and all that stuff."

Ma Green's eyes were sparkling as she shared this news with Rev. Peters.

"When? How? What do you want me to do?" he stammered. "Isn't Jesus just going to return and take care of business for us? Why go to all this effort to shake things up like that?"

Dough turned slowly toward Rev. Peters, enjoying the reaction, "Pete, Pete, Pete, all in due time. For now, let's eat and get you back home."

"No! No! No!" Rev. Peters responded. "I have come all this way through hell and back to receive your little secret message on the end times, and all you have to tell me is that you all are moving into our sanctuary? I need more than that."

Pico chimed in, "First, this isn't the fuckin' end! How many times do we have to tell you that? All that hocus-pocus shit you've got crammed up in your head, you've gotta let it go! Second, this is the new beginning. The Creative is making all things new! Third, it ain't none of our shit. It will happen with or without us. Fourth, this is all moving fast, and we are just moving with the Breath. We don't know the day or time. We know that many of us will be there, and we are going to need your support."

"So, you don't have any idea when, or how, or what I need to do?"

Roo, who had been carefully listening throughout this whole conversation, stood up to gather the now-empty bowl.

Roo looked at the Reverend, "You'll support us, right?"

Everyone got up from around the table and began moving toward the doors.

"Wait! Where are you all going, and how am I going to get home?" Rev. Peters was growing frustrated.

"Tim will help you get home, Pete." Dough offered in the form of comfort.

"Who is Tim?"

The group barely heard the last question as they offered pleasantries, handshakes, and hugs. One could tell that these folks had been "through it" together. There was a love for one another that was palpable. Rev. Peters was envious of their bond but was also frustrated no one was offering a plan to get him home. He had a bunch of things to consider, and thinking about how to get home was overwhelming. He worried about confronting his wife, staff, and congregation. Everyone was going to write him off as nuts! Ma Green, Pico, Stevie, Roo, Roxie, and Margret turned to the Reverend and waved goodbye. Ma Green was the last to actually walk out the door and simply said, "See you soon, Pete!" Dough was the only one who didn't leave, and the Revered was getting a little emotional.

"Well, Pete, we have had one hell of a day! I am so thankful that you decided to come, and I hope you had an incredible experience. But now, it's time for me to head in another direction. I'm going to turn you over to Tim to help you find your way back home." He reached out and grabbed the Reverend by the shoulder and pulled him close. "I will see you again soon. What a trip!"

Rev. Peters was at a loss for words. At the least, he thought Dough might accompany him back since he brought him to the Gathering in the first place. He didn't understand why he would leave him now, but he surrendered to Dough's hug.

"I have no idea what this is all about. I have no idea what I'm supposed to do. But, I have experienced such beauty, horror, suffering, liberation, and joy on this journey with you that I can honestly say something has changed."

"It's the mind change," Dough softly replied.

"I guess," Rev. Peters responded as he moved away from Dough.

Dough smiled and began to chuckle at the Reverend, "You're a mess! And, you smell terrible!"

Standing just outside the open doorway leading to the street was a small, shadowy figure. The person couldn't be more than four feet tall.

"There's Tim!" Dough shouted, pointing to the figure.

Both Dough and Rev. Peters walked out of the room and into the street. Standing there was a diminutive man. He wore a full beard that took some time to grow, as it touched the upper part of his chest. He had substantial gauge earrings, which made his earlobes look massive. He also had piercings in his ears, nose, and eyebrows. If Rev. Peters' mother were around, she would have sworn the guy came straight from the carnival. The reason he thought of that was that to his mother, everyone with earrings and tattoos were carnies who were considered one of the lowest of all modern people groups. At least, according to his mother.

Tim also had tattoos all over his body. His arms were covered with what appeared to be skulls, dragons, demons, and other horrifying images. Vines intertwined around his neck to look as if they were choking him. The tattoo on his cheek appeared to be a gang symbol—two lines of equal lengths forming a cross. In the upper right quadrant of the cross, there was a skeleton key, in the upper left an old oil lamp, on the bottom left was a skull, and the remaining quadrant had a raven. Tim was wearing an old black leather jacket and worn blue jeans. And he sported a fantastic pair of motorcycle boots, complete with platinum buckles on the side. Tim looked like a rough character, which made Rev. Peters wonder why Tim was the guy to take him home.

"Tim, this is Pete. Pete, this is Tim."

The Reverend spoke first. "Nice to meet you, Tim."

Tim just nodded. Dough seemed to have a glow of accomplishment about him.

"OK, you two, I'm gonna let you go. Make sure you get him to the right train, Tim."

"I will!"

"So, you do speak." Rev. Peters offered to break the ice.

"Yep!" Tim replied. "The train station is about three miles east of here. Where are you going?"

Rev. Peters almost forgot where he needed to go, partially because he was considering if he wanted to follow this crazy dream out or just run and hide in a hole.

"I live in Bakerville."

"OK. Then we need to get you on the Green Line."

Rev. Peters just kept walking, following Tim as he made his way through the maze that made up the old warehouse district.

"How long have you been a part of this community?"

Rev. Peters was making an effort at small talk. By now, he had moved beyond exhaustion and on to loopiness. He had no real sense of time anymore, and it just seemed like this adventure had occurred in weeks, not hours.

"I guess I've been here most of my life. I don't keep track. It just causes too much distraction, always worrying about time. I used to have a watch, but I threw it out a long time ago." Tim chuckled. " . . . a long 'time' ago. That's funny."

Rev. Peters was beginning to see another side of Tim. Rough on the outside, but a jokester on the inside.

"The watch binds my life," the Reverend offered.

"Why's that, Pete?"

"Well, I have schedules, and schedules for schedules, and meetings I need to schedule, for stuff that makes me feel like I'm staying on schedule."

"Sounds like a real shit show to me."

"Yes, it does, Tim. Maybe, when I get home, I'll get rid of my watch too."

Tim smirked and chuckled under his breath. "So Pete, I hear you're a pastor. How'd that all happen?"

"Well, I guess it was a calling."

"Guess?" Tim questioned.

"Well, yes. I guess. I'm not sure anyone can have absolute certainty about a calling. Maybe the best way I can explain it is that it's the only thing I can imagine doing."

Tim looked up at him, "Doing what?"

"Well, you know, ministry."

"What does it mean to do ministry?" Tim pressed.

"You know, getting people to come to know Jesus."

Tim interrupted the Reverend, "So, ministry is the work of convincing people they need Jesus? For what?"

Rev. Peters was confused. "What are you talking about? My call is to be the pastor of a church. To care for people and love them as Jesus did. I am also supposed to help them grow in love with God and each other."

Tim smiled, "And you need a watch for that?" He continued, "I'll ask again . . . ministry is getting people to love God and each other? For what?"

"For what? What do you mean?" Rev. Peters was growing a little edgy in his response.

Tim continued, "For heavenly rewards? So they don't go to hell? So they can feel better about themselves? So they don't have to suffer? So they can maintain a certain level of prosperity, meanwhile feeling good enough about their relationship with Jesus that they don't have to give a shit about anyone else?"

"Yes!" Rev. Peters responded. "As you said, it's a shit show!"

There now was a silence between the two as they walked along. The Reverend was a little offended by Tim and how he was pushing him. *How dare he immediately start passing judgment on the people from my church and me. That little ass.*

"We are almost to the station Pete. It's been great walking with you. I hope I didn't piss you off. I'm just sick of all the theological glam and spiritual masturbation that goes on with all of us religious types. I include myself in that definition because I am seriously screwed up and have a long way to journey. I appreciate your honesty, and I will see you again. Listen, you're a good person, and you've got some serious days ahead of you. So hold on! Ain't nothin' playin' out like we all thought it would."

At that, Tim pointed to the station, handed Rev. Peters a token, turned on his heels, and disappeared into the night.

The station was old and in need of repair. It was well-used by the community. It had brought the working poor and service industry folks over from the other side for many years. The place smelled of urine, and it was unkempt. Rev. Peters, in his filthy hospital pants, Lil' Piggy Mart T-shirt, and high-top sneakers fit right in. Several people were waiting for the train, and for the first time that day, he saw the time: 11:37. *Holy crap! By the time I get home, it will be tomorrow morning.* Then he thought about what Tim had said about time. If you don't know about it, you don't worry as much.

Rev. Peters found a seat on the loading deck and fell asleep. He awoke to the sound of screeching train wheels and brakes. For a moment, he was thankful that he didn't have another horrible nightmare. As he sat up, a couple of quarters and a crumpled-up dollar bill fell from his chest. "What the hell!" he muttered. To be sure he wasn't dreaming, he slapped himself. When he felt the pain, he knew he was awake. The train's doors opened, and as he entered, he looked for a seat farthest away from anyone. Unfortunately, it appeared that everyone wanted to be in the same car he was and they had secured their seats before he could, and it was standing room only.

In a sarcastic tone, he mentioned under his breath, "There are only eight other cars on this train, people!"

He moved toward the door to see if he could switch to another car when the lady sitting next to him said,

> "Oh brother, you're in the right car!"

> "Excuse me?" Rev. Peters replied.

> "You ain't gonna want to leave this car. In a few stops, this is the car that picks up the Prophet!"

> Rev. Peters looked at the lady straight in the eye, "Ma'am, the last thing I need is more prophets!"

Before he could make a move, the doors closed, and the conductor called out,

> "Please be seated or grab the handrail if you need to stand. The next stops are Exchange, Carter, and Deliverance."

> "I guess you're gonna meet the Prophet now whether you like it or not!"

The train was mesmerizing, and Rev. Peters kept fading back and forth between twilight and sleep. At one point, the lady next to him woke him to get his head off her shoulder. It was super embarrassing because he had drooled a little on her coat. As disgusted as he was, having to sit next to all of "those" people, he realized it was even worse for them to sit next to him.

"Next stop Deliverance," the conductor called out.

"Here we are!" said the lady next to him. "The home of the Prophet."

Rev. Peters was finally curious enough to ask her more about the Prophet.

"Oh, he rides this car every night, and everyone crams into this car just to hear what he has to say."

Rev. Peters looked at the car door as the train began to come to a stop.

"Is he dangerous?" Rev. Peters questioned.

"No . . . just . . . well, you'll see!"

The car came to a complete stop. Outside were a few more people ready to get in the car, but nobody got off. And there he was—the Prophet—a tall, dark-skinned man with unkempt hair and terrible teeth. He wore a gold chain around his neck with a huge ankh dangling at the bottom. He was neatly dressed and had a bunch of bracelets around his wrists. A sizeable purple cloak draped across his shoulders, and he had a little propeller cap strapped around his chin sitting on top of his head.

Rev. Peters turned to the lady, "I'm guessing this is him?"

She just shushed him and turned her attention back to the Prophet. He stood in the middle of the train with his head bowed. As the train started moving, he remained fixed in one spot, not even phased by the train's momentum.

"Next stop, "Homer," the train conductor proclaimed.

Once the train reached full speed, the Prophet opened his arms wide. His cape expanded, making his presence known to everyone in the car. The Prophet looked up to the ceiling and breathed deeply.

"Come Breath! Come Breath!" he recited in a deep, gravelly voice.

Then he sprang into action, crouching down and moving in a swaying motion. He made his way around the car, looking into the eyes of all those gathered there that night. As he made his way back to the first person in the car, he took his hands and clapped them together in front of the person's face. The person jumped and then giggled to cover their fear. He looked them in the eyes and made his proclamation,

"You're IN!"

The Prophet continued to move around the car, focusing his attention on one person at a time. With each stop, he would offer his verdict. Luckily, everyone he gazed at to this point was in, which got Rev. Peters thinking. How many times had he been told by parishioners, pastors, and parents he was "out"? Growing up in a relatively conservative church, the focus was always about getting it right, perfect, and not being "out." He chuckled as he considered what "IN" and "OUT" actually meant. Sure, there was a lot of theological and biblical language used. Still, it only really amounted to whether a person was like us or not. To put it bluntly, if most Christian folk were held to their own judgmental standard, nobody would be in. Rev. Peters started to get a little anxious as the Prophet drew closer to him. All the condemning voices, teachings, and attitudes of the past were screaming in his head. He caught himself thinking, *Please let me be IN! Please let me be IN!* The prophet moved to the lady next to him, the one who told him he needed to stay, and he thought, *I think she might be out.*

The prophet looked into her eyes, "IN!"

She exclaimed, "Hallelujah!"

Now it was Rev. Peters' turn. Sweat began to bead on his brow. His heart was racing, and his right leg was jiggling. *This is the stupidest thing ever!* He knew the man was crazy and that this verdict was meaningless, but something drew him to this judgment.

The Prophet shuffled over in front of the Reverend and bent down to look into his eyes. Rev. Peters looked right back at him. He wanted to be confident, show no fear, and be as cool as he could be. After all, he was the religious specialist in the car! The two men's eyes met. The Prophets eyes were dark, almost black, and you couldn't make out a pupil. His skin was wrinkled but tightly drawn across the skeleton just below the surface. His lips were chapped and peeling.

"IN!" he shouted.

Rev. Peters shot up out of his seat and screamed, "YES!"

The Prophet was taken back by the exuberance. Rev. Peters grabbed The Prophet and gave him a big hug.

"I'm In! . . . Yes! . . . I'm In!"

He began to cry, and the lady sitting next to him put her arm around his shoulders and whispered, "Now, aren't you glad you stayed."

It was clear The Prophet wasn't expecting anyone to take him that seriously. The enthusiastic response left him so disconcerted he didn't conclude his judgment work and slipped straight out of the train at Homer.

The lady comforting Rev. Peters said, "I guess he can dish it out but can't take it. I thought for sure he would be dancing that he produced a convert."

Rev. Peters laughed and then explained, "I apologize. I have been so focused on getting home that I didn't even introduce myself. I'm, well, Pete."

The woman smiled at him, "I'm Delorus. Nice to meet you, Pete. I told you this was the best damn car on the train. If you're ever this way again, you can always see the Prophet in this car. Just look for the Green Line number 144."

"I will," the Reverend responded, "I am just amazed at how good it felt to have someone . . . a stranger, a prophet . . . tell me that *I* was in!"

"Oh honey," Delorus affirmed, "I have come to see the Prophet many times, and it always feels good to know that while everything else in the world can be telling you you're out, the Prophet' knows you're in!"

"You mean everyone is in?" Rev. Peters questioned.

"Yep! I've never heard of anyone being out in this car. Not even my ass-hole brother-in-law, and that's saying a lot!"

"Bakerville!" the conductor announced over the intercom.

Rev. Peters got up and wished Delorus well.

"Thank you so much for encouraging me to stick it out on #144!"

"Glad to be of service, Pete!"

He stood up slowly and walked to the sliding doors. The train came to a stop, the doors opened, and he exited the car. The few people waiting to get on the car moved far out of his way. He turned to them and shrugged, uttering, "Rough day!" Those starring at him gave no response and averted their eyes in hopes that this "vagrant" might not ask them for money. He walked down the platform, opened the exit door, and walked onto the street. Standing there, looking in the direction of his home, it started to rain.

CHAPTER 12

WHEEEE-ERRRRRRRR

The rain was cold and refreshing. Droplets hit his head and soaked into his clothes; he could feel the water running down through his hair, onto his face, neck, and back. It had to be well past midnight, and while exhausted, the rain brought a renewed energy. Rev. Peters wasn't one for getting wet, but this felt more like a cleansing. He held his arms out with his palms turned up toward the sky. The Reverend tilted his head back to catch the rain more directly on his face. As it came pouring down, he could feel the dirt from the day wash away. He found himself enjoying it so much that he started strolling. His slow march to his house was also part reluctance; he dreaded having to face his wife. Jenny was a great person, but she had a temper, especially if triggered by something foolish. As he walked, he started rehearsing what he was going to say. "Hey, honey, have I got a story for you!" or, "I don't want to talk about it right now; I've had a super long and trying day!" or, "I'm so glad to be home, and I missed you so much! How's Mickey doing?" or, "I was kidnapped, and they threw me out on the street!" He could think of nothing that would ease the anticipated confrontation, and all the Revered wanted to do was go to bed and sleep it off.

Rev. Peters' home was only a few blocks away, and as he shuffled down the middle of the street, he thought about how secure he felt in his neighborhood. Never once, in the twelve years they lived there, did he ever feel threatened or at risk. The streetlights were all bright and well-lit. They had a strong neighborhood watch, and most families were well-educated professionals. The Peters' neighbors were both doctors, and across the street, were a lawyer and construction contractor. The houses were well built and maintained. The only real annoyance was that a few cats that occasionally wandered between yards would have a "good time" just outside the Peters' master bedroom window. Neighbors kept their lawns nicely tended and even though the Reverend chose to stroll down the middle of the street, they did have nice sidewalks throughout the neighborhood. Children played freely and rode their bikes all over the place. Last year, the hottest topic of discussion in the community was how to keep the squirrels from invading the bird feeders in most of the back yards.

The home Rev. Peters lived in wasn't his own; he lived in the parsonage provided for him by the church. Guidelines designated the number of rooms needed, proper upkeep, appliances, utilities, and lawn care. It was a part of the "pastoral salary package." While it would seem to help reduce living expenses, it didn't help much with finances. Pastors have to pay taxes at the "fair market value" of rental homes in the area. Well, the fair market value of the parsonage Rev. Peters was living in was quite a bit more than he could afford if he had to purchase something on his own. So, the good Reverend lied on his taxes and put down what he thought a "fair market value" should be. Most of his colleagues received housing allowances, which was a much more cash beneficial opportunity for clergy. Parsonages didn't help clergy members establish any equity from their homes to use toward their retirement or pay off significant bills. In the old days, many retiring clergy were having to purchase their first home when they left the church.

His church had bought the home in the early '90s. It was a good size, and the church did a great job of keeping it up to date and in good shape. Rev. Peters appreciated their neighborhood and how lovely the home was but resented living in a home that wasn't his. It was tough to make a parsonage your own, and the church's trustees always wanted to pop in to check it out. Most church members were very conscientious of the pastoral family's privacy. Still, occasionally you'd get a new "Trustee Chair" that felt it was their job to monitor all behavior at the house. "After all, this is the church's investment! We have to keep it around for a long time!" In the last church he served, he received a housing allowance before the "rapid decline" just before his current appointment. The Peters bought a cute little house in a neighborhood that better fit their lifestyle. It was about twenty-five miles away from the church, so there was very little interaction with "church folks" during the week.

Jenny didn't like church folks much, and Mickey didn't like people at all. Even now, things are still changing as many churches no longer have paid clergy or are only employing them part-time. In many ways, this change was a blessing as it shifted the focus from preservation toward serving the world. It also freed clergy to offer a more prophetic voice since their livelihood was no longer dependent on tithes and offerings. Rev. Peters was one of the last hold-outs of the rapid decline. The decline had been coming for many years as most churches lost touch with the needs of the new generations of people rising and living in their communities. Most people no longer saw the necessity for a community that still lived as if it were the 1970s.

Back in the heyday of the American church, the church was the center of the community. It was the social media platform people needed to stay connected. Once technological advances gave individuals the means for interpersonal communication, giving and receiving information, and entertainment to happen in the palm of your hand or even implanted in your head, the role church played diminished significantly. The international pandemic that hit years ago didn't help either. It forced people to stay at home, and over time they began developing new habits. Few churches survived much longer after that, and those that did had large endowments that kept the 25-75 members still showing up happy as remnants of a tradition long gone.

Rev. Peters' thoughts shifted again as he contrasted his home and neighborhood, church and work, with the warehouse district the Others called home. Here he was, in his thoughts, critiquing the home provided for him, in a neighborhood that was the safest in town. And yet, the Others were happy. Rev. Peters shook his head as his privilege struck him hard. And yet, he wasn't happy.

The Reverend had finally made it to his street, Elysium Drive. As he turned to walk down the street, he heard a car coming up from behind him. Rev. Peters began to move out of the center of the road to give the vehicle enough room to pass.

The "Wheeee-errrrrrr" made him jump, and along with the alert, a bright light pointed directly at him. *Shit!* From the car, a voice came through the speaker gently so as not to disturb the sleeping residents. "Put your hands on your head and slowly turn around."

Rev. Peters did just as the officer told him. He stood there for several minutes before an officer approached him from the car.

"Sir, state your name and your business here so late at night."

Tired and bewildered, the Reverend offered his best at the moment, "I'm Rev. Michael Peters, and I live here!"

The officer shined his light in Rev. Peters face. Illuminated, in his full glory, in the middle of the street, only a few hundred feet away from his home Rev. Peters was stopped. Sneakers, bloody hospital pants, dirty and bloody Lil Piggy Mart T-shirt, and a fantastic hairstyle still reminiscent of his hospital stay.

"Sir, do you have any identification on you?"

"No, I do not! I was taken from the hospital by a man and dragged around town. I could not bring any of that with me."

The officer shifted a bit. "Sir, we received a call from someone in the neighborhood that a vagrant was wandering the streets acting a little unusual. You fit the description."

"Listen, officer . . .," Rev. Peters stammered, "I live just five houses down on the right. I am just coming home from a very long day. Might you have heard of a pastor being taken from the hospital early in the morning yesterday? That's me. I'm the pastor! I'm the pastor!"

"Sure you are, sir. I know you're not technically doing anything wrong, but to sort this out, I'm going to have to take you in."

"No!" Rev. Peters shouted. "I'm frickin' almost home! I live right there, just down the street. My wife and son are there waiting for me."

"I'm sure they are, sir, but since you don't have any ID, I can't walk up to some house and wake people up just because you say you live there. I mean, look at you!"

Rev. Peters looked down at his pants, dirty with bloodstains, and then he ran.

"Stop right there! Freeze!"

As Rev. Peters ran, he could feel pressure in his chest again, like the episode he had several days before. He was running as hard as he could and began to scream,

"Help! Jen—"

ZAP! Electrical charges surged from the Reverend's buttocks up throughout his whole body. He couldn't speak and fell hard on the pavement face-first, his 250-pound body collapsing in a mound. His body was jerking about when two officers jumped on top of him, grabbing his arms and pulling them to his back. He was unable to speak. They cuffed him, read him his rights, and then proceeded to pull the Taser darts out of his now tender ass. Both of them picked him up and moved him toward the squad car. Several lights from the immediate houses around him came on. One neighbor opened the door and shouted, "Is everything all right, officers?"

> "Yes, we are just going to take this gentleman down to the station for further questioning. Please go back to sleep; everything is under control."

Rev. Peters tried to say something, "Dorctra Blah..veh!"

He was trying to shout "Doctor Blevins," but he couldn't form his words. The officers opened the back door, shielded his head, and ushered him into the back seat.

Once settled in the vehicle, the officers told Rev. Peters that they would be taking him downtown and he could share his story there. After recording several reports of the incident, they put the car in drive. They proceeded to drive right past the Reverend's home. He was not feeling well, but his speech was returning to him.

> "Officers, you are both making a huge mistake! I'm the pastor of First Church, and you just drove right past my house. What in the hell do you think you're doing? I wasn't doing anything wrong!"

> The officers ignored his comments and simply said, "We'll be at the station soon."

The squad car was new. It still had that "new car smell." New vinyl and plastic. The vehicle had all the modern devices. It had cameras mounted on all sides of the car facing outward and toward the interior. It had a voice-activated computer system that spoke directly to the officers while driving. Those changes came about as technology allowed voice activation to replace the onboard computer officers depended on years ago. The new cars could also drive themselves. This feature could be turned on or off, depending on the situation.

In most cases, officers would have the cars drive them back to the station so they could work on their processing paperwork during the drive.

Rev. Peters tried to soften the officers up, "So, where are you boys from?"

Still no response, just the same old "We will be at the station soon."

It was time to give in to the situation. Rev. Peters thought about his day and how he had traveled with Dough from the hospital and only heard police officers after the young boy was shot in the playground. He realized that he never once saw a police officer or sheriff's deputy in the warehouse district. *But, fricken walking in my neighborhood . . . then I see the police!*

The Reverend stared out the window of the car as he passed all the streets he had just traversed. He began to laugh and laugh hard. Both officers were caught entirely off guard.

"Sir, what is so funny?"

Rev. Peters just kept laughing, and then between his chuckles, he stated, "Wait until you hear the story I'm going to tell! It's flippin' nuts, and all I can do now is laugh!"

"That's fine, sir, but could you please keep it down? We need to pay attention to our Shelah."

"Who's Shelah?" Rev. Peters blurted out with a laugh behind it.

"Shelah is our computer."

"Really? Well, you tell Shelah to look up Rev. Michael Peters!"

At that, Shelah responded, "Rev. Michael Peters is the pastor of First Church and has been reported missing by his wife after apparently leaving the hospital of his own free will."

The Reverend beamed, "See! I told you so!"

The two officers asked Shelah a further question, "Where does Rev. Michael Peters live?"

Shelah responded, "The Rev. Michael Peters lives at 1360 Elysium Drive."

Rev. Peters began to laugh even harder. "You two are so in trouble! But I completely understand. I look like absolute shit. You have no ID, and lord knows I wouldn't want the two of you dragging a blood-stained, filthy vagrant to my door in the early morning. And, I did run. Which gets me thinking, why the hell did I run?"

"No worries, sir, that happens more than people think. It is the one thing that causes some of the most egregious police work. Most cities have banned using guns on a runner anymore. Our town still allows us to use Tasers, well, as you know."

"I always wondered what being Tased felt like. Now I know! Listen, guys, I'm sorry for giving you a hell of a night."

At that moment, the police officers pulled over into a parking lot to call down to the station to seek guidance on what to do with Rev. Peters. The Reverend, still handcuffed in the back seat, listened intently. The conversation the officers were having outside the vehicle was clearly turning in his favor. He thought about how the night went down and how easily something as innocent as walking home could turn into a complete takedown and arrest. He also thought about how lucky he was that the police department didn't allow officers to use guns when someone ran away. With horror, it dawned on him, *I could have been shot!* On any other night, if he had been walking through his neighborhood dressed in decent clothes, nobody would have even flinched. That thought gave him pause. After all he had been through that day, if he had been shot, nobody would ever know what had happened. They would have asked why he was dressed like a clown, why was he covered in blood, dirty, smelling like dog piss, and looking like a loser. They would have wondered who did he kill. Questions and rumors would have arisen about his escape from the hospital and the justification for having to shoot him. The town leaders would have come up with something to cover their asses, probably something having to do with a psychotic episode.

"Holy Jesus!" Rev. Peters shouted.

The two officers finally got back into the car.

"Sir, we are extremely sorry for this mix-up and hope you will forgive us."

Rev. Peters looked at the two young men, "As I said, I'm as guilty as anyone in this divine comedy. Don't worry about it, but could you please take off these god-awful handcuffs?"

The two officers scurried out of the car and immediately opened the back door to let Rev. Peters out. They removed his handcuffs and allowed him a minute to stretch.

"Those things are super uncomfortable!" Rev. Peters offered.

"Sir, we would be glad to take you back to your house now."

Looking at the ground for a moment, the Reverend slowly lifted his head.

A devilish smirk came across his face, "Nope, gentlemen! I'd like you to take me down to the station."

CHAPTER 13

FRIDAY THE 13TH

Riding down to the station, Rev. Peters had difficulty staying awake, but it wasn't easy to get comfortable. Squad cars aren't known for their amenities, and the back seat isn't a luxurious ride. It had to be at least 3:00 a.m., and he couldn't even remember what day it was. Curiosity got the best of him, and he asked the two officers what time it was. The officer sitting in the passenger seat looked at his watch. A flurry of digital light splashed across the ceiling of the squad car, and then his watch stated, "The current time is 2:45 a.m."

"Thank you!" Rev. Peters acknowledged, "And, could you tell me what day it is?"

The officer twisted his head just enough to offer a silhouette of his face and then spoke over his shoulder, "It's Friday the 13th!"

"OK!" Rev. Peters responded.

He chuckled at that and thought, "*If yesterday was the 12th, I sure hate to see what the 13th is going to bring.*"

Rev. Peters wasn't a very superstitious person and held the number 13 in high regard. He and Jenny were married on June 13th. His father was born on July 13th, and his high school basketball number was 13. He had to fight to get the coach to allow him to have that "cursed" number, but the coach caved because he was a pretty good shot. At that moment, he also took notice of the features of the young police officer sitting in the front seat. The officer was probably in his mid-twenties and had high cheekbones and a prominent chin. His skin glistened with the passing lights from a long night and morning on the beat. He had also been sweating a little after exerting himself chasing and tasing Rev. Peters. His hair was dark, and he had a burgeoning mustache. His ears were average size, but you could see minor scars at the center of each of his earlobes. "Earrings!" Rev. Peters said to himself in a "discovery" kind of way. He wondered about the young man—Why a police officer? Does he have a family? Had he always wanted to be a police officer? Or was he looking for a steady job and had this opportunity? He considered asking but didn't have the energy.

Halfway across town Rev. Peters drifted off briefly. It wasn't a deep sleep but a numb sleep—the kind where your mind shuts off, but your body can't find its rest. He was also experiencing a skin reaction from a day of sweat, dirt, blood, and piss. A "skin reaction" is a kind way of saying he was breaking out in a rash. The rain had helped a little, and was enough to offer him a second wind and take the first layer of filth off his body, but he still needed to scrub the remaining grime away. I guess one could say that it wasn't a complete baptism.

While he was sitting in the back of the squad car alone, waiting for the officers to decide his fate, he had begun to smell himself pretty well, and he was glad he was the only one in the back of the car. It was a putrid sweet stink that would have been attractive to flies and other vermin but not so much for human interaction. The only other time he recalled having smelled that bad was on a youth mission trip with youth from his church many years ago. The place they stayed on the trip had no warm showers, only a hose sticking through a wall, drawing from some cistern sitting on top of an old roof. The water was so cold no one on the mission team took showers; instead they just used up a couple of boxes of baby wipes to bathe. Thinking back on that trip, it was no wonder that none of the native people would hang out with them or invite them to participate in any events or games. They stunk! A combination of baby lotion with pubescent B-O. It was a deadly cocktail. Jenny demanded that Rev. Peters drive himself home and come back and get her after he showered. The exciting thing was that no one who went on the trip thought they smelled that bad. If anything, they all came home feeling a sense of accomplishment—not from what they did for others during the mission trip, but from surviving a week without their usual comforts.

"Reverend!"

A voice awoke Rev. Peters from the front of the car. He was just about to dive into a deep sleep, and now he was thrown right back into consciousness.

"What?" the Reverend shouted.

"So, you're a reverend, right?"

"Yep," the Reverend offered a bit more begrudgingly.

"Can I ask you a question?"

For a split second, Rev. Peters contemplated whether he had committed some grave sin that had led to these past twenty-four hours. Maybe the dualistic universe he had spent most of his ministry deconstructing does exist. Good things happen to people who do good, and bad things happen to those who do wrong. Then again, he couldn't think of what he had done that was so wrong it would warrant such a day as he had just experienced.

"OK, shoot," he replied as if he had been hitting the bottle hard.

"I have questions about God, suffering, Heaven, and Hell. I mean, those things are real. I mean, you believe that the Bible is true. And, if it is true, we are all in a heap of shit if I remember the things people have told me over the years. I get worried about it after seeing all this darkness every day, without stopping, without answers. You start thinking that this all might be chaos with no rhyme or reason to it."

Rev. Peters was tired. There wasn't an actual question in there anywhere and he didn't really have anything else to offer, but he didn't want to discourage the young officer.

"Listen, um . . ."

"Robert, my name is Robert."

"Listen, Robert; I don't believe in the Bible. I believe that the Bible is a gift. It points to the complexities of how humanity has wrestled with its understanding of God, and how God has revealed Godself throughout history. There's a lot of shit in the Bible, and there is no way someone can approach it without first admitting to that fact. Thousands of years, thousands of documents, hundreds of thousands of translations, additions, over 750,000 variants, removals, abuses, and, yes, beautiful nuggets of truth. It invites us on a journey. The Bible is like a travel log linking our story with those who have gone before us. Does that help?"

Robert turned his head over his left shoulder again, "Nope! It's too late for all that shit. I need a yes or no answer."

Rev. Peters smiled, "Well then, I can't give that to you, and that's part of the problem; certainty is the opposite of faith."

"Thanks for trying." Robert offered as the sleepy pastor decided talking wasn't getting him anywhere either.

When the squad car pulled into the station, Rev. Peters noticed that his chest was getting tight again.

"Hey, guys? I actually might need to go back to the hospital."

"What seems to be the problem?" the officer driving the car asked with authority.

"Well, I left the hospital after they thought I might be having heart problems and . . ."

Without hesitation, the leading officer was on the radio.

"Dispatch, this is Officer Danner, Car 25, we have a situation."

"Thank you, Car 25; please report."

"The passenger is having chest pain and we'll be taking the rider to the hospital."

"What?" Rev. Peters shouted.

"No worries, sir, we will get you to the hospital in no time. Better to have you checked out than to have a problem at the station."

The more Rev. Peters thought about it, the more it made sense, and at least he would finally end up in a room with a warm shower, new clothes, and a bed! The police car sped through the city with sirens wailing. Rev. Peters thought about all the people his ride to the hospital was waking up prematurely. Street lamps and the lights in buildings flew by in a blur. As they approached the hospital, Officer Danner turned off the sirens and pulled into the emergency room entrance. The double doors of the ER slid open. Several nurses came out with a wheelchair, opened the car door, helped the Reverend into the chair, and took him to the hospital. He didn't even have time to say goodbye to the officers and felt a bit put off by that. After all, they had shared some intimate moments.

As he was being transferred to a gurney, one of the nurses, covering her nose with her arm, said, "Where in God's hell have you come from?"

All Rev. Peters could say was, "God doesn't have a hell."

"OK, smarty-pants, we need some information. The only information we got from the police was that they were bringing in a transient person who was having chest pain."

"Yeah, well," the Reverend breathed out, "I am Rev. Michael Peters, and I was here just twenty-four hours ago and was undergoing some testing related to my chest pain. I had passed out at my office and ended up in here. Then a man invited me to go on a journey with him, and I left. After a very long day, I had more chest pain, so the officers brought me here instead of the station. Oh, and did I mention they Tased me in the ass?"

The nurse continued her interrogation without flinching, "Who do I need to contact? Do you have insurance? Who is your doctor? Have you had heart problems or tightness in your chest any other times?"

He did his best to answer but just wanted to go to bed. They wheeled him into a room and helped him up on a table. They removed all of his clothes and offered him a new hospital gown.

"Excuse me? Can I please take a shower and get all this testing done tomorrow?"

"No, Rev. Peters, we need to get this done right now."

With that, they placed him on a heart monitor, stuck him with a needle, and connected him to a drip IV. The nurse did a final check of everything she'd connected and finally spoke to him.

"The cardiac team will be meeting with you in a moment."

Rev. Peters just threw his head back into the pillow and fell asleep. It couldn't have been more than a few minutes when he felt a firm nudge on his arm. He opened his eyes, and standing beside him was Margret.

"So, you're back again?" Margret spoke with a soft, comforting tone. "I guess we had better get to figuring out what is with all this chest pain. I do not think it's another heart attack, as you probably would have dropped on that journey you took with Dough. But somethin' is going on and we need to know what it is."

Rev. Peters looked deep into her eyes, "Margret, I feel like I'm never going to get any rest. I'm so tired, and I don't know what the hell is going on! I am so angry and confused, and frustrated, and, . . ."

"Shhhh." Margret placed her hand on his shoulder. "Take this time for resting because in a few days we are going to need you ready to go."

Rev. Peters practically shot up out of bed, but Margret held him down.

"There ain't no way in hell I'm going to do anymore. I'm done! There is nothing else! All this shit about the new beginning, the Others, the Breath, and my participation in it all is bullshit! I'm sorry; you're a nice lady, but I've just been dragged all over kingdom come for some fantasy. A fantasy embraced by a community that lives in many abandoned warehouses and worships lights that shoot through a roof that can't even keep the rain out! There isn't a damn thing that's going to change! You are all living in a dream world if you think a bunch of losers from the wrong side of town will be the great liberators of the world. Hell, some of those folks can't even tie their shoes, let alone talk with a real human being.

"It's like you have all embraced this romantic idea that all will be right! And, this is going to all take place when a bunch of homeless folks, who have no real ability to fend for themselves, start moving out and inhabiting the places that do! It's all in your imagination, and it isn't real! It's not even possible! There is no way on God's green earth that change is going to happen through the weak! And, there is no way in hell I'm going to be a part of that! What a sucker I have been! Why would I even possibly think that this could lead to something? I must be in bad shape to find such an invitation to be appealing."

Margret had held her tongue and let him go on and get this off his chest, but she'd finally had enough and raised her hand with force, stopping the Reverend just as he was gearing up for more.

"Pete, you are a part of that! It ain't a matter of your choice!"

Rev. Peters was angry, but it was subsiding. He never was someone who could hold on to anger, which made him such a good pastor. Some might have called him a pushover or, at the least, too forgiving. It was both a strength and a weakness, but in the politics of the church, it equaled survival. Not rocking the boat too much, and being a good friend to everyone secured your longevity. But he found more and more he was expected to never say too much and constantly affirm whatever agenda the person standing in front of him was espousing. His face was still red, but his anger was turning into embarrassment. Margret sat down beside the examination table and didn't say a word. It took the Reverend several minutes before he could muster something up to say to her. He was feeling guilty about yelling.

"Margret, I'm sorry for being such an ass! I'm just exhausted, and I don't know what end is up or down at the moment. All I do know is that I need to sleep!"

Margret stood back up and placed her hand back on his shoulder.

"It's all right, Pete. I was expecting that rant a lot sooner. Every single one of us who has become a participant in the work of the Breath rants regularly. I will say, though, that while this work of following the lead of the Human One is hard, it's not nearly as hard as continuing to live in a world that doesn't give a shit about you!"

Rev. Peters looked at her dark face and could see tears running down her cheeks.

"I'm sorry, Pete. I shouldn't be crying all over you!"

"That's all right, Margret."

He could tell she was offering herself in all sincerity, and that was his experience with everyone who was a part of the Others. The work that she and the Others are all about was not just a fantasy but a genuine hope! Through the leading of the Breath, what they received, discerned, and lived was as real as the light that filled the Gathering—as real as the people who appeared in the beams of light that evening. It streamed in and rested on every person there. The rust was eating away the barrier that once kept the light from entering.

The door to his room pushed open, and several medical types came scurrying around getting things ready for what appeared to be a procedure. Margret knew most of the people working that night and nodded to the Reverend,

"You're in good hands, Pete!"

She winked and then walked out of the room.

"OK, Reverend Peters, we are going to take you down to the Cath lab."

A nurse began to unlock the wheels on the exam table while others disconnected him from the monitors and laid the IV bag on the bed next to him. Another nurse with a clipboard walked beside him and explained many things he received with a nod but not with much comprehension.

"Do you understand everything I shared with you, Reverend Peters?"

"Yes! But I've already had a heart cath!" the Reverend answered.

"Well, Reverend Peters, they're ordering another one."

After a series of winding halls and an elevator ride, the crew arrived at the Cath lab. They shifted Rev. Peters onto another exam table. A tall doctor entered the room and immediately took her place next to Rev. Peters.

> "Reverend, my name is Doctor Matthews, and I will be doing your procedure this morning. I'm going to be putting you under a mild sedative."

> "Praise Jesus!" Rev. Peters shouted. "I am finally going to get some sleep!"

The doctor looked perplexed. She had never seen someone so excited about having a heart catheterization.

"Excuse me?" she replied while injecting some medication into his IV.

"Doc, I'm just so happy that you are going to knock me out!"

"Well, Rev. Peters, I'm not so sure this is something worth celebrating. After all, you might be having heart problems."

"I know, and I want you to do the best job you can in figuring out what's causing all this, but if you knew the past couple days I've had . . ."

Darkness.

CHAPTER 14

THE SMELL OF HER

A smell filled Rev. Peters' nostrils as he started to wake from his sleep. It was a floral bouquet, and it was familiar. He continued to lie still, not bringing attention to the fact that he was awake. He needed time to process and think through the first few words he would say. He kept his eyes tightly shut and continued to breathe as if enjoying one of the best moments of sleep in his life. The aroma continued to permeate the room; it was Jenny's perfume. He began to think that she must be there to comfort him since she went to the trouble of spritzing before leaving the house. If she were pissed, she wouldn't have gone out of her way to be so welcoming. He breathed her in thoroughly and remembered all the times that smell, the smell of her, brought him so much joy and pleasure. It wasn't your ordinary scent, and it was finding its way through all of his senses.

He was also listening closely to the way she walked around the room. What was she wearing? The distinctive "click-click" was not the sound of the comfortable shoes she typically wore; it indicated a shoe that required some technique to wear. *High heels!* Rev. Peters thought. Now he knew she wasn't there to scold him but welcome him back with concern but not anger. A slight smile crept across his face, but he immediately squelched it, realizing how much he was enjoying this blind taste test. He still wasn't quite ready to open his eyes. The Reverend needed to consider longer the best approach to entering the world and the encounter with Jenny.

A yawn and a stretch with a warm, "How ya doing, sweetheart?" or, maybe open his eyes and softly say, "Jenny." The only other possibility that came to mind was waking and asking, "What are you doing here?" He quickly discarded that option, realizing that while that might be the way he felt about their relationship, maybe this crisis could bring a new day and new life to their marriage. They were struggling with being married. Rev. Peters wasn't sure what he had to offer to the relationship anymore. After turning fifty, the physical drive just wasn't the same. He found himself wanting to go straight to bed rather than try to force something that wasn't going to be fulfilling for anyone. Back in the day, they couldn't keep their hands off each other, but then a kid, life, and age got in the way. Jenny was also feeling the pressure of pretending they had something that could make it until "life do us part." Communication often focused on their son, Mickey, church, and Jenny's work at the bank. Back in the day, they used to talk about their hopes, dreams, adventures, and future. Now the future had arrived, and it wasn't that exciting. To be honest, both were thinking about ways to escape rather than end well together. It was sad but true.

Several of Rev. Peters' closest friends told him that he needed to talk to his doctor about his aging lack of sexual desire. They shared with him that modern medicine had a whole host of concoctions to bring the "boom" back into the bedroom. Every time they brought it up, the Reverend would turn red and change the subject. It wasn't like he was afraid of sex or thought it was dirty; he just never thought he would be the one needing help with it. While their sex life was dismal and was moving toward hopelessness, Rev. Peters knew there were much deeper issues at play than simply bad or no sex. Both he and Jenny had been moving in different directions for quite some time. Jenny loved the world and all that it had to offer. On the other hand, the Reverend was seriously wrestling with what he called illusions. When they were younger, the physical drives and desires helped perpetuate a certain level of adventure and mystery in their lives. It was something they had in common. They both liked sex with each other. If things were getting boring, stressed, at odds, or the world had become routine, they could always escape into the flesh and find some satisfaction in being together. Now, while sex was still something he desired, it wasn't filling those ever larger gaps.

Rev. Peters had spent countless hours cautioning against the traps of placing too much emphasis on the physical with couples who came to him seeking pre-marriage counseling. Now he was wrestling with it himself. He would tell them, "You have both got to learn to discover the mystery in the other! Strengthen your love by recognizing all the gifts your partner brings to the marriage and spend time adoring them. Listen well, and desire the best for the other, and they will desire the best for you. The sex, well, that's all wonderful, but it isn't the thing that makes a marriage last!" He knew all of this and had preached it his whole life, but the application wasn't there. For as many who came to him wanting to get married, just as many came to him seeking a divorce. In each situation, a gap emerged as the marriage progressed, and they could no longer recognize the person next to them anymore. The origins of such separation have many starting points, but the seed is always in unrealistic expectations. The couple began with the false narrative that God was somehow a divine matchmaker providing them with their perfect partner, or they assumed that over time they could change the imperfections to make them the perfect partner. Often, they never saw growing old coming. Whatever the starting point, unhealthy expectations set upon the other in the relationship eventually grow into some form of resentment and ultimately loss.

Rev. Peters and Jenny both grew up in relatively mainstream evangelical households in the '90s. The evangelical church was having its day conquering the American landscape, selling a Christianity of prosperity and magical blessings. This evangelicalism found incredibly creative ways to sell its message through media. It was personal, political, and violent. The product was built and packaged for consumption. The heavy emphasis on personal salvation made Jesus accessible to everyone and gave the born again individual permission to turn away from some of the more glaring systemic evils in society. "Why do we need to deal with things like racism and human inequity now if Jesus will make it all right when the end comes?" Conservative evangelicalism was more concerned with the escape plan to God's perfect alternate universe than working toward making things better on earth. "Care about the environment? Why? It's all going to be incinerated by God." "Trying to work for peace among all people? Why? There will always be war and rumors of war! And, we're all getting out of here anyway." As long as you have Jesus, everything else will be sorted out and fixed in the life to come if you get there.

The church expanded to employ all platforms and invested enormous budgets in the quality of production. Television, magazines, books, radio, and music all with a "moral" message flooded the streets, communities, and local churches. Who would have ever thought that an apocalyptic theology of a violent end, and the damnation of the majority of all the world's people, would have become so popular?

For those who maintained purity and obedience to God, there would be an unimaginable blessing. But Hell awaited those who rebelled and never received God! Music held a heavy influence amongst the teenagers of the day, and desperate youth directors and parents who wanted Christianity to be cool again would send them without even considering the content. Despite contrasting theological teachings, churches of every denomination were sending their kids to concerts that espoused incredibly toxic teachings. Although identified by its stylistic categories throughout the ages, the Christian subcategory of music was now determined by religious preferences. From the "Jesus Movement" of the '70s to the adaptation of modern genres that emerged, Christian music began to flood the market and bring its message to the world, and they were prevailing. Not only was it influencing the arts but even more horrifying, politics.

Within this Conservative evangelical world view, the goal of perfection was elevated as the highest standard. Sure, everyone was dirty scum worthy of condemnation to hell, but once you met Jesus, the ideals and goals changed. "Immediate sanctification" was the term several youth directors used at Bible studies that Rev. Peters used to attend. He had no idea at that time what they were talking about, but he knew whatever it was, it was "immediate." No one talking about all this "God-ordained" language would ever say an unhealthy perfectionism drove the teaching, but it did. Rev. Peters and Jenny grew up in that Christian cultural moment through which God was the divine puppet master, and everything was in line with his sovereign guidance—even the person you were going to marry. One pastor at their college used to preach, "There are no divine mistakes, and nothing is left to chance! God has foreordained all that is to happen, and you're just lucky if you're amongst the ones to be accounted for!"

Jenny and Rev. Peters met at a Christian college where the young students were constantly reminded that maintaining purity would bring them in line with God's will and the perfect person God had intended for them. Young women were asked to pray and ask God to reveal their ideal companion to them. They were encouraged to imagine what that relationship would be like, and were told it would be beautiful. What they didn't tell them was that these extremely horny, sexually repressed young men who had been identified as their perfect partners would be fondling, groping, and having sex with them every moment they could get. Which, for the most part, probably wasn't what they were imagining. Young men, well, they were told that their perfect gift would be revealed and unwrapped on their wedding day, and then they could do whatever they wanted. "Whatever they wanted!" This meant that fondling, groping, and a wild variety of sexual acts were waiting to be revealed to these young men, just like what those women demonstrated in their porn magazines.

Then there was the tragedy of those who were born of a different orientation. Whether that be gender identity or attraction, if ever it was revealed a person liked the same sex or felt they were born in the wrong body, you were immediately whisked away to get the demon of homosexuality cast out, and the "gay prayed away!" Countless Christian Gay Camps were established all over the country, and particular organizations were formed to help guide those bound by homosexual lust to experience conversion. Conversion therapies were also offered in most conservative evangelical churches or counseling centers with the premise that same-sex attraction was a sin and "Jesus could make them right again." This therapy never worked, and at one point, the most significant conversion therapy centers in the United States shut down and acknowledged the inefficacy of their programs and the enormous harm it had caused those who were encouraged to suppress their true identity. Many of the young people caught up in this toxic teaching and movement ended up forcing themselves to live a lie and convinced themselves that they should play the part of a straight person. They accepted the lie that God doesn't make mistakes, and being gay is a mistake. Others were excommunicated from churches, called abominations, and heralded as demons. The result of these teachings didn't bring about healing, wholeness, and new life. It only resulted in more broken people, broken marriages, and even suicide. Those who were strong enough in their faith could find healthy affirming congregations to be a part of and even thrived in their faith. Many others turned away from the established church and found community with those similar to themselves.

It was an unrealistic, overly romanticized notion of divine game playing, which ultimately led to thousands of disastrous lives and abusive marriages. If you're told the person you're going to marry is perfect, what a surprise it is when they aren't. When the marriage ceremony is all about arriving at perfection, it leaves nothing for the journey ahead. Marriage is not about perfection but an openness to the beauty of human imperfection. The marriages most likely to last grow in the mystery of the "other" and find delight in the "other." People grow in love; they never arrive there. Rev. Peters knew all of this, yet he and Jenny were in an unhealthy marriage, and he didn't know how they could make it better.

The smell of her was so much a part of the room that now he could barely notice the scent any longer. Listening carefully, Rev. Peters reclaimed his senses from his more profound thoughts; he also noticed that the noise from her shoes had stopped. He assumed that meant she was sitting down or, worse, standing over his bed. If she was over his bed, her presence there would startle him, so the Reverend considered whether he should roll over on his side to transition from darkness and his mind to the well-lit room and Jenny. He also didn't want to shift in his bed because he knew that might trigger Jenny's response, and he wanted to get in the "first word." In the distance, he could faintly hear the voices and commotion of those walking by his room in the hallway. The only other noise he heard was the constant beeping of whatever machine he was hooked up to. *I'm just going to say her name*, he told himself as he slowly began to count backward to open his eyes. *Here we go . . . 10, 9, 8, 7, 6, 5 . . .*

As he counted down, the more nervous he became. He remembered a nurse telling him during one of his many hospital visits with church members that nothing raises a person's blood pressure more than the visit of their spouse. He often chuckled when he visited a church member and their spouse was in the room at the same time. He would glance at the blood pressure monitor to notice if he could see any change.

... *4, 3, 2, 1* ... Rev. Peters made it to 1, but the name just wouldn't come out. He tried, but he was such a wimp when it came to confrontation; he would prefer just avoiding Jenny! Realizing that he needed to get this confrontation out of the way, he slowly opened his eyes and immediately squinted as the light blurred his sight. No one was standing over him, so he mustered,

"Jenny?"

"Who's Jenny?" a voice replied.

CHAPTER 15

PICASSO

"Well, well? If it ain't our good man Pete waking from the dead!" Pico exclaimed, with a flare only she could exhibit without it feeling like an act.

As the Reverend slowly turned to look at who was sitting in the room, he pondered how long Pico had been sitting there. It was her perfume that woke him and her scent that got him thinking about sexual things.

"What are you doing here, Pico?" Rev. Peters offered with a bold but direct statement.

"I'm here because I care about you, Pete! We all care about you. You're part of us now, and we don't let anyone hang low by themselves. Margret watched you for a while, but then the word got out to all of us on the other side. Dough swung by in the middle of the night, and then I made my way here early this morning."

"Where is Jenny?"

"Oh, she's fine. Margret sent her home about a couple of hours ago to try to get some rest. It appears . . ."

"Why is she not here?"

"Well, Pete, she was here, but I don't think you need to be concerning yourself about that at the moment. She's coming back."

The Reverend was befuddled. He was hoping it was Jenny he would wake up to and not Pico.

"Where did you get that perfume?"

"It's my favorite, and I have been wearing it ever since I made the change."

"That's exactly the stuff my Jenny wears!"

Pico raised an eyebrow and gently cradled her chin in her open hand, "Well, your Jenny's got good taste! It's called—"

"Moondust!" Rev. Peters stated, "I buy it for her every year."

"Every year?" Pico looked at him curiously.

Rev. Peters returned to his back and stared up at the white, tiled ceiling suspended above him.

"So, How long have you been here, Pico?"

"I've been here for the past three hours, and I must say I'm getting a little hungry."

"What time is it? And, how long have I been out?"

"It's 9:03 a.m., and you've been sleeping a long time."

"What!?" the Reverend shot up in his bed.

"Careful now, Pete! You don't want to irritate anything!"

Rev. Peters was confused. The doctor told him that the sedative would wear off within hours after the procedure, but obviously, that wasn't the case.

"Is there something majorly wrong? Do I have heart problems? Why was I asleep for so long?"

Pico shifted her legs in the chair and gracefully crossed them in a new direction. Pico was elegant and moved like a woman who'd been practicing for the runway her whole life.

"I know very little, Pete, and, honestly, I think it should be your wife that gives you all the news."

"Tell me. We are, after all, family now!" Pete responded in a snarky tone.

"OK! You're fine. Overly stressed and in need of a vacation."

Rev. Peters allowed his shoulders to release a little with Pico's affirmations that he was OK.

"And?" the Reverend questioned.

"And, you need to take a break from the church and spend some time in therapy."

"And?" the Reverend offered a final inquiry.

"And, you shouldn't be running around town with a bunch of crazy people you don't even know until all hours of the night."

"So let me get this straight. My heart is fine, and I am only stressed."

"Yep!" Pico responded.

"I am also not supposed to be hanging out with you people?"

Pico smirked and then politely coughed out, "Whoever said that?"

Still a bit confused, while somewhat relieved, Rev. Peters asked, "So why did I sleep so long?"

Pico shifted her legs once again and placed her hands on both sides of the chair. "Because you were fuckin' tired!"

Rev. Peters pondered all he had heard for a moment and still thought it was ridiculous. His long nap was related to stress, days of complete sleeplessness, arrests, and a collard diet. Yet, he was content with the verdict because stress was curable. He sat up in the bed and shifted his legs around, dangling them off the side. He was dressed in a new hospital gown, and while he was no longer wearing the terrible clothes he arrived in, he still was not completely clean.

"What a frickin' crazy few days! I haven't had this much adventure for a long time!"

Pico smiled, "Oh, you're gonna have a lot more!"

"More? I've already been to 'the other side' and—"

"Now you wait a minute Pete! You walked across town once, spent a few hours in a new neighborhood, and got to know only a handful of people. You ate Ma Green's collards, experienced one Gathering, found your way back to the hospital from whence you came, and think you've been to the Other side? You don't know shit, and if you think this is a game, you have another think coming! Every person who has made the warehouse district their home has been fully beaten down, broken, and abused in one way or another—their lives held together because the Breath and depth of the Spirit drew them to a place where, for the first time in their lives, they no longer had to pretend, try to fit in, and play the game of the privileged.

"Those who had been abandoned, excluded, banished, and cast aside all found a home with each other. They were able to embrace a belonging bigger than themselves. They were able to receive that in ways those caught up in the illusion of material success cannot comprehend. It takes humility, dammit! Humility and a casting away of the pride and systems that seek to preserve power. Those who have made their way to join us have no strings attached; they are free, and they know they are loved. Not because any one of us is perfect, or we have some super leaders that have the charisma to make for change, but because we all see ourselves as the change. And, that shit never ends! You have just skimmed the surface, my good brother; hell, we all have! It's relationships, and that is the work of a lifetime, and maybe even more if what I read in a novel once is true."

Rev. Peters had no idea how to respond to Pico's outburst and immediately felt that he should have just kept his mouth shut. He found himself staring at the floor and feeling shame. Pico was right. He didn't have an experience anything like those new friends he met just a few days before. He was invited into their world, just as he was, with all his privilege and position, without judgment, and no strings attached. Oh, except that he was a part of this great new beginning everyone kept referencing but never stopped to define. He slowly lifted his head to meet Pico and looked deliberately into her eyes before speaking again.

"I'm sorry, Pico. I didn't mean to downplay or belittle all the good people and things going on through the Others."

Pico stared right back at him and slowly spoke, "I forgive you. There's a lot of work to do!"

Rev. Peters got up out of the hospital bed, stretched, and, even though he was connected to tubes and cables, felt taller and, to his amazement, restored. Once he got the blood moving a bit, he plopped down in the other chair in the room beside Pico. The jubilant transformation almost made Pico feel uncomfortable. The Reverend was now invading Pico's space by sitting so close.

"So, Pico, tell me about yourself. Who are you, and how did you end up with the Others?"

Pico was hoping Rev. Peters' wife would walk through the door at that moment, but she wasn't granted a way out of answering his questions. She pressed her hands into the arms of the chair as if to stand up, but then slowly allowed her body to slip back into the cushions supporting her.

"You want to know about me, do you? Well, I guess I can share. It's a long story and one you've probably never heard before."

The Reverend squirmed a bit to get comfortable and then replied, "Shoot!"

"Okay. I won't bore you with the details, so the short version is this: I grew up in a home in the suburbs with two parents who loved each other, and a brother and a sister. I am the oldest child in the family. We were raised in the church and spent more time at the church than we did at home. Every night was a revival, study, prayer service, worship opportunity, and fellowship event. The church was our life, and my family was fully committed to it. I sang in the choir and assisted the pastor in the service. I would light candles, read scripture, and help in any way I could.

"My momma told me it was a blessing to be asked and even more to serve. I could also preach. The pastor would often get to the middle of his sermon, and in a 'full-on Holy Spirit moment,' hand the mic over to me to 'bring a word.' I knew the Bible and could quote the scriptures like no one else. My poor younger brother wasn't quite as adept in memorizing the Holy Word and was jealous of all the attention I would draw to myself. In so many words, I was the honored child amongst my siblings and the other kids at church. And, then I became a teenager."

Pico tucked her leg under her and turned more toward her audience in preparation for a shift in the story. Rev. Peters was riveted.

"When I was younger, I always knew something was different about me, but I always attributed it to my intelligence. I wasn't like the other kids and had no interest in some of the other little boys' games. By the time I reached puberty, the difference had started to become clear to me. While I was a boy in all my parts, I wasn't a boy inside. At first, I thought I might be gay, but the more I considered my feelings and image of myself, I knew it was more complicated than that. So, I suppressed those feelings as best I could and played the part. But that was tolerable for only so long.

"I was a woman, and while my parents were away, I would wander into my mother's closet and try on her clothes. Those moments made me feel free, like I was who I was supposed to be. As soon as I would hear the sound of the car or my siblings coming home, I would strip off the clothes and carefully place them back in the closet so nobody would ever know . . . until one day when I didn't strip them off fast enough. Everyone was out of the house, and I told my parents I wasn't feeling good, so they would leave me alone. Once I felt the coast was clear, I immediately went to my mother's closet and put on the full wardrobe. The family was going to be gone for a while, attending a revival service. Those things could last for days. I stood in front of the mirror and admired my feminine self. What always seemed funny to me is that I never viewed this as playing dress-up, but rather being who God had made me.

"Then, unexpectedly, I heard the car pull back up into the driveway. I tried to strip the clothes off quickly, but in my hurry to remove the undergarments, I tripped and fell face-first into the floor. It was too late. My father had come back for his coat and was standing in the door. He grabbed me by the neck and pulled me to my feet. 'What in the hell are you doing? Are you some kind of sissy now?' he shouted. I tried to answer, but the words wouldn't come out. 'Answer me!' Nothing came. 'I said answer me!' he growled at me. My father threw me to the ground and kicked me in the gut while yelling, 'Ain't no son of mine gonna be found alive wearing women's clothing!' He took off his belt and began beating me. With every lash, he would scream, 'You're a Christian, damn it! You're no fairy! I'm going to beat this demon right out of you!' By the time he finished, all I could do was lay there in the agony of the pain. I didn't dare cry. I sucked it up. I wasn't going to let him see me weak."

Rev. Peters' mouth was open and could feel within him every bit of the story. Pico had tears welling up in her eyes but maintained her composure.

"So, Pete, you want me to keep going?"

The Reverend felt ill-equipped for this, clueless of where to start, but offered his best response, "Wow, Pico. I only want you to share with me what is comfortable for you. You've offered more than I would have ever disclosed, and I am sure this brings back painful memories."

Pico looked gently at the Reverend, "There are a few more things I'd like to share. But, some will have to wait until another time."

Now, Rev. Peters was hoping that his wife Jenny would be running late. He wanted to hear more about Pico's life and realized this could take some time.

"If you have more to share, please, share!"

Pico shifted around again in her chair, but this time took a more confident position—leg crossed again with elegance and class, her hands propped on her knee in a tasteful but 'Don't mess with me!' fashion.

"I left home at seventeen, but the details on that part of the story are probably for another time. Before my departure, my parents sent me to a wide variety of camps, pastors, prophetesses, and counselors, all trying to pray the demons away. That built more resentment, and the real tragedy is that I believed I was damaged goods and that God didn't want me, let alone love me!" A tear escaped Pico's eyes at this point and streamed down her cheek.

"I left quietly, in the middle of the night, while everyone was asleep. I went down to the bus station with the only money I had and bought a ticket for the next bus out of town. It was a ticket to New York City. New York was a mixed blessing. To make a long story short, I was homeless for a while. It was horrifying living on the streets, and I did things for money that I'm not proud of. I made a few friends though some of my friends didn't make it. Two were murdered, one died of hunger, and others just disappeared. But, eventually I found community and one day a tall, beautiful light brown woman stopped me, looked me in the eyes, and asked if I needed a mother. I was saved.

"In New York, there were other misfits like me, and they all found refuge in each other. I was given a place to stay and encouraged to grow into the fullness of all God intended me to be. There were parties, balls, and support. The love we shared for each other and the desire to see each other succeed was incredible. Sure, we hated each other from time to time, but at the end of the day, we all knew what it was like to be 'cast out' and 'brought back.' It is the first place I experienced a truly loving community. It was the church, not like the institution, but actually. What I also regained was my faith. Faith in the Human One. Not the God of uniformity and conformity but of unity and non-conformity. It was also the community that was able to see the giftedness in me and encouraged me to pursue those gifts. When I look back at my time in Mothers House, I realize there was no judgment on me as a person but only support for my gifts. If you wanted to make Mother upset, not using the gifts God gave you was the way to do it! Mother wouldn't put up with destructive behaviors, but it was never a battle against identity, just a celebration of living into one's fullness."

Pico paused for a moment and stood up. She straightened her skirt and stretched her arms way above her head. She was very tall and, when stretched out, was quite intimidating.

The Reverend shook his head, "I have heard about communities like the one you described, but I've never actually met someone who experienced it! It's fascinating to me how you survived and thrived. Please keep going, if you have the time."

Pico walked across the room to the built-in desk on the far side of the room. She pushed aside some paperwork and sat down on the edge.

"Giftedness. That's what we celebrated. In the house we had incredible dancers, singers, and cooks. Others were book smart and good with finances. All of us loved competing together at the balls as the best-looking dames in New York. I wasn't completely sure what my main gift was and pondered whether maybe I was just average. Mother used to look at me and say, 'You just keep exploring, and something will rise to the surface.' I had gotten a job down around the corner from our apartment at a local coffee shop. It was the first place I was my complete self, amidst a public who didn't completely know how to handle a six-foot-six woman. I could tell when a customer was uncomfortable and, I'll confess, I'd shit around with them. The amazing thing is that the longer I worked there and got to know people, the more I began to feel like I fit in.

"You know, the ultimate dream of any child who wrestles with gender identity is to be accepted for the gender they know to be their truth, and I felt that at the coffee shop. On Tuesdays, a man would come into the shop and order an Americano. While waiting for his coffee, he would set up a table easel next to the window facing the street. He would bring a little blank canvas each week and a few tubes of paint and sit there while drinking his coffee, painting what he experienced in the street that day. I watched in amazement. I was fascinated by how he worked the brush, mixed the paint, and interpreted what he saw.

"As the weeks moved on, I got to know the man; his name was Roger. He would let me sit next to him as he painted, and he answered the questions I asked. I learned about his life, his wife who had passed away, and his fears and hopes. Roger and I were buddies. Early in our relationship, Roger asked me what my name was, and all I could offer was the name I took after leaving home. I was born James, and when I left, I took on Jamie. When I told him my name, he just shook his head, 'Nope! You're no Jamie. I sense something much more meaningful than that. Something that tells us who you are and how you can change the world.' I brushed him off as a dreamer and never really thought much about the conversation. Then one day he came into the shop, set up his supplies, asked me to come over, and told me to paint."

A knock at the door interrupted Pico's story, much to Pete's dismay.

"Rev. Peters?" a voice shouted from outside, "Is it OK if I come in?"

"What's this for?" Rev. Peters responded.

"I'm here to check your vitals and get you ready to head home. I called your wife, and she is on her way to get you."

The Reverend wasn't ready to go home; he wanted to hear more of Pico's story.

"I need a little more time. Can you give me fifteen to twenty minutes?"

"OK, but we are gonna need to get you out of here pretty quickly."

The door to the room remained shut, and Pete and Pico had a little more time to finish the story.

"Tell me more about your name, and what did you paint?"

"Patience now, Pete! You can't rush a good story."

The Reverend shifted and settled again in his chair. Pico remained seated on the desk. This time she had shuffled further on the desk, allowing her feet to dangle just above the ground. *Wow! She had super long legs.* Rev. Peters noted.

Pico continued, "I sat down in front of the little canvas and asked Roger, 'What in the hell am I supposed to do?' Roger handed me a brush, squirted a few colors on the palette, and told me to paint what I saw and felt. The second I touched the brush to the paint, I knew I could do it. Not just paint but see. See beyond shape and color to the story unfolding before me. As I looked out the window, I saw a young woman leaning against a pole with her head hanging down. You could tell she was sad, and as I focused on her, everything else on the street disappeared. And it happened! I was painting, and within an hour, I had captured the beauty and the pain of that young lady. Roger looked at the painting and smiled. Then he looked me in the face and said, 'Your name is Picasso! For just as he once said, *Everything you can imagine is real!*' So, from that day on, I was Picasso or Pico for short."

A million more questions were flying through Rev. Peters' head. He wanted more time and to hear more of Pico's story, but he knew at any minute Jenny would be walking through that door, and he would finally have to return home. He sat for a moment with that last thought, ". . . *have to return home? Home? Where is my home?*

He snapped out of it and dove back in with more questions for Pico, "So what happened after that? What happened to Roger? What . . ."

Pico laughed, "I've never really had anyone be this into my story! . . . OK, so, when I finished the painting, Roger told me that whatever I do, always find someone to give it away to. So, I got up off my seat and walked across the street to the young woman. She was sitting down on the sidewalk, and as I approached, I could tell she was afraid. I asked her where she was from and how long she had been out on the streets? She told me that she had left home, was alone, and had run away. I handed her the painting and told her that I had painted this earlier and wanted her to have it. She took the painting and held it up to her face. Tears were rolling down her cheeks, and she gazed at the girl in the painting. 'She's so alone!' the girl said softly. 'Yep. I replied. Would you like to come home with me and meet my family?' The girl was shocked by my invitation, and maybe overjoyed that she wouldn't be alone anymore. I picked up her bag and grabbed her arm, and we both went back to the coffee shop. As we walked through the door, I noticed that Roger was no longer there. 'Yo, Jon, have you seen Roger?' I asked. Jon was too busy putting mugs away to respond, but all Roger's stuff was completely gone—all but one thing. Sitting on the chair was a canvas sitting facedown. On top of the canvas was an envelope.

I opened the envelope, and there was a check and a note that read, 'Dear Picasso, Please take this gift and buy the supplies you need to paint the world and use the rest to go to school.' The check was for $75,000, made out to cash, and in the memo: Picasso. I couldn't believe what I was seeing! I never would have imagined anything like this could have happened to me! After all, I was told I was damaged goods. After settling myself a bit, standing alongside my new friend Nila, I picked up the painting. It was me, and I was beautiful! After that day I never saw Roger again and I found my gift. I am an artist!"

CHAPTER 16

NO PLACE LIKE HOME

"Wow! What a story!"

The Reverend was completely captivated by Pico's experience.

"New York, community, giftedness, $75k, and a new life. It's just amazing how it all came together, and you are such a good storyteller."

Pico blushed a bit and couldn't look Rev. Peters in the eye.

"A life story is easy to tell," she dismissed in humility.

The Reverend straightened, "So, what happened next? What did you do to grow as a painter? What did you do with the money? And, how in the hell did you end up with the Others?"

Pico hopped off the desk and gracefully landed on the floor. Her heels made a unified sound as they hit the tile floor at the same time.

"Well, Pete, I believe it's time for me to go."

"No!" The Reverend responded, "Just a little more. Please!"

Pico was outwardly starting to get annoyed with the Reverend.

"Let's save it for another day . . . and, Pete, we *will* have another day."

Rev. Peters relented, and his reluctant submission to her departure was reflected as his shoulders fell and his demeanor shifted from exuberant to crestfallen. He begged for a concession.

"Just one more question, and then you can go. How did you meet Dough?"

As Pico reached for the door handle, she turned her head, throwing her long dark hair over her shoulder.

"I met Dough at Harvard."

"What?" Rev. Peters shouted, still unable to comprehend Dough's time there, and now awestruck to learn of Pico's as well.

Pico had planned to leave that hanging as she made a hasty exit. She flung the door open to find Jenny about to come in. Jenny looked at the six-foot-six woman and was not at all sure what to make of her.

Pico said with guile, "You can come in, ma'am. I'm finished."

She pushed past Jenny and moved quickly down the hall. Jenny was left standing at the door for a moment.

"Michael?" she queried with a single word as she looked over her shoulder in the direction of Pico's departure.

"Hey! Come on in!"

Jenny walked into the room cautiously, as if other surprises were lurking around the corner.

"Michael, who was that?"

The Reverend squirmed a bit but made every effort to keep from making too big a deal out of Pico's visit, as he knew there was a lot to unpack.

"Oh, that was Pico. She volunteers to check in on patients to see if everything is all right."

"Oh?" Jenny replied with suspicion. "That is one of the tallest women I have ever seen."

"Yep!" The Reverend confirmed, "She is a very tall lady!" and then, in an attempt to shift the attention away from a difficult topic, he said, "It is so good to see you! What an incredible, crazy few days I have had!"

As he moved in to embrace her, she pushed him away.

"You need to take a shower before we start hugging each other. I'm glad you're OK, but it might be a good idea to clean up a little more before we go."

Rev. Peters wasn't shocked by her response; after all, he'd had little more than a sponge bath for days. Jenny grabbed a seat in the chair where he'd found Pico when he awoke. Rev. Peters noticed the striking differences between Pico's presence and Jenny's. Jenny was small in stature and rather plain. She never wore any color and kept her hairstyle and makeup rather conservative. While she wasn't much for being a pastor's wife, she certainly dressed like one. Pico was bold, vibrant, colorful, and hardened by the world. Pico wasn't afraid to be herself, and everything about her was an expression of who she was and wanted to be. Jenny's appearance came across like she was trying to hide something, or at least blend in. Conversely to Pico's boldness, Jenny didn't want the world to recognize her. Instead, she allowed herself to disappear. Rev. Peters retook his seat on the bed and continued to look at Jenny, and wondered what was bottled up inside.

"I'm sorry, Jenny, for scaring you like this. I'm not sure what got into me, but I needed to go!"

"Go where?" Jenny asked, baffled by her husband's behavior.

"Well, that's a long story, and I had better take your advice and get in a shower before we head home. Did you bring me any clothes?"

Jenny held up a shopping bag with the Reverend's clothes and toiletries in it.

"I would have brought a suitcase but figured we were only a few miles away from home."

He could tell that Jenny was hurting inside, wondering what this departure, journey, and crazy medical emergency was all about. He sympathized with how she felt and couldn't imagine what he would have gone through if she had been the one who disappeared.

Rev. Peters took the bag and reached into the bathroom and turned on the water in the shower. It quickly became hot; the steam billowed to the ceiling and began to cloud the mirror just inside the door. He closed the door behind him and stripped off the gown before stepping into the stall. The water pressure shooting out of the head was forceful and pounded his skin, running down his head, over shoulders to his torso and legs. He could feel the water in ways he had never experienced before. He breathed in the steam from the water, taking it deep into his lungs, tasting a hint of the minerals and chemicals the water had picked up along its journey to his body. The shower itself had an industrial design, lined with stainless steel to allow for it to be disinfected quickly and efficiently. There were also several shower heads, rails, and access points that could meet the needs of a wide variety of patients. He picked up the soap and held it to his nose. It was lavender. He drew in the cleansing aroma and then proceeded to lather his body. Shampoo would follow, and as the soap all ran away, he thought, *Maybe today will be a normal day. I'm gonna let everything rinse away.* When he had finished, he grabbed a towel, which was satisfyingly starched and scratchy. It was better than any cheap hotel room towel, each of the fibers abrasively brushing against his skin, making him feel fully cleansed. He was enjoying every moment of every experience, and his senses were heightened more than any time he could ever remember. Maybe the intensity was related to gratitude or appreciation after having gone without for so long. He considered, *I can't ever remember appreciating a shower quite this much before.* Once he was dry, he moved over to the mirror that was now completely fogged up. He wiped the mirror with his towel, providing just enough of a glimpse of himself to complete the act of getting his shit together. He slowly pulled on his clothes, combed his hair, put on his deodorant, and straightened his eyebrows that were constantly calling for attention the older he got. As he opened the door, another scent waltzed in with the hospitalized air: Moondust.

Jenny was still sitting in the chair on the other side of the room. It didn't look as though she had moved at all since the Reverend went to take a shower.

"So!" Rev. Peters announced, "Are we ready to head home?"

Suddenly, Jenny started to cry. "Where were you, and why would you not tell me about it? I was worried sick! First, you end up in the hospital for potential heart problems! Then, you left of your free flippin' will with some stranger. Are you fuckin' crazy! And, not even a call, or text, or message . . . nothing! I am so hurt and pissed and disappointed in you. Then, you're brought back to the hospital looking like a homeless person after being picked up by the police, Tased, and experiencing more chest pain. I . . . I . . . I don't even know what to do with all of this!"

Rev. Peters knew this was coming, so he slowly took his seat back on the edge of the bed.

"Wow! You know a lot more than I thought! How did you find all this out?"

Jenny looked up with her deep brown eyes, "Ms. Margret told me. I was here right after they brought you back from the procedure, but you were completely out, and there wasn't much but rest that would have revived you. Margret came in to sit with me, and I just spilled everything out on her. She reassured me that you had learned your lesson and that the days ahead would be better."

"What?" Rev. Peters questioned, "Margret said that? Ms. Margret is a part of it all. She's one of the Others! Listen, Jenny, this adventure is more complicated than just sowing my oats or having a mid-life crisis. This moment has a call and purpose that I find undeniable. I wasn't forced, but I definitely felt compelled to go. My life——"

"That's exactly it! It's all about *your* life Michael; but what about mine? What about Mickey's? I don't think you care about us. You work all the goddamn time and don't ever do anything fun with us. Maybe I want to run free all over town on crazy adventures! Maybe I want out of this boring existence! Maybe I want more out of life!"

The Reverend just bowed his head. There wasn't going to be a way to reach her in this moment.

"Let's go, Jenny. Let's get out of here and head back home. When we get there and have a good meal, I will share all the details of what happened over these last few days and what is still to come."

Margret and the nurse assistant came to the room with the wheelchair with perfect timing to execute his request.

"I don't need that." Rev. Peters commented.

"It's hospital policy. Sorry boss," the young man replied.

"Rev. Peters, it sure was good having you and nice to meet your lovely wife," Margret said, handing a tissue to help her in trying to cover her tears.

As she helped the Reverend into the chair she instructed, "You two get some rest and make sure you listen well to each other tonight or tomorrow, or whenever you talk about the events of these days. And, you need to promise me you will talk."

Both of them nodded and the young man wheeled him out of the room. He remembered that night with Dough and the adrenaline that rushed through his body as they made their escape. Rev. Peters wondered what Dough was doing right then and when he would see him again. He contemplated Ma Green's statement at the end of his visit—that they would be moving into his church. Rev. Peters had a lot to process and even more to share with Jenny. Then he remembered his church. What was he going to say to them? The elevator doors opened, and the nurse assistant rolled him in and stopped in the center. He was facing the back wall of the elevator and Jenny took her place beside him. The elevator groaned into motion and down they went. Rev. Peters was dragged back out of the elevator and turned toward the lobby doors. Jenny told the assistant she could run to get their car and pull around to the entrance. The assistant told her they would be waiting just inside the doors. Just as Jenny walked out, Dough walked in!

"Come on! We need to go!"

Rev. Peters almost flipped out of his chair, and the assistant didn't know what to do.

"Do you know this man?" the assistant asked.

"Yes!" the Reverend answered, "But, I am not going anywhere but home!"

"Come on, Pete! Another adventure!"

"Not for a long while! And it would be best if you got out of here. My wife is getting the car. If she comes back and finds me gone, I'll never be allowed back home. I'm not going anywhere!"

Dough looked at him with a slight smile, "No place like home, eh, Pete. Where is that, by the way?"

Rev. Peters stood up out of the wheelchair and got right up in Dough's face.

"I am going home with Jenny, and you are going to leave me alone."

Dough looked right back at the Reverend and began to laugh.

"I'm just pullin' your chain, Pete! I just wanted to say goodbye and let you know I'm glad you're OK."

Rev. Peters face turned beet red, "You are a total asshole! Don't you ever play that game with me again."

Dough pulled himself back from the Reverend a bit, "I'm sorry, Pete. I thought we were closer than that. Go home and get some rest. Tell Jenny the whole story and regain some of your strength. There is a lot more to come, and the Others are going to be moving—"

Jenny pulled the car up and laid on the horn to demonstrate her impatience. Dough shifted and proceeded to walk down one of the side halls, leaving Rev. Peters without the one thing he was eager to hear. He turned in the direction of Dough, who was now yards away,

"Wait! When are they coming?"

Dough turned and shouted, "Soon!"

Jenny unlocked the doors, and the nurse assistant opened the door for the Reverend. The car was relatively new and still had that new leather smell. It was the smell of success and stability.

"No more walking!" Rev. Peters sighed.

"What did you say?" Jenny asked.

"Oh, nothing. I was just saying I am tired of walking."

"Who was that man you were talking with? Was that one of the Others? Or, was that just another homeless person you were making friends with?"

"That was Dough, and he is a part of the Others. He's the one who asked me to go with him and walked me across town to the other side. He is the one who came to get me and bring me to the Gathering, which is a collection of misfits from all walks of life. That super tall lady you saw leaving when you arrived this morning . . . she is one of the Others as well. Ms. Margret . . . also with the Others. They brought me to them to let me know—"

Jenny interrupted, "That you are the chosen one and going to help liberate all the poor and oppressed people of the world. You have magic powers that exceed all the normal pastoral super-powers, and they need you to help save them. That the end is coming, and you have been chosen above all other god-fearing men to lead it all!"

Rev. Peters was taken aback by her snarkiness, "Nope," he calmly responded, "but, they're moving into our church."

There was silence for a few minutes after the Reverend's last comment. Then Jenny opened up.

"So let me get this straight: They took a sick man out of the hospital and dragged him across town to proclaim that they had decided that they were going to move into our church. What in the Sam Hill is that all about?"

Rev. Peters continued, "They have been called by the Creative, which is their word for God, and have received a vision from the Breath, which is their word for the Spirit, to embody the truth of the Human One, which is their language for Jesus, to inhabit those places that need liberation and usher in the new beginning."

Jenny was perplexed. "They're nuts! You followed a few nuts across town, and they are trying to draw you into their cult and steal our church."

"No, I don't think they're nuts. They've got their shit together!"

"What does that mean, Michael? What the hell does that mean? You're the pastor of a church. You've got people to care for. You have a salary, a place to live, a pension, and health insurance. You're successful and one of the few that survived the dark years when churches were all collapsing after the pandemic. Sure, it will never be the same, but can't you just ride it out? Why do you feel the need to be a hero? Nothing you're going to do will change anything! Come on, Michael, have some common sense!"

The Reverend looked down at his lap and thought deeply about what Jenny was saying. She was afraid; he was scared.

"I'm not trying to be the hero. Hell, I didn't ask for this! I went because Dough asked, and I felt I was missing something. Sure, it might have been a waste of time, but earlier that day, just before I passed out at the church, I was thinking about how empty my life in ministry has been over the past ten years. I have just been going through the motions and fulfilling my duty to maintain the institution, its buildings, and the budget. Years ago, when everything hit the fan, and the church found itself confronting the truths of her sins, many people left because of their political allegiances and self-centered attitudes about faith.

"Our brick and mortar made it through on the endowments handed down to preserve such an institution. Many of my colleagues are now working other jobs for a living or even left the faith. First Church isn't going to make it much longer, and even many of the new incarnations of the church are too homogenized to make any real difference. That's what appeals to me about the Others. They don't care about the frills and are truly free to embody something new. I saw it for myself. As challenging as the journey was for me that day, it brought me a sense of hope. That's all I got! And, all they are asking of me is to open the doors of the church and let them in."

Jenny shifted in her seat as she pulled into their neighborhood. Rev. Peters could tell she was uncomfortable with all of his comments.

"It was right here that I got Tased!" he blurted out to change the subject.

"You were this close to home?"

"Yep, it was a total nightmare. Hilarious now that I think about it. Before it all happened, I was just walking down the street, enjoying the rain, and thinking, *No place like home.*"

CHAPTER 17

CALL IN THE NIGHT

The Peters' house was modest, but a good size. The neighborhood they lived in had a homeowners' association, which laid out all kinds of rules and regulations about how your lawn should look, what colors you could paint exterior parts of the house, and even what plants you could plant in your yard. The neighborhood also required everyone to decorate for the major national holidays—Christmas, Halloween, and the 4th of July. It was exciting the first couple of years, but then waned into a chore in the years that followed. Jenny and Rev. Peters used to love to celebrate the holidays, but the HOA transformed them into something resembling Scrooge. Their house was made of red brick and had a dark green shingled roof. The windows were large and painted with white trim. The landscaping surrounding the sidewalk to the front door was well kept and included a few little figurines. The front door was large and painted a dark green that matched the roof.

Rev. Peters automatically reached into his pocket for his keys as he approached the front door.

"Damn!" he exclaimed, realizing that he didn't have his keys.

"No worries, I picked your keys up after your hospital break."

Jenny fished her set out of her purse and unlocked the door. Stepping inside, the smell of the Peters caught his nostrils. It was a blend of lasagna, cinnamon candles, and teenage boy.

"We're home!" Jenny cried out in hopes of getting a response.

"I'm back!" the Reverend called to him, hoping for some answer.

As they walked through the foyer, past the dining room, they could see the top of Mickey's head scrunched into the couch. He was playing a video game. Rev. Peters placed his hand on his son's head, and Mickey shrugged to remove it without losing control of the game.

"I'm back!" Rev. Peters announced again.

Without taking his eyes off the screen, Mickey shouted, "Who cares!"

Rev. Peters would have taken that with a grain of salt and written it off to a pubescent teenager on any other day. This time it hurt. He walked around the couch and stood in front of Mickey, then he sat down in the chair opposite him and just watched him play the game.

Mickey's eyes, affixed to the characters on the screen, were set. With every character's movement, his tongue would jet in and out of his mouth. He used his tongue as a form of balance, reminding Rev. Peters of his athletic days. The Reverend was a tongue-wagger too. He stared into his son's eyes and saw his mother. The hews of green and deep brown made them unusually beautiful and mysterious. His hair was thick, curly, and dark brown as well. *What a handsome kid!"* the Reverend thought as he studied him. *I wonder why he is just sitting in here all day. The world is his to claim!* With every move of the game, his leg would twitch, as if throwing it around somehow impacted the events on the screen. He was wholly absorbed. Rev. Peters continued to stare at the kid and wondered what might be going through his head. He thought back to the day Mickey was younger, dependent, and loved being with them. The Reverend remembered all the times they went on trips, laughed, and enjoyed growing up together. He also remembered all the times he said, "Can you wait until later? Not now, son. Maybe we can do that tomorrow."When relational hopes are dashed too many times, other relationships rise to fill the void. He remembered his grandmother always saying, "Idle hands are the devil's toolbox," or, "You are only a gift if you're giving to others," which made him wonder if maybe Mickey's teenage isolation wasn't just Mickey's issue. Deep down inside, he knew that both he and Jenny were culpable for creating such a climate of disconnection, but you never want to admit it. *Hell! I'm a pastor dammit!*

It was over an hour that Rev. Peters stared at Mickey until Jenny broke his thoughts with questions about dinner.

"What do you want to eat? Do you want to throw something together or have it delivered?"

The world shifted drastically in the way meals were prepared and consumed during and after the last health crisis. Grocery stores transformed into meal delivery services. Restaurants focused more on delivering their food, saving money from dining room overhead costs, and being dependent on people showing up. Sure, a few high-end places were able to continue a sit-down dining experience, but they were few and far between. Most meals even came prepared for you. Just warm them up or pop off the lid. One would have thought that after moving through over ten years of radical shift and change that people might return to putting some effort into their lifestyles rather than remaining so dependent on companies and businesses to feed them, but entitlement is a tough demon to cast out.

"I don't know."The Reverend responded, "Let's just have something delivered."

The next question was always the same, "Ok, what do you want?"

"I don't know?"

"What do you want, Mickey?" Silence.

"How about Chinese?"

"No, I had that yesterday."

"Ok, how about barbecue?"

"No, I'm not in the mood for barbecue!"

"Then what do you want?"

"I don't know; what do you want?"

This is how the conversation goes until—almost 99% of the time—Rev. Peters just makes a decision. When addressing their continual indecisiveness regarding what they were going to eat on any occasion, Jenny would always blame the Reverend for never making up his mind. Typically, this would send Rev. Peters into a fury because he was the one always making the final decision. He was also aware that their conversation was born entirely of their privilege. They had a choice to eat whatever they wanted, whenever they wanted.

They finally agreed on Thai food. After ordering, Jenny went back into the kitchen to get out some plates and utensils. Rev. Peters followed her in.

"Are we going to talk about this more?" Rev. Peters inquired.

Jenny set down the silverware and leaned against the counter, "I don't know what else we need to talk about. You had a little fling, and now it's time for us to get back to normal."

The Reverend grabbed her hands and held them tightly, "Everything is not going back to normal. I'm not happy. You're not happy. Our son is a mess. The world sucks, and being the pastor of a church is sucking the life out of me. There is no life here right now! And, something is happening!"

Jenny started to cry and pulled her hands away from the Reverend.

"Are you wanting a divorce? Is that what you are saying?" Jenny shouted and turned back toward the kitchen counter, rubbing her eyes to push away the forming tears.

"No! I don't want a divorce. I want us to be alive again. Enjoy life again. Not just go through the motions. To stop arguing over menial things. And to be involved in things that matter!"

"So what are those things, Michael? Are those things like the indigents you are hanging out with? Is living poor on the street what matters? Is scaring the heal out of a perfectly decent man and asking him to walk across town after passing out what matters? It's like I don't even know you anymore!"

Rev. Peters bowed his head, took a deep breath, and calmly spoke into the situation.

"I love you. I want the best for you and Mickey, but I can't keep on living out the same old, same old. It's like being sucked into the ship. Hell, it's like I'm on the couch so focused on winning and maintaining, that I have forgotten about anyone else. I'm devoid of any fulfillment or life. I'm just being. We're just being!"

Jenny turned quickly, "You listen to me, mister! I like our life, and you've got a home provided for you, health insurance, car payments, a pension, and we are going to need to pay for Mickey's schooling. You must play the game. It's what everybody does. The 'same old, same old' is what we do! It makes our life possible without any problems. Don't you love our life? Don't you love having what you need, getting what you want, going where you want? Don't you like being a pastor and having people look up to you? Isn't this all that life is anyway? You, we, us, we're on the right track. Aren't we?"

The Reverend sighed, and the doorbell rang.

"That was fast!"

He shifted his attention away from the conversation to collect himself enough to be presentable for getting the food. He walked to the door and looked at the video screen. It was a delivery person. He opened the door to a short gentleman wearing a black hoody and supporting a rather long beard and mustache combo.

"Mickey Peters?" the delivery person asked.

"Nope! I'll get him," Rev. Peters replied unequivocally.

He marched right into the living room and ripped the earbuds out of Mickey's ears, and shouted,

"Your *damn* food is here, your *highness*!"

Mickey jumped back, "What the hell? You're an asshole!"

Then he pushed his way past the Reverend and went to the door, grabbed his food, and marched straight to his room.

"I'm the asshole?" Rev. Peters shouted. "That little jerk ordered food without even thinking about us. Why do I even bother? *This* is the goddamned life you want to live? Not an ounce of gratitude, empathy, or compassion. Just feed the fuckin' machine!"

While he raged, Jenny set the table in preparation for the arrival of their food. Rev. Peters simply returned to the chair in the living room opposite the couch.

"My whole family hates me," he grumbled. "They don't get it. And I don't get it either. Maybe I am stuck."

Just then, the doorbell rang again.

"I'll get it!" The Reverend shouted.

He approached the door a second time and looked at the video screen. It was another delivery person. This time the person was rather tall, thin, and possibly female.

"Thai King!" the voice shouted just outside the door.

Rev. Peters opened the door slowly again, almost as if he was worried there might be another surprise.

"You OK, sir?" the delivery person queried.

"Yes, I am. Thank you for bringing our food. How much do I owe you?"

"It's covered," the delivery person explained.

"What? What are you talking about covered? Who covered it?"

"I'm not permitted to divulge that information, sir. Have a good night."

"Wait!" the Reverend shouted, "How about a tip?"

The delivery person turned their head and looked over their shoulder, "It's covered."

As he closed the door with the bag of food in his hand, he wondered who could have done such a thing. He was accustomed to having his meals paid for when they used to go out to dinner a lot. Members of his church, or community, would treat him for all of his excellent work as a pastor. He always appreciated the gift but prided himself on figuring out who was the generous benefactor and would eventually send them a thank you note. This gift was different, though. It was takeout. Who would know him at "Thai King?" Oh well, it was free, smelled delicious, and he was famished.

Jenny and the Reverend had just dished up their plates and sat down at the table when his phone rang.

"Damn it!" he responded. "I'm not going to get it right now. Let's eat!"

Both of them sat at the table in silence. The only noise was the sound of the utensils meeting the plates and their glasses hitting the wood after taking a drink. It was an odd, active kind of silence—a silence that indicated the only thing that mattered about life was eating. The Thai food was excellent and comforting. The tom kha gai soup, full of chicken and coconut milk, smelled of sweetness like new spring grass and its scent rose with the steam from the top of the bowl, wafting up into the sky. Rev. Peters found the soup brought him some peace. He especially appreciated the complexity of the spices and the layers of flavors.

"This is incredible soup!" he stated emphatically to Jenny.

"It's all right," she offered thwarting any enthusiasm he might bring to the evening.

Usually, he was the first one finished with their meal, but he was savoring it on this night. He had just lifted the last spoonful of soup to his lips when the phone rang again. Jenny looked at his phone as she walked into the kitchen.

"You're going to want to get this, Michael. It's Joel."

Joel Newcome was the Church Leadership Chair and responsible for ensuring everything was "running aright," as he always used to say. Rev. Peters always dreaded talking with Joel because there wasn't anything he ever had to say that was encouraging. Joel was his Leadership Chair, but he was a soul suck! The youth director at the church used to say, "If Joel ever attended a children's birthday party, all the balloons would fall straight to the ground!" which got Rev. Peters pondering once again as he walked to pick up his phone. *How did someone like Joel get placed in leadership at the church?* He tried to remember when Joel was asked to serve, but to his surprise, he couldn't recall how it happened. Was it a coup? Maybe he was always the Chair. He couldn't remember, but he always had someone like Joel serving at every church he served as pastor. These were people who never received much respect or place of power in their lives, so they had to take it out by offering their service where gaining control was easy—the church or their homeowner's association. The Reverend took another deep breath and picked up the phone.

"Joel, my good buddy! How are you doing?"

"Well, I'm fine, but it's you I'm concerned about. What's been going on with you this past week?"

Rev. Peters quickly walked outside so Jenny wouldn't hear his conversation. It was a beautiful night out on the front porch. There was a slight, cool breeze indicating that the season was about to make a change. It was typical of pleasantries before the storm. A few days of absolutely perfect weather only to be followed by a downward trend and worsening conditions.

"Well, Joel, I was in the hospital, and now I'm out. The doctors said I was dealing with stress."

"Stress my ass." Joel retorted, "You only work on Sundays! Ha, ha, ha."

"Yes . . .," Rev. Peters wanted to punch him. "I know we pastors have it pretty good. Only dealing with life, death, salvation, souls, crisis, natural disasters, sermons, studies, board meetings, difficult people . . ."

"I get it; you pastors supposedly work hard."

Joel was a business owner in his working life before retiring. He was mildly successful and believed nobody worked harder than he did. When Rev. Peters asked for a renewal leave from the church a few years back, Joel laughed and immediately belittled the good Reverend for being weak! Rev. Peters never took the break, which was an indication that maybe Joel was correct—he was weak.

"So, when are you getting back to work? How are we going to cover the story that you were gallivanting all over town, half-naked with a bunch of homeless people?"

"Now, Joel, I was not gallivanting, nor was I half-naked. I was with some interesting and tremendously gifted people."

"Right!" Joel interrupted. "Listen, Rev, we've got an image to maintain in this community, and you are not helping us bring in new members by not being very professional. I like you, but I hope this is an end of this type of behavior?"

Rev. Peters felt his blood boiling. He was so pissed and wanted to cuss Joel out. He wanted to let him have it and give Joel back some of the pain he was causing at this moment. Joel represented everything wrong with the church. He couldn't believe that someone, anyone, could be so callous and unable to be empathetic. He was always there for Joel, yet all Joel could offer was a judgmental critique in his time of need. All he could focus on was "maintaining our image." What a total jerk!

Rev. Peters finally managed to respond, "I do appreciate you calling to check in on my health Joel. Thank you for caring so much about my family and me. Knowing that the church has leaders like you . . . well, I'm at a loss for words."

"Anytime, Reverend. I'm glad to help keep us moving forward and not becoming disrespectful or disgusting in the community. God knows we need to take care of all those beggars that have been hanging around the church. It just looks tacky, and parents don't want to bring their children to a homeless shelter. By the way. You might consider carrying a gun."

"What?" Rev. Peters replied with shock. "You want me to carry a gun? Are you flippin' nuts!"

"Nope, I just don't want anyone at the church to be a soft target. The last thing we need is for some coward to come in and shoot up the place when we could prevent it. Tough times need tough people willing to make tough decisions!"

At that, Rev. Peters decided it would be best to end the conversation. "Good night, Joel."

"Goodnight," Joel returned, "Let's keep running aright."

Rev. Peters hung up the phone and thought, *What does he think 'running aright' even means?*

With that final thought, he turned out the porch lights and went back inside.

CHAPTER 18

NOTHING

After dinner, Jenny had immediately gotten up from the table, thrown away her plastic dining ware, and headed for the bedroom. Rev. Peters sat down at the table alone and stewed over his conversation with Joel and finding very little space to share his feelings with Jenny. His wife was exhausted, and the past few days had left her feeling empty. Rev. Peters was tired and hoping to participate in the ritual of making up once they settled into bed. Hurriedly he cleaned the table, threw his plastics away, wiped down the table and counter, placed his glass in the sink, and dimmed the kitchen light. He walked down the hall to their room, carefully listening as he passed Mickey's door. Nothing.

As he reached his bedroom, he opened the door only to find Jenny already asleep. He quietly shut the door behind him, and then tiptoed into the bathroom to get himself ready. He was relieved to be home, but it was a stressful place. He slipped out of his clothes, washed his face, and slid between the covers. At first, he just laid on his back to see if there would be any response from Jenny. Nothing. He rolled over on his side, facing her body turned away from him in a semi-fetal position. Extending his arm, the tips of his fingers touched her back.

Her skin was smooth and warm. He gently rubbed her back and ran his fingers in a circular motion. Rev. Peters needed physical contact. Every night they went to bed, he would rub her back to affirm they were still connected. As he gently scratched and rubbed, Jenny just laid there. *Certainly, she feels that,* the Reverend hoped. He rubbed a little more firmly and extended his range from her upper back down to her lower back. He was hoping she might respond, even if it was, "Go to bed, Michael!" Nothing. So he returned to his back, kept his hand on her back, and closed his eyes. Rev. Peters fell asleep quickly.

The Reverend's eyes slowly opened as a strange feeling disrupted his sleep. He rolled over to look at his clock, which read 3:30 a.m. *Holy shit! Why am I awake?* He reached out to touch Jenny once again. Jenny wasn't there. He patted the top of the sheets to make sure she hadn't squirmed to the edge of the bed. Nothing. *Maybe, she's in the bathroom.* Minutes passed, and Jenny didn't return. Then, an hour passed, and still no Jenny. He pondered whether he should get up or not. Maybe she was sick and having some trouble. Or, maybe she was sitting up thinking things over. Rev. Peters didn't believe the string of events over the past few days was enough to lead Jenny to an existential crisis. Sure, she might have been upset he didn't call her, or that he left the hospital without telling her, or that he was talking wacky about the Others, but that was all. He just inconvenienced her a bit and made her worry, but nothing worth getting up in the middle of the night over. The longer he lay in bed, the more suspicious he became.

"Jenny . . .," he quietly whispered as if someone could hear him across the house. Nothing. The Reverend pushed the sheets off and slid on a pair of shorts. He looked in the master bathroom. He walked down the hall, but the house was dark. He looked in the kitchen. Again, nothing. He looked out on the porch. He opened the garage door, and Jenny's car was gone. A tear ran down his cheek as the reality hit him that she'd had enough. Where could she have gone? Picking up his cell phone, he touched the screen to call and there in bright letters read:

I'm OK, don't try to call.

I just need some time.

I'll call you in a day or two.

Rev. Peters put down his phone and went back into the kitchen to make himself a cup of coffee. As the coffee steeped, the fragrance filled the room. "Coffee!" he mumbled to himself. Once it brewed, he poured a cup and went out the back door to sit on the porch.

The early morning air was cool but not too cold. Some might argue it was the perfect temperature. It had a fresh scent to it, as if all the plants were finally able to exhale and enjoy the world apart from all the humans. There was a slight breeze, and it was dark. It was also amazingly silent; every living thing was resting. The Reverend pulled out a chair from under their table. The chair screeched as he pulled out, startling him and causing him to immediately apologize to Mickey, as if he was standing right beside him. The porch table was a place of many fond memories. It was the place of many family dinners, gatherings with friends, euchre, and an occasional whiskey and cigar. It was a place Rev. Peters could decompress. Many notable guests found their way to the Peters' porch. After an event at the church, or some teaching or study, guests would join the Peters for some home cooking and conversation. Bishops, Theologians, Scholars, and Missionaries had all joined the Reverend on the porch to share their insights and intuitions about the faith and world.

Rev. Peters lifted his coffee to his mouth. His senses immediately lit up with the brilliance a little caffeine can bring. "Ah! Coffee!" he muttered again. As he sipped the coffee, occasionally, he heard something that sounded like someone was flipping paper. *Thap, Thap, Thap,*

Thap, Thap, Thap. It would repeat and then stop. The Reverend turned his ear to the sound in hopes of figuring out what might be the cause.

Maybe it's coming from the air conditioner, he considered. The sound reminded him of summers as a child riding bikes in the neighborhood. Every summer, his friends would fold a piece of paper and attach it to the forks on the fronts of their bikes so that as they rode, the spokes would hit the paper, making a *Thap-ing* sound. He sat in the silence, waiting to catch it again. *Thap, Thap*.

"Hmm," he pondered, "Maybe a bug? A big bug?" He stood up from his chair and pushed his seat back. With that movement, it set whatever was making the noise off, "*Thap, Thap, Thap, Thap, Thap, Thap*. The *Thap-ing* was fast and consistent and just long enough for Rev. Peters to fix his eyes on the culprit. A dragonfly!

Hanging on the ceiling, this enormous dragonfly was trying to find its way out. The light from the house had illuminated the white ceiling of the porch just enough to confuse the poor creature. It had mistaken the ceiling for the sky, and it was exhausting itself trying to find a way to breakout. Rev. Peters immediately opened the screen door and pulled his chair right under the dragonfly.

"Come on, you little sucker."

He reached up to assist the creature to freedom, but it simply dodged his advances and flew down to the other end of the porch.

"Dammit! Don't you want to get out! You're going to die in here!"

Thap, Thap, Thap, Thap.

Pointing to the dragonfly, the Reverend exclaimed, "You stay right there!"

He jogged back into the house, through the kitchen, and into the garage. He paused for a moment as he became aware again that Jenny was gone. He looked into the corner and found the kitchen broom. Grasping the wooden handle, he yanked it out of the bracket where it hung. He jogged gingerly back out onto the porch to rescue this poor ancient dragonfly. The Reverend thought it must be old for a dragonfly because it was huge, bigger than most he'd seen darting around the yard at dusk, and it had arrived at its full maturity.

"Stay there, dragonfly!"

He spoke gently to the creature, hoping that his kindness would convince it to fly out the door. He raised the broom and slowly moved it just behind the dragonfly's body. When it came within inches, the creature flew. This time it set its course right at Rev. Peters, who threw the broom down and ran away. After the dodge, he laughed at himself.

"It's a damn bug! What are you running from?"

The dragonfly proceeded to bounce on the ceiling, anxiously looking for a way out. It would rest every couple of minutes to save energy for the next effort to gain its freedom. Eventually, the dragonfly came to rest close to the place the Reverend had their first encounter. He could tell that the creature was tired and didn't have much fight left in it.

The Reverend climbed back up on the chair and was able to get relatively close to the dragonfly. The closer he got to the insect, the better he could see how spectacular it was. It had some of the most beautiful colors and patterns on its body the Reverend had ever seen. He thought, *If this thing were the size of a person, we'd all be dead. It's a perfect war machine.* He tried to get a closer look at the huge eyes that made up most of the dragonfly's head. They were mirrored and reflected all the colors that were in their surroundings. Gigantic eyes to see and guide this killer through the air as it picked out the tiniest flying insects to dine upon each night. Eyes that could navigate away from any object or predator moving quickly toward the creature. The Reverend moved his hand up behind the insect to scoop or push it toward the door. This time the dragonfly just sat there staring back at him. *I wonder what it's thinking*, he entertained. Rev. Peters thrust his hand across the ceiling with one swift motion, and the dragonfly dropped and dodged his advances. *Thap, Thap, Thap, Thap.* The bug flew with all its energy, as if to break through the ceiling containing it.

> "You damn insect! Can't you see I'm trying to save you! You are going to die out here! The door is open! Get out while you still can."
>
> *Thap, Thap, Thap, Thap.*

With a burst of energy, he grabbed the broom and swung it in the air, trying to scare, direct, or bat the dragonfly in the direction of the open door. Nothing was working. The creature would dodge right, left, around, and even below. Nothing was going to save the dragonfly, except maybe the dragonfly.

> The dragonfly once again came to rest, and the Reverend sat back down in his chair.
>
> "Maybe if I turn out the light, it will realize that the ceiling isn't the sky and find its way out?"

He took another couple of sips of his coffee and got up to open the door. Reaching around the door frame just inside, the Reverend clicked off the light switch. Darkness! He closed the door and stumbled a bit, trying to navigate his way back to the chair. He sat down and took another healthy swig of coffee.

> "OK, mister, if you want to live, you're going to have to figure this out for yourself. All I can do is open the damn door and hope your senses kick in."

As Rev. Peters' eyes adjusted to the darkness, he could see the stars growing ever brighter just outside the screen door. The darkest place in the entire backyard was on the porch. "*Thap, Thap, Thap, Thap.*

"Come on! You can do this!"

He picked up his mug once again, but he had already taken the last sip.

"Damn it! There's never enough."

He thought about getting back up and making another cup, but the early morning sleepiness had set in. Jenny would always comment on how much coffee the Reverend could drink and still fall asleep, and this even minutes before going to bed. He could go right to sleep after drinking a whole pitcher of "truck stop delight." It was mind-blowing to Jenny but didn't appear to be a big deal to Rev. Peters. Jenny would say, "If I drank that much coffee, my heart would explode!" The Reverend would chuckle at her.

Rev. Peters looked around to see if the dragonfly was still hanging around. He couldn't see its figure silhouetted on the dark ceiling above him.

"Yes! Maybe it worked!"

He stood up and walked around the porch, paying close attention to see if his new friend was still hanging around, possibly on the screens. It appeared that the dragonfly had gone.

"Alright! At least something good has happened today!"

He turned on his heel and headed back to the door to turn on the lights for a final check. "Crunch!"

"No!" he jumped back in disgust and bent down to see what might have made the noise. "Please, don't let it . . ."

It was. There on the cement floor was the old dragonfly. It had given everything to try to break the ceiling, but it was just too much. No matter how many attempts to get the creature to change its course, head in a new direction, find freedom, it just couldn't move away from what it thought was the sky. It was banging against that ceiling all night. Maybe even days. The Reverend felt another tear coming to his eyes.

"How can we get free of the ceiling? How in the flippin' HELL does anyone get out of this alive? We're just bangin' our heads against the ceiling. Damn it!"

The Reverend bent down and scooped the dragonfly into his hand. He no longer feared the insect. Now lifeless, he could look at it even more closely. "Beautiful!" he uttered as he sat back down in his chair and stared.

The most noticeable thing about the creature was its enormous eyes. They appeared to be every color, and the complexity of the eyes was a work of art. They consisted of what appeared to be thousands of eyes all gathered into one massive optical thaumaturgy. *No wonder you can never catch these suckers!*

Deep-set into the shiny exterior coating of the eye were colors of green, yellow, blue, black, and red in a wide variety of shades and hues. Incredible in every way, and yet unable to find the door on a star-lit night. The irony was confounding. Its body was long and hard.

Whatever kept this tiny dragon going was hidden deep within. The wings were another spectacle—twice as long as the body, two wings on each side, attached along its rugged thorax. The wings were translucent for the most part, with black brush strokes dispersed as camouflage throughout each wing. Rev. Peters held the dragonfly up to the starlight, which revealed the intricate display of veins. The veins gave strength to the wings, enabling the tiny dragon to dart and fly like no other creature on earth. The legs were the only thing that gave the

Reverend the creeps. They were long, skinny, and alien. Each connected to the bottom of the thorax with what appeared to be mechanical joints. *These are tiny robots*! he thought again through his discovery. Then Rev. Peters carefully flipped the insect over on its back to take a closer look at its mouth. The Reverend had remembered learning about dragonflies years ago in biology class. These creatures were amongst the oldest still living on earth. These creatures were designed for survival and killing. There in the palm of his hand lay millions of years of evolution designed to survive in a violent and competitive world, equipped with some of the greatest weapons and machinery, and stuck on a middle-aged pastor's porch, unable to escape.

Rev. Peters walked back into the house carrying the body.

"I wonder if we'll be around as long as these little suckers."

He pulled out the chair at the kitchen bar and set the little creature on the countertop. He walked over to the coffee pot and poured himself the last bit that was left then shuffled back to the chair to sit with his new friend and ponder the exhausting morning. He found himself talking to the little creature.

"You know, I feel like I'm hitting the ceiling all the time! Did you know she left in the middle of the night? I don't know if anything is worth it anymore. I just want to know what it means not to have so many damn strings attached! Hell, I'm just a pawn, and I feel like I'm getting played. I don't even know how to help anyone anymore! I can't even help my own family! Damn it!"

"Who are you talking to?" a voice sounded from behind him, startling him and causing him to spill the last coffee in his cup.

"Damn it, Mickey! You scared the shit out of me!"

Mickey paused; he wasn't used to the colorful language his father had been using recently.

"I'm sorry, dad? I didn't mean to scare the *shit* out of you!" he said with a grin.

The Reverend realized he was talking with his son and needed to figure out how not to screw this moment up.

"I'm sorry, Mickey, it's been a tough couple of days. What are you doing up so early?"

Mickey realized that he had let his defenses down and considered turning and running back into his room when he saw the dragonfly sitting on the counter.

"What's that?" he asked.

"Oh, that's my new friend."

"Are you OK, Dad?"

"No!" the Reverend responded with an exasperated tone. "She left, Mickey."

An odd silence hung in the air as both of them stared at the dragonfly.

"I'm sorry, Dad, but I knew it was coming. She isn't happy, and I'm not sure anyone would be able to pull her out of it."

Rev. Peters looked at Mickey and realized that this young man he thought was wasting his life consumed by games was becoming an adult.

"Mickey? You knew it was coming? . . . And, I'm talking to a dead dragonfly!"

Then he started to laugh. He started laughing so hard he almost fell out of his chair.

"Dad, you're kinda freaking me out right now."

The Reverend put his hand on Mickey's shoulder.

"You would not believe me if I told you the shit I've experienced these past few days. It was flippin' nuts! And, it called everything out into the light. The screen door is open, and the question is, will I keep hitting the ceiling or fly out into the glorious night."

Mickey was looking at his father curiously, "I have no idea what you are talking about. I'm going to leave you and your little buddy so you can continue your conversation."

"No!" the Reverend exclaimed, "We are going out to breakfast!"

"No, we aren't. I've got school."

Rev. Peters smiled, "Not today! Come on, Mickey we are going to find a real dive and have a super breakfast."

Mickey had no idea what to make of his father's spontaneity, but he was enjoying it!

"OK?" Mickey stated cautiously.

"Alright, then go get dressed; we're leaving in fifteen minutes!" the Reverend announced, and he saw Mickey smile.

CHAPTER 19

CUSSING

Mickey ordered the "World Waffle Wonder," and the Reverend had the "Dad Stack." It had been years since the two of them had gone out to eat together. The practice used to be one of their favorite things to do together during the week. While Jenny enjoyed the company of both the boys in the family, she was not quite as fond of their love for eating at the most suspect dives they could find. "World Waffle House," WWH for short, was located on the other side of town. Rev. Peters noticed it when he was escaping the hospital with Dough.

The place smelled of fried bacon and old coffee. The seats were the "WWH" traditional burnt orange, and the vinyl was cracked in places from years of wear. The site was full of interesting customers. Several young people were sitting in the corner working off a night on the town. Two older women were seated across from each other, drinking coffee and intently sharing news from around the neighborhood. Middle-aged men and a few colorfully dressed ladies were sitting at the breakfast bar eating, staring, and reading the newspaper. Behind the breakfast bar, the cooks were hurriedly preparing food and shouting orders across the restaurant. The place was freezing, and condensation was dripping down the large glass windows. "World Waffle House" was always cold to help keep the staff and customers awake. It was an institution proud of its eclecticism.

"How'd you find this place?" Mickey asked as he slowly and intentionally lifted the waffles, placing slabs of butter between the warm cakes.

Rev. Peters was still a little shocked that Mickey was so amenable to go, "I saw it when I was walking across town the other day."

Mickey nodded as if he had heard something about his excursion. He looked his father in the eyes as he simultaneously and artfully poured the syrup over the waffles in tiny circular motions.

"So what was that deal all about? Mom said you had slipped a gasket and wandered off with a cult group."

"Well . . . ," the Reverend began as slowly as the syrup was pouring over the waffles, "it's complicated, but yes, I went with a gentleman who had something to share with me. And, it was one hell of a journey."

Rev. Peters pulled his waffles apart into sections, laying them independently around his plate. He then took the pats of butter and carefully placed each in a symmetrical fashion around his waffles. Once he had navigated the buttering process, he set the first waffle in the center and grabbed the syrup Mickey had just put down. Slowly he poured the syrup, beginning in the center and then building outward until he just let it drizzle off the edge. Once he poured the syrup, he took the next waffle, placed it on top, and repeated the process until all five waffles were perfectly buttered, syruped, and stacked.

"Holy Jesus! This is gonna be sweet!" Rev. Peters offered as an opening prayer for the indulgence the two of them were about to partake.

"So, Mickey, these people I met live in this part of town. They call themselves the Others, and they are preparing themselves to bring the good news of new beginnings to the world."

"So, they're all 'whack cases!'" Mickey responded, shoving a forkful of waffle into his mouth.

The Reverend finished chewing, and then took a long sip of coffee, "Coffee!" he offered as part of the morning liturgy. "Well, 'whack cases' might be a bit extreme. I found some extremely intelligent, well-organized, incredibly diverse, genuinely hospitable, and enormously gracious people. They share all things and focus their energy on gifts and celebrating those gifts for the good of the community."

"Sounds like a false utopia to me. There isn't such a place, and if people are trying to convince you that they have answers about the end of the world, I would hope you of all people would raise a red flag."

After offering the comment, Mickey stabbed his fork through another layer of gooey, buttery waffles. Rev. Peters just sat there watching Mickey eat. He was contemplating, *Is this, my son? Is he talking to me? And, as if he cares about me.*

Arising from the momentary reflection, he spoke softly, "You know, I never heard a mention of the end of time, just new beginnings. They wanted me to come and see their worship service they call the Gathering, and it was nice, powerful at moments, but nothing that made me levitate off the ground or anything. If anything, it was rather simple. But there was a moment I saw something in the light pouring through the holes in the roof. People were standing in the beams but not in the room!"

"That's scary shit!" Mickey shouted.

Reverend nodded in agreement with his mouth full of waffle, "You'd think it would be scary, but it wasn't. They all were in God's future! The experience really could never be captured in writing or even pictures; it's something you'd have to experience."

"I want to go!" Mickey blurted out.

"Really?" Rev. Peters was stunned. "OK, I think we can do that."

The two of them finished off their breakfast. There was not a waffle or drop of syrup left on Mickey's or Rev. Peters' plates. The Reverend mused, *Like father like son. Well, except for how we prepare the waffles and, well, eat them. But, we both love them.* For a moment, Rev. Peters became overly aware of how unique, different, special, and beautiful Mickey was. Mickey was not something for him to control, manipulate, or conform, but to delight in. For the first time in many years, the Reverend found himself admiring his son. Mickey was also surprised by this adventure his father had thrown at him. He loved being with his dad when his work didn't consume him. He had even built up a resentment toward the church, God, and God's people for being terrible to his dad and what he believed was stealing his dad away from him. Yet, here they were traveling across town, skipping school, and eating delicious waffles together. He watched his dad finish the entire plate and, once again, his dad was cool.

"I want to meet these Others," Mickey stated again.

"Oh, you will soon. They're coming to live in our church."

"What!" Mickey laughed and snorted at the same time. "Joel Newcome and the trustees are going to flip! They wouldn't even let our little band play a concert in the social hall, and they are constantly calling the police to haul off vagrants from the property. I can't wait to see this! When is it going to happen?"

"Slow down. There's a lot more to this than horrifying the church people."

"What more could be better than that?" Mickey kept chuckling. "It's about damn time someone had the balls to stand up to those privileged cowards!"

Rev. Peters had never heard Mickey speak this way before, and he liked it.

"I never knew you felt this way about the leaders at the church?"

"Are you crazy! All they're interested in is preserving what's theirs, not welcoming, including, and liberating anyone! They're a shit show!"

"Mickey!" Rev. Peters scolded.

"Oh, come on, Dad! Like you've never heard that word before. We are sitting in Waffle World. I've already heard that word used a hundred times by the cooks."

"Yeah, but you shouldn't use that word; it's not appropriate."

"Why is that?" Mickey questioned.

"Well, society says it's inappropriate, and it means vulgar things."

Mickey stared back, "Blah, blah, blah, from the man who says 'shit' all the time, and even a couple of 'fucks.' Let alone, when you try to substitute words. Is it any different? You say 'buck' and 'frickin' all the time!"

Rev. Peters didn't have a response to Mickey's last comment. Mickey was making a good point. What is the difference? Society? Position? Or the violence? The Reverend looked back up at his son.

"It has to do with violence, Mickey." Feeling confident in his defense, he continued, "Do I commit harm with the words I speak? Are they being used as a weapon? Are they intended to tear down, discourage, hurt, or abuse?"

Mickey's eyes settled in on his old man, "I agree with you, Dad; if they harm, that's not right. But, when they don't cause harm, they're 'frickin' OK."

His statement still made Rev. Peters cringe. Just then, almost jumping over the top of the barrier separating their booth from the one directly behind them, a figure stood up and shouted, "Pete!"

"Shit!" Rev. Peters screamed.

Mickey couldn't stop laughing. He had never seen his father jump so high and scream that loud before, and his heart was racing too. The Reverend was now lying down on the booth bench, exhausted from the jolt.

"I'm sorry, Pete. I couldn't help myself. I saw you two sitting there when I came in the side door and just had to make a big entrance."

Mickey couldn't keep his eyes off the man.

From almost under the table, Rev. Peters' voice muffled, "Mickey, this is Dough and, Dough, this is my son Mickey."

Dough immediately extended his hand, "Well, I'll be, the son of Pete! I am honored to meet you."

"Who is Pete?" Mickey questioned.

"Oh, Mick, that's your father. We got tired of all the titles, and he didn't look like a Michael to me. So, I started calling him Pete."

"Well, that makes sense," Mickey responded sarcastically.

"I like you, Mick; you've got an edge to ya. And, after hearing your theories on the violence and proper use of cuss words, I think you'll fit right in with the Others."

Mickey beamed, "I want to see the Others!"

Dough leaned over the divider before jumping to the ground and sliding into the seat next to Mickey.

"Well, my brother, if you've seen one of us, you've seen them all!"

The Reverend was finally pulling himself back up to a respectful position.

"Can you please stop scaring the shit out of me?"

"See, that's the proper use of a cuss word," Mickey jokingly offered.

"Shut up, Mickey!" Rev. Peters responded.

"Now that's a violent use of language," Dough offered.

The Reverend turned red, "You too!"

Mickey was infatuated with this new friend. He was tall, mysterious, and had a sense of adventure about him. Mickey was also impressed that his father left the hospital to take a trip with Dough.

"Hey!" Mickey cried, "I saw you a couple of times in our church parking lot."

"Yep, that was me. I was waiting for your father. It took a couple of months, but eventually I was able to have a conversation. Every time I would try to approach him, he would walk quickly away. It was like I had the virus or something."

"No," Mickey resounded, "He just thought you were homeless and begging for money. That virus is called privilege."

The three of them sat in silence for a moment until the server stopped by the table to offer them all a little more coffee. The server handed a mug to Dough and filled them all to the top. The three took hold of their warm mugs and sipped. "Ah, Coffee!" they all proclaimed in unison. Rev. Peters broke the liturgy of ingesting and inhaling the sweet nectar of coffee,

"So why are you here, Dough?"

Dough sat up straight, "I was going to ask you the same thing. These are my parts, ya know!"

Rev. Peters felt guilty for assuming that Dough was following them. Mickey was trying to avoid any further conflict and kept sipping the hot coffee, burning the roof of his mouth.

Dough put his coffee down, and confessed, "OK, I was following you."

"I knew it!" the Reverend exclaimed. "I knew it, knew it, knew it! And here I was feeling guilty for thinking those thoughts in my head.

"You were thinking those thoughts?" Dough shot back. "Well, anyway," Dough continued, "it's time. The Others are making their way to First Church, and Ma sent me to let you know. How convenient that you all came to me."

Mickey was smiling, "The shit is gonna hit the fan!"

Dough looked over at the young man, "Now wait a minute! Ain't no shit hitting any fan. We are coming to invite everyone into the story bigger than themselves. Love is the bigger story. It's being present and embodying good news so that everyone comes to know they belong and are all becoming. We, the Others, have been striving to live this way, imperfectly and beautifully, for over ten years now, and it's time."

Mickey was intrigued again with everything Dough had to say. "So, Dough, are you talking about the end times? I love the end times!"

Dough flinched a little and responded, "No! Not the end. Always a beginning. There is no end. It's all about living . . . living a better story. People get so caught up in thinking everything will be purged, burned away, destroyed, and only then will God's wrath be appeased. But, that's the way human beings would end things, not the Creative! Not the Human One! Not the Breath! I believe that sometimes life gets so hard it's easier for folks to imagine its demise rather than working for the better."

Mickey was silent, and Rev. Peters was caught up in Dough's words.

"I've gotta get back to the church!" the Reverend shouted.

"No, you don't!" Dough asserted, reaching across the table and grabbing his hand. "Sit and enjoy this time we have together."

Mickey had never smiled this much in his life, and he also reached across the table, "Stay here with us, Dad! Enjoy the moment!"

Rev. Peters settled down and sank back into the seat.

"What are they going to do to you, Pete? Kick you out? The Others will be there when you get back," Dough asked.

Then, Rev. Peters thought about Jenny. What was she doing? When was she coming back? He was so caught up in the delight of being with Mickey that he had forgotten for a moment that she had left.

"Whatcha thinking?" Mickey asked.

"I was just thinking about your mother. Where is she? Will we ever be able to get things back together? When is she coming home?"

Mickey got up from his seat and moved over to slide next to his father.

"I don't know when or how; I'm just glad that we were able to come to be together at World Waffle. Mom will be alright. She needs to sort some shit out. I think if she saw us now, she would have passed out!"

"That would be correct!" Rev. Peters chuckled.

Dough was pretending like he was ignoring their conversation to give them a moment.

Then he offered his condolences, "I'm sorry, Pete. I know this shit is hard. You're not alone."

Dough then turned to Mickey, "So, Mick, what do you do well?"

Mickey had never been asked that question before, but he felt like he had something to contribute.

"Well . . .," Mickey began, "I am super good with computers and technology. I hacked into my first corporate system when I was twelve!"

"What?" Rev. Peters responded in horror.

"Don't worry, Dad, I was able to avoid the Feds! I am also good at making friends online. I play a lot of games basically because life has been pretty boring. Online I meet kids from all over the world, and the gaming platforms are so real you can pretty much disappear in digits."

Now Dough looked intrigued, "Tell me more about this world. That is something I'm not familiar with."

Mickey straightened up again and faced Dough with purpose. "It's an amazing world which ultimately gives you everything you want. Looks, strength, wealth, property, and sex."

"Sex? You never told me about the sex!" the Reverend stated bluntly.

"Calm down, old-timer! It gives you everything you can't attain in this world and a community to connect. Everyone I meet online strives to reach the next level, gain more lives, find more treasure, and garner more special weapons. And, if you die or fail, you upload yourself again."

"Sounds kind of like a hope-filled hopelessness," Dough replied.

"To be honest," Mickey spoke humbly, "I'm tired of it. They can never program a game world big enough to fill all the voids! I just want to be real."

Rev. Peters and Dough looked at each other, and then looked to Mickey and said, "You are real!"

The server once again interrupted the moment. The young woman placed the bill on the table and gently patted it. The Reverend picked it up. It read, "Food is free! The Others." Rev. Peters looked at Dough, and Dough just shrugged his shoulders.

"Rachael is a part of the community, and everything is free when you're part of the Others."

"Is there anyone who is not a part of the Others?" Rev. Peters questioned.

Dough chuckled, "Well, we're going to meet them right now. I'm just hoping that everyone will be able to see each other."

Mickey chimed in, "If food is free, I'm with the Others!"

Dough chuckled again, "You sure are. You sure are."

CHAPTER 20

INHABITING

Rev. Peters checked his watch as he walked out the door of World Waffle. It was 9:00 a.m. Mickey and Dough followed him, talking, laughing, and having a good time together. It warmed the Reverend's heart to see Mickey engaged, interested, and enjoying life. Together they walked out into the parking lot to find their car.

"You want a ride, Dough?" Rev. Peters asked.

"Nope, I like walking. It takes a little longer, but it's better for you. Thank you for the invitation, though. I'll walk you to your car, and then I have to split."

Mickey sauntered, and his head bowed as if contemplating a proposal.

"Dad?" Mickey posed hesitantly. "Would it be OK if I went with Dough?"

For a moment, the Reverend fell silent and didn't know how to respond. His first thought was, *There's no way in hell I'm going to let you wanderer off with anyone! Your mom has already had enough of me.* Then a second thought came to mind. *Why not?*

They reached the car and Rev. Peters looked at Dough, "I apologize on Mickey's behalf; he shouldn't have just invited himself to go with you."

"That's quite all right." Dough responded. "I would love to have Mickey come along with me. I can't promise when I might get him back to you, though. Are you all right with that?"

Rev. Peters thought a second further, "Yep! You can go. You keep him safe, Dough!"

"I will. I took good care of you, didn't I?"

The Reverend smiled, "Well . . .,"

Dough and Mickey hopped off away from the car and headed toward the warehouse district. Mickey was almost skipping. He was so excited to join Dough on this adventure, and Rev. Peters' heart pounded a little thinking about how he would explain it to Jenny. The Reverend opened the door to the car and slipped into his seat. The car started the second he put his foot on the brake and hands on the wheel.

"I hate this new technology! The damn cars are too smart! . . . Reverse!" Rev. Peters shouted, giving the car a command.

"Sorry, I will reverse in a moment. You have an incoming call."

"Answer." Rev. Peters shouted.

He always felt like the voice command technologies could never completely hear him.

"Hello!" Rev. Peters answered.

"Rev. Peters, this is Grace and, I need you to come to the church immediately."

The Reverend was worried about getting this call, for he knew it was coming.

"Grace, can I assume you are calling because there are a bunch of new people at the church?"

There was a moment of silence, and then Grace replied, "Ah, yes, sir. How did you know?"

"Well, Grace, they are all friends of mine, and they are welcome."

Following the statement, he took a deep breath, knowing that Mickey was right, the shit was gonna hit the fan!

"Sir, the people have all been very polite and kind. And, sir, there are a lot of them! It's Mr. Newcome that I'm worried about. He is freaking out!"

"You sit tight, Grace. I'll be right there."

As he hung up the phone, he inhaled and then loudly exhaled as if to cast the stress away. "Newcome!" Rev. Peters muttered.

It took fifteen minutes for the Reverend to get to the church. He pulled into his designated parking spot with the sign sitting before him, which read, "Rev. Michael Peters - Senior Pastor." Such authority, and to think that he was special enough to have a space always reserved for him. At any moment of the day or night, Rev. Peters had a place to park his car that was his own. He opened the door and began his walk into the inner courtyards of the church property. There were people all over the place. Some were sitting on the ground with blankets. Others were trimming bushes and picking up garbage from around the property. As he made his way past the office door, he knocked on the glass just to let Grace know that he had arrived but didn't have enough time to chat.

As he drew closer to the sanctuary, he could hear screaming coming from within. It was loud and violent screaming. He tried to focus on the screaming, and all he could make out was, "G . . . Out! This . . . Not

. . .Place!" As he approached the door, he paused and inhaled deeply. Then he let it all out and opened the door. Joel Newcome immediately turned when the Reverend entered the room and screamed,

> "Well, it's about time you got here! Your church is going to hell in a handbasket, and you were nowhere to be found. Whatever happened to office hours? These vagrants have invaded our church and won't leave. I have asked them politely, and they told me *you* invited them! Is that true? I sure as God hope it isn't true!"

With all the pastoral acumen possible, Rev. Peters gently grabbed a seat in one of the open pews facing Mr. Newcome.

> "Joel. I do not understand why this is causing you to get so angry?"

Mr. Newcome's fists clenched in response. Rev. Peters thought, *Maybe that was't the best initial response.*

> "I am angry because nobody is listening to me and these vagrants think they own the place!" Mr. Newcome shouted.

Rev. Peters focused more intently on defusing the situation.

> "Joel, come sit down here and let's talk about what is going on."

> Again, Mr. Newcome's fist clenched even harder, "There is no way in hell I'm sitting down. This is no time for calm; we are being invaded. Who knows where these people are from or what kind of criminal activities they are associated with? They will not leave, so I'm going to have to call the police."

> "Well, Joel," Rev. Peters offered a little more forcefully this time, "you can't have them forcibly removed if I invited them."

At that moment, one might have thought a small nuclear bomb went off in Mr. Newcome's head. His face turned beet red, and his hands clenched tighter than might seem possible.

"I am not going to tolerate this level of disrespect, Michael! These people are invading our space, and they need to go! Who do they think they are anyway? And, have you lost your mind! I AM CALLING THE POLICE!"

Mr. Newcome turned on his heels and briskly walked out of the sanctuary. As he walked through the door, a gentle voice from among the crowd of people said, "Thank you!" Rev. Peters recognized the voice. He turned to scan the crowd of people and sitting toward the back was Ma Green.

"We are here, Pete! And thank you for welcoming us!"

She stood up and began making her way toward Rev. Peters.

"How many of you are here?" Rev. Peters inquired.

"Well, maybe a little over a hundred. You're not the only church the Others are inhabiting."

The Reverend looked around the room. He recognized a few of the people from his limited time on the other side. Eve, the young woman he met who was in the wheelchair, was waving at him from the other side of the room.

"Ma, I am so sorry for the way Mr. Newcome treated you."

Ma grabbed Rev. Peters' hand and held it firmly, "No worries. They are going to fight, and we are going to love."

Rev. Peters placed his hand under Ma Green's and started to cry.

"What's this all about?" Ma asked him gently.

Rev. Peters wiped the tears from his face, "I don't know what I'm doing. It's like I am a part of this thing, only I have no idea what this thing is? I like you people, but I have no control of the boat. When you said, they are inhabiting more churches than mine, what are you talking about?"

Ma Green listened carefully and waited patiently before responding. "Is that all you needed to say?"

Rev. Peters nodded.

"I know this won't make any sense or offer any more clarity, but we aren't sure we know why we are being driven in this way either. We know that it's like breath—a force that arises from those who know what it means to seek justice, love mercy, and walk humbly. Those who have set aside their desire for power, privilege, position, and prestige have heard the voice inside calling us to act. That action is happening now and will continue, not just in this place, but all over the world. It's the beginning of the end of violence, death-dealing that has driven human existence throughout the ages. It is the proper response to the death of the Human One who made it possible to move away from those destructive narratives by breaking the cycle and surrendering life for life. By moving into the places that claim to be in control, we have something to offer. Love and relationships that heal, redeem, and restore! It is, after all, all about moving into the neighborhood."

Rev. Peters just stared at her, and with all the honesty he could muster, said, "I have no idea what you are talking about. But, I trust this movement more than anything else I have encountered. Hell, I even let my son go hang out with Dough!"

"You did what?" Ma abruptly responded. Rev. Peters looked a little shocked by her reply. Ma continued, "Well, you might be bailing your son out of prison later tonight."

The sirens came a lot faster than the Reverend expected. Within seconds, several police officers were moving into the sanctuary, hands on their pistols.

"We need to speak with Rev. Peters."

Rev. Peters waved his hand in the air and graciously excused himself from Ma Green.

"I'm over here."

Two officers all moved closer while several remained at the back of the room.

"Are you the pastor in charge of this facility?"

Rev. Peters grabbed the back of one of the pews, "Yes, I am."

"Sir, we received a formal complaint from a Mr. Joel Newcome that vagrants are inhabiting the facilities, and he has filed a 'no trespassing order'."

The Reverend shifted a bit, "Well, you can tear that up, for I invited these people to gather here."

The police officer shifted in his stance. "Sir, you do know that we have a city ordinance that nobody is allowed to inhabit a church or business to spend the night or permanently live."

"I did not know that," Rev. Peters replied. "So, I guess our youth can no longer have any lock-ins, and missionaries are not allowed to stay in the church either?"

"It appears to be that way, sir. I'm sorry, Pastor, I don't make the laws; I enforce them."

Rev. Peters was getting a little agitated. He had been in this town a long time and never once heard of that ordinance. Now they were reaching deep into their statues to try to move these people. Rev. Peters repositioned himself again, searching for a response that would quiet the storm for a moment.

"Officer. First, they haven't spent the night yet, and I'm not completely sure of their intention. Second, due to the separation of church and state, I don't believe you can move someone who declares 'sanctuary.'"

The officer laughed, "Sanctuary! Hilarious! You know that has no merit in the modern world and carries no legal backing." Then with a loud voice, the officer commanded, "Let's round them up and get them out."

The remaining officers grabbed those in the sanctuary by their arms to escort them out of the building.

Most people allowed their bodies to go limp and would cry out, "This house is for all people!" and "We haven't done anything!" Rev. Peters was aghast. He couldn't believe what was happening.

Then with a loud voice, drawing from a place he had never drawn before, he cried, "Stop it! In the name of God, stop it! You have no authority to remove these people from this place! Let alone, I believe it's happening all over town. Are you going to arrest everyone?"

The commanding officer looked toward another officer who seemed to have been just getting off his radio. The officer who was on the radio nodded to the commanding officer to affirm what Rev. Peters had been saying. At that moment, Rev. Peters picked up his phone and found the number for City News 2. He dialed the number quickly.

When the news office answered the phone, Rev. Peters proclaimed, "You might want to get a reporter down here! The police are arresting innocent people from the church!" He hung up, not waiting for a response.

The officers stopped their pursuit and started letting people go.

"Sir, you have turned this into a complicated situation, and I hope you know you are obstructing justice."

"What?" the Reverend blurted out, "Justice? Try military action; but definitely not justice. I will ask you to please leave the church."

The officers didn't offer another word, but all nodded to one another and then proceeded to exit the sanctuary. Rev. Peters was so excited by the event that he screamed, "Yes!" after they walked through the door and then began applauding wildly. But he was the only one. Those gathered in the room with Rev. Peters were all staring at him and his enthusiasm.

"Thank you, Pete," Ma Green stated, "for standing your ground and drawing on your courage and the Breath to guide you through all of that. I will say, as exciting as that was, and as wrong as it was for them to try to remove us, they are human beings. Nobody is winning or losing in this. If we do not invite them into the love that's bigger than ourselves, they will never find their place in it. There will be struggles ahead, and epiphanies, and hardened and transformed hearts. Our work is to invite everyone to see beyond to a new day. Even those who don't want to enter."

Rev. Peters was feeling a little deflated and embarrassed. "Ma, I didn't mean to make this about a victory over them, but it just felt so damn good, and I was proud of myself!"

"We, and I believe I speak for us all in the room, are proud of you too."

Rev. Peters bowed his head and knew that this was just the beginning of the tensions. He began to wonder at what point more of the leaders at the church would be showing up. The hour was growing closer to the end of the workday, and Mr. Newcome would more than likely be back, but this time with the trustees. Ma could sense the tension in the Reverend and immediately shifted the focus in the room.

"Who is good at cooking?"

Several hands shot into the air in response to Ma's appeal.

"Good!" she said, "Pete is going to show you all to the kitchen."

"I am?" The Reverend responded.

"Who has brought the produce from the gardens?"

Several more hands shot up.

"Spectacular! You will need to bring all of that to our cooks as they get ready to prepare meals. Lastly, who are our runners that will be traveling between the church and the other side?"

Ma Green was getting all the parts organized and workers in place to be productive.

"Pete," she called, "You can't focus on the negative or even the violence of the moment. You have to look ahead toward the future. You have to focus on the people, the relationships, and the gifts they share. Even those you don't like, for many times they will be important down the road. Mr. Newcome, I believe that's his name, is just as beautiful and in need of a new beginning as any of us!"

Around the room, people were hustling about and leaving to different parts of the church. Still, others remained in the sanctuary and set up stations for a wide variety of activities and crafts. Rev. Peters chuckled as it reminded him of Vacation Bible School. He showed the cooks to the kitchen, shared with several new friends where all the bathrooms and showers were located and gave Ma Green a key.

"I don't need that!" she scolded him. "These doors need to be open. There will be many more coming."

Rev. Peters took the key back and placed it in his pocket. "So what's next, Ma?"

"Well, Pete, we offer presence and let the world join us. The Breath will do the rest."

Rev. Peters was tired and decided to sit in the middle of the sanctuary to catch up on his thoughts and rest a moment. He sat there watching the Others all scurry about and was amazed at their desire to serve and give. He thought, *I wish our church members would work that hard!* As soon as the thought passed, Eve rolled up next to him with a bowl of kale soup. It smelled delicious, and the Reverend was hungry. He grabbed the warm bowl and thanked Eve for bringing it. He held the bowl on his lap, allowing the steam to carry the scent of the spices up into his nostrils. He breathed it in, and even though he had yet to take a sip, he could taste it. It reminded him of the big holiday dinners his family had while he was growing up. Oh, how he missed those gatherings. Both of Rev. Peters' parents had passed away several years back, and he and his siblings never really gathered like they did when his mom and dad were alive. His mother would spend the whole day, along with whoever wanted to help out, preparing the meals. The smells were wonderfully overwhelming at times, and there were efforts to snatch a bit of whatever was cooking in the oven or covered on the counter. Rev. Peters always made several attempts to grab something, but his mother would catch him and scold him. "Michael Dale Peters! You get your hands out of my cooking. It's coming, be patient." The meal, the smells, and the longing to be fed reminded Rev. Peters of that great scripture passage from the book of Hebrews 11:1. "Faith is the evidence of things hoped for and the conviction of things unseen!"

CHAPTER 21

WHAT'S THE USE?

After a considerable amount of time hanging around the church, Rev. Peters was ready to head home. The afternoon continued to be a flurry of new faces, filling spaces, and working on a wide variety of projects, activities, and conversations. Everyone was genuinely excited to be there and had confidence that this effort was worthwhile. Rev. Peters still found himself confused in light of the actions taking place. He was even shocked with himself as he reflected on how he was so confident and aggressive toward those who wanted to extricate the Others. He had never raised his voice or stood in opposition to a sheriff's officer! A couple of familiar faces eventually showed up at the church while still observing what appeared to be random chaos. Nurse Margret stopped by to see how things were going and offer any support that might be needed. She caught Rev. Peters' eye from across the room and gave him a wink.

"You've got some company gathering outside, Pete!" she shouted across the room.

Roo and Roxie, whom the Reverend had met at the council meeting following the Gathering, also walked by. Roo shouted, "PETE!!!" Rev.

Peters waved awkwardly as if he was in a parade and addressing the public celebrating his presence. Just then, when Rev. Peters decided it was time for him to leave, everyone who was on the church property started streaming back into the sanctuary. It was a noisy invasion of the space as adults, youth, and children gathered, talking and laughing. The spirit was pure, and their desire to be together was palpable. As they all took their seats in the pews, Rev. Peters heard one lady sitting a few rows behind him state,

"It's been a hell of a long time since I last sat in a pew!"

The young girl sitting next to her asked, "What's a pew?"

Everyone around her laughed. Prone on his hands, ready to propel himself onto his feet and leave, Rev. Peters decided to settle back down. Ma Green walked up in front of the gathering, lifted her hands, and closed her eyes.

"Who meets us in this space?" Ma asked.

"The Creative, the Breath, and the Human One!" the community responded.

Ma continued, "This is not Ma's place, the church's place, your place, or any particular people's place. This is the . . .," the liturgy paused for a response,

"The One who is life's place."

"Does anyone have authority over you?" Ma offered.

"No, not one!" they all shouted.

"So, what is it that guides you?" Ma asked boldly.

"Love!" they shouted even more loudly.

"What?" Ma Green questioned.

"Love! A story bigger than ourselves!"

The whole crowd of people of all ages erupted in applause and shouts. Ma Green walked back out into the room and took a seat next to Rev. Peters. As she was sitting down, a thin young man walked up to the front. He stood up straight and spoke, making every effort to catch the eyes of everyone in the crowd,

> "When you attempt to live by your own plans and projects, you are cut off from The Human One; you fall from grace. Meanwhile, we expectantly wait for a satisfying relationship with the Breath. For in The Human One, neither our most conscientious efforts nor blatant disregard amounts to anything. What matters is something far more powerful: faith expressed in love." ***

Ma Green turned to the Reverend, "You heard that one before Pete?"

Rev. Peters thought about it for a moment, and then he remembered, "Yes! I know the 'faith expressed in love' part. It's Paul, and I'm going to guess Philippians."

Ma smiled and explained, "It is Paul, but it's in Galatians. Rodney, who just read, loves the translation of the Travelogue called 'The Messenger.' He edited a bit for our context."

"I knew it was 'The Messenger!' That dude got it right."

Ma sat up straight and whispered to Rev. Peters, "You know Pete, most of these young people have never been in an 'official' church sanctuary before. They have been taught that being together makes the difference and not the facilities. Yet, I can tell they are intrigued with the symbols, colors, stained glass, and fancy furniture. The older kids and young adults have all been taught that places like this only exist to justify themselves and their participation in systems of oppression."

"You're teaching them what?" Rev. Peters spoke in a low but direct tone. "Ma, you have taught them that the church is here to maintain the oppression of people? We aren't about that at all! And, if anything, I think that might be the problem! By pointing the blame at us, there will only be bigger walls erected and not healing. I thought you were all about unity."

Ma's smile faded, and the corners of her mouth tightened, "Rev. Peters! You know damn well that's a lie! It's an effort to simply pull back to the places you are most comfortable with rather than acknowledge the truth. *This* and everything that has contributed to *this* was built on the backs of privilege. You, yourself, are trapped in it. You can't preach prophetically because you know people will leave. If you spoke the truth, most of your extremely generous givers would take their money and run down the street to the next comforting church. The struggle is that maintaining that corruptible system has no breath and, therefore, no life in it. But, in acknowledging the truths around how we treat each other and naming those systems and ways we participate in perpetuating those systems, the Breath comes back to us. We begin to understand what it means to be free!"

Rev. Peters was struck by every word Ma shared and was left speechless. He thought about all the battles in the church over his twenty-five years in ministry—LGBTQIA rights and their full inclusion in the life of the church; the denomination's "anti-racism" task force and writing policies to help bring greater freedoms to all people, primarily black and dark-skinned people; how he wasn't afraid to speak boldly about corrupt politicians who build division and spread lies. He thought about how he had advocated for farm workers and helped them gain simple human rights. The more he thought, the more frustrated he became. It was anger. How dare Ma accuse him of being a racist? And that was precisely what she was doing! He just turned his attention back to the front of the stage as another young person stood up and raised her hands in the air to offer some form of benediction. Rev. Peters bowed his head as he had done so many times before. He felt like giving up and thought, *What's the use?*

Once the benediction was over, Rev. Peters lifted his head, and Ma Green grabbed his hand,

"I pissed you off, didn't I?"

The Reverend turned red and brought his attention back to Ma. As he looked at her face, he saw the depth of color in her eyes. They were brown with striking flecks of green. They were full of experience, compassion, and life. Some might even say Ma's eyes were a bit wily. As he stared, she spoke to him in a calm, compassionate voice.

"We all have a lot to learn. Each of us comes in and out of our racism and prejudices toward each other. None of us are exempt, yet we are being invited to name it, identify it, and do everything we can to work against that darkness. We are to work against anything that creates language, actions, attitudes, and policies that create inequity. The drive is toward solidarity and a greater unity that does not abandon the beauty of our diversity. It is actually uniformity that most of the world believes is unity. But that's a lie! If everyone is to sit across the table, those sitting on top of the table must first come down. Coming down is what causes the tension. Coming down is what got you all stirred up!"

Rev. Peters grabbed her hand more firmly.

"You're right, Ma! It's going to be hard!"

"Yes, it is!" Ma comforted, "The good news is we are not alone. Remember several years back when there was a movement toward a more equitable society? We held marches and protests, court cases, and justice work, talking about equality while never addressing the chains that hold such oppression in place. Well, that was a start, but soon the consumerist culture drove that good work right into the ground."

Letting go of Ma's hand, the Reverend stood up.

"Thank you, Ma. This was church."

Ma nodded and stood up next to Rev. Peters.

"Now you go on and get home. I heard you've got a little work to do with Jenny."

"Yes, I do. Not sure how that is going to work out, but I'll try."

Rev. Peters stepped around Ma and started walking toward the doors of the sanctuary. As he approached the large wooden sanctuary doors, he could see lights coming through the crack. It wasn't pure light, as the beams that cascaded down on everyone at the Gathering, but blue and red lights as in law enforcement. He placed his ear along the crack of the door, hoping nobody would push the door open to see if he could hear what was going on outside. Slowly, he opened the door. In front of him was a line of squad cars, all with their lights flashing. Officers were blocking what looked like a crowd of people trying to get to the church.

"Please stand back! This is private property and nobody will be allowed to enter!"

The Reverend was aghast! He looked around to see who was supporting this effort from the church. Indeed, someone had called the Sheriff's department. There were also Police cars sitting there as well.

"Excuse me!" Rev. Peters shouted. "Hey!"

He ran toward the officers, all facing the crowd standing on the other side of their line.

"Hey! What do you think you're doing?"

Two of the officers turned and placed their hands on their guns.

"Stand back, sir!" one of the officers shouted. "We are here to protect private property, and these people have trespassed.

"Who reported them?" Rev. Peters asked forcefully.

"I did!" Joel Newcome shouted from behind Rev. Peters.

"Joel, you son of a bitch!"

"Watch it now *holy* man!'" Joel retorted, "You're supposed to be a witness to others!"

"They're about to witness you getting your ass kicked!" the Reverend volleyed back.

"Pete!" A voice shouted from the crowd. "Do not succumb to their violence!"

Rev. Peters looked around to see who was shouting at him. There, on the side of the officer blockade, were Dough and Pico.

"Don't do it, Pete!" Pico shouted as well.

Joel Newcome chimed in as well, "Yeah, Pete . . . if that's what you go by in the ghetto. Stand down, and you might consider packing all your stuff because, after this, you're through!"

Those words! Those words! "You're through!" came rushing down like the healing "Balm of Gilead." They entered Rev. Peters' soul like rolling waters of justice and a righteous ever-flowing stream. At that moment, he was free. He no longer needed to care about the institution, but the people who longed to make love real in the world. He turned toward the officer who was addressing him at the time.

"Officer, I'm the pastor of this church, and I am asking you to leave."

The officer turned to Rev. Peters and briskly responded, "Sir, I wish we could, but this isn't just a response to the trespassing; it's coming from the Mayor."

"What?" The Reverend was shocked. "The Mayor has ordered this?"

"Yes, sir, Reverend Pete."

Joel rolled his eyes, "His name is Michael!"

"Shut up, Joel!" Rev. Peters reached out and grabbed the officer's arm, "Why would the Mayor do this?"

"Sir, if you don't let go of my arm, I will have to arrest you for assaulting an officer."

"Bullshit!" The Reverend responded.

"No, Sir!" The officer stated, "Let go, or I'll have you arrested."

Rev. Peters let go of the officer's arm and stepped back. It was like he had lost all control.

"What about separation of church and state?" Rev. Peters offered.

The officer turned briefly toward him and said, "That's why we haven't crossed the sidewalk, sir."

"Aha!" Rev. Peters proclaimed, celebrating his momentary victory. "I knew you couldn't touch those folks in the church."

"Oh, we can, sir, especially since Mr. Newcome has deemed them as trespassers. But, we would be arresting half the town. This isn't the only unrest happening in town. We're here to make sure not too many more people get into places and spaces they don't belong. Like your church!"

Rev. Peters was even more confused than ever. He looked toward the other side of the squad cars, and there, waving and motioning him to come over were Dough, Pico, and Mickey. He turned to the officer, and with a much calmer voice, asked,

"Would it be all right if I went over there to see my friends?"

The officer responded, "If you cross the line, you aren't coming back."

The Reverend started walking toward Dough, Pico, and Mickey.

"Sir!" The officer shouted, "You won't be allowed in if you cross!"

Rev. Peters kept walking and murmured to himself, 'You just watch me!"

When he reached the other side of the blockade, Dough and Mickey gave him a big hug, and Pico grabbed his hand. Pico looked Rev. Peters in the eyes.

"It's tough getting in trouble for doing nothing wrong!"

Rev. Peters started laughing. They all started laughing.

"Let's get in some more trouble for nothing!" Mickey shouted.

All around them were many people who were headed to the church. They wanted to join the Others. All of them just stood there staring at the officers and trying to enter into polite conversation.

One member of the crowd asked, "And what exactly are you keeping us away from? Church? Last time I could remember, the church was begging folks to come in!"

The four started to walk away from the crowd a bit to find a place a little quieter.

"What in God's name is going on?" the Reverend asked.

Dough lifted his head up, looking into the sky, "That's exactly it, Pete. It's all in the Creative. I have no idea what we are doing now, supposed to do next, or will be doing in the future. We just know that we are change agents and need to be in the places that we aren't supposed to be."

An even more confused look came across Rev. Peters' face. "You don't have a plan?"

Pico grabbed his hand again, "No plan but presence. Just be present and force the tension!"

"Pete, this ain't no predestination shit," Dough offered. "This is relational shit! This isn't a coercive effort but an open effort to reach beyond ourselves and those who need to get to know us. The Creative is all about new beginnings, Pete. The Breath would have it no other way. It just took a shit load of time for us to get to this moment. Humans can be a bit slow."

Mickey was just standing there, taking it all in, and wondering if his dad was going to ask him to go home. Rev. Peters looked around at the crowd of people that was slowly growing.

"I appreciate you all taking care of Mickey, but the two of us need to go home."

"Dad," Mickey humbly requested, "can I stay with Dough and Pico?"

The Reverend looked at Mickey and then the two of them. They all had smiles on their faces, like elementary students who just snuck out of class.

"Sure."

Rev. Peters turned and started walking home.

"Aren't you going to get your car, Pete?" Dough shouted.

"Nope. They won't let me back . . . for now!"

CHAPTER 22

THE NEWS TODAY

Walking was good for Rev. Peters. He needed to clear his head and get his bearings on all that was going on. He was also hoping to catch Jenny at the house. He had been texting her every few hours but never received any texts back. As he was walking down the sidewalk, he noticed the old border trees that had been planted hundreds of years ago when the city itself was just being born. The Reverend had never really seen them before. He knew that they were there but hadn't really paid close attention to their detail. Old trees with thick bark. Limbs twisting into the air, reaching out for the sun, covered with dark green leaves. He stopped in front of one particular tree for a moment and thought about all that tree had experienced. "If only trees could talk," he murmured to himself. But maybe they can. He noticed places where the branches had broken off due to significant trauma, a storm, a saw, or a collision. Wondering what type of trees these were, he pulled out his phone and opened his "plant identifier" app. He carefully aimed his phone at a healthy branch filled with leaves.

"Bloop!" the phone notified, "West Indian Mahogany."

Wow, that's a huge, old tree. Apparently, hundreds of years ago, someone had brought these trees to town to line the streets for shade. They had been there the entire time and further back than any human history Rev. Peters could recall. The city was formed in the early 1800s. That meant these trees had experienced chattel slavery, the Civil War, World War I, the roaring 20s, the Great Depression, World War II, the Korean War, and the Vietnam War. Through the space program and rapid advancements in science, the trees have been standing there and witnessing horse-drawn carriages transition to automobiles. These trees survived pandemics, drought, tornados, hurricanes, and fires. They have stood alongside women seeking equal rights, the Civil Rights movement, the LGBTQ+ community progress, and Black Lives Matter. They have weathered many presidents and politicians and still hold their place.

Rev. Peters was focused on another tree that hadn't faired so well. The Reverend walked over to the trunk that remained. The trunk of the once noble tree was still sticking up out of the ground. It was massive and missing its top. Rev. Peters attempted to put his arms around the trunk to understand how wide it actually was. His hands couldn't even reach halfway. He estimated its width, "Probably 18-20 feet around!" He imagined what happened to the old giant. What was it that ended its reign along the street? "All things must come to an end!" he quipped. "But all things begin again." Out of the old tree a wide variety of other living things were growing from the wood that still remained. Insects and little creatures inhabited spaces throughout the old trunk base. It even looked like some new tree shoots were coming up out of the ground. "What we think is dead is actually contributing to life!" he mused out loud. Rev. Peters remembered reading a book long ago about how trees actually speak to each other, have feelings, and even travel.

When he was reading the book, he remembered thinking it was a bit kooky. Now, standing in front of these massive creatures, he started to feel unity, like he was a part of something with them. He placed his hand on the old trunk and focused his attention on the rough bark under his hand.

"Speak to me," he requested in prayerful reflection. He sat there for a good fifteen minutes, just waiting and hoping that something would happen. Nothing happened. Or did it? He released his hand but could still feel the rough bark that was now imprinted on his palm.

"I'm sorry for all the shit you've had to deal with from us humans. I'll try to be more aware of my non-human kin."

Rev. Peters stepped even further away from the tree and then set his sights on the journey home.

Quite a few people were walking in the direction of the church, passing the Reverend. He was the only one walking away from all the action. Some of them said hello or offered a polite nod, while others just scampered past, not even acknowledging his presence. Rev. Peters pondered how a few of them probably thought he was a nut case talking to trees and all. He kept walking as quickly as possible, hoping to speak with Jenny when he returned home, and then get some rest. The excursions with the Others were tiring, and the Reverend knew there would be more to come. As he walked, his reflection on the prolonged presence of the trees and their silent contributions throughout the centuries made him pause and raise a new question in his mind. *Why is it always a new beginning and never an end?* He thought about comments Dough, Ma Green, Pico, and others had made over his journey. Never once did they talk about the end of things, always beginnings. They never viewed violence and suffering in the world as a sign of the end, but only as signs of how much more work needed to happen to live into this newness. They viewed the future as open and not manipulated or coerced by forces bigger than themselves. They always approached life as if a greater power was walking alongside them the whole way. It was not "gloom and doom" but "hope and relationship."

Rev. Peters thought about the trees and what those ancient creatures had to say about the state of things. The most destructive force in the world is people. People cause the vast majority of suffering worldwide, whether through the horror of war, economic exploitation, blatant disregard for the planet, or just their own self-centered attitudes about rights, liberty, and private ownership. The things most people wish to escape from in this world are actually the hell created by people. The trees know this as they stand watching for generations. One cycle of idiots after another lay claim to what they believe is theirs, only to give it to the next generation of idiots to repeat the process all over again. It's going to take an intervention, a second coming of the highest degree, to get humanity to step outside itself and find its place in the whole. It is the only way to find the harmony that can be identified in all life and move away from our own projections of how we believe God, or gods, will take care of business. Maybe, the truth around the new beginning will be an outbreak of a greater understanding and relationality with the world and all the Creative has set into motion. Maybe, the unity comes in knowing we are all of the same substance. Perhaps, the trees are the wisest of all creatures, just waiting for the parasites to run their course and free the beautiful world again to know peace.

His thoughts helped the time pass quickly, and before he knew it, he was standing in front of his house. The lights were on, and he suspected Jenny might be home. He walked up to the door and reached into his pocket to grab his keys, but they weren't there. "Shit!" he uttered in exasperation. He didn't want to have to knock on the door and explain himself once again. He turned around, considering whether he should just leave and come back another time, but that would be ridiculous. Walking back to the door, he raised his arm to knock when Jenny opened it.

"Michael? You just scared me to death!"

She had startled the Reverend too. "I'm back and accidentally left my keys somewhere."

Jenny stepped back just inside the foyer to let Rev. Peters in.

"We need to talk, Jenny. I know there has been a lot of crazy stuff going on in our lives, but we just need to talk."

Jenny was standing there in the entry, but it was clear she was not planning on staying for long. Just behind her was the suitcase she was carrying.

"Are you leaving me, Jenny?" Rev. Peters asked gently.

Jenny lowered her head and then looked up at the Reverend.

"Michael, it's just not working. I just don't love you anymore or the things that you love. You are in this really weird place, and I just can't surrender all we have made together for some crazy pipe dream of a better day! We had a better day! I don't believe you have my best interest in mind anymore, and I definitely don't have the same feelings for you anymore."

Rev. Peters wasn't prepared for this, even though he knew on some level it was coming. Even the Others had a sense this was coming.

"Well, Jenny, I wish we could have worked things out, gone to counseling, talked more about this before you decided to leave. That being said, I'll give you your space and pray that we might be able to make amends in the future."

He had an almost guilty feeling come over him that he wasn't mourning her departure quite the way he had expected. Maybe, he had already moved on as well.

The two stood in the doorway for what seemed to be a long time when Jenny broke the silence,

"Where is Mickey? I didn't see him in the house and wanted to say goodbye."

"Mickey!" Rev. Peters muttered, "Well, Mickey and I had a great time, and we are actually on speaking terms again. He's over staying at a friend's."

"What, friend?" Jenny asked in an accusatory kind of way.

"A good friend of mine. He's in great hands."

"You let him go with your homeless buddies, didn't you!"

"Well, Jenny, first they aren't homeless, and second you were gone!"

"Michael Dale Peters, you'd better get that boy back to this house, or I'm calling the police!"

The Reverend's face grew red and hot for the second time of the day, "You listen to Me. Mickey is finally enjoying life and is off that couch and out of the house. He is with one of the most careful and beautiful people I know and will end up at the church sometime later tonight."

"Later tonight? It's 10:00 p.m.! And, the church is the last place I want him to be! Have you heard the news?"

Rev. Peters was dumbfounded, "What news?"

Jenny grabbed her bag and pushed the Reverend aside.

"You go watch the news for yourself! I'm out of here, and that boy had better be home safely; there will be consequences. Michael, I am concerned about you. You're not right, and the folks you are supporting aren't right either. I heard what happened earlier today at the church and then there was the blistering phone call I received from Joel Newcome when he was looking for you. You have a great job, family, pension, and a faithful community! Isn't that good enough?"

Jenny moved quickly past Rev. Peters and to a car waiting for her on the other side of the street. Then drove away.

Rev. Peters didn't know what to do. His emotions were running all over the place. It was a day of courage, new freedom, and loss. The way things had been were no longer. The newness to which he had been so attracted still had a long way to go before it would feel complete. At the moment, Jenny was not his priority, so he tried to breathe deeply and decide what direction he needed to head next. Nothing else was standing in his way. He walked into the living room to turn on the TV and see what Jenny was talking about.

"Sari, turn on City News 2."

"I'd be glad to," Sari, the computer command, replied.

The screen grew bright as the news anchors were on location. It was dark outside, and there was an abundance of red and blue lights.

"Cathryn Sidel here for City News 2."

Rev. Peters thought, *This must be serious for Cathryn Sidel to come out on location this late at night!*

Cathryn continued, "An amazing stream of events is happening all over our city, country, and world! It appears that massive numbers of people are finding their way to local churches, synagogues, mosques, parks, national monuments, and other public gathering areas. They do not appear to be doing any damage to the properties, but are just moving in."

A smile came over Rev. Peters' face.

"What in kingdom come is going on here?" Cathryn continued, "Local authorities are doing their best to keep people from invading private property. Other locations they have left open as they lack the number of officers needed to patrol. There are also other people gathering in opposition to the current events. Church members, community leaders, and some political activists are setting up in front of these facilities discouraging those trying to make their way in. With me right now is a man opposed to this movement of primarily lower-income minority people. Sir, what is your name?"

"Ma'am, my name is Roger Clayton, and I am here to help stop this abuse of rights! It is a breach of common goodwill! My partners and I are a part of a group called 'V' and we stand up for life, liberty, and the American way!"

Cathryn stepped in closer to the gentleman, "Thank you, Roger! Can you share with us why you believe your presence is important here tonight?"

"Well, ma'am, it's just not right. If we let just anyone invade private spaces, then it's a slippery slope to other infringements of personal rights. See, my buddies and I have come to protect and defend private rights. We are willing to support our military and law enforcement with deadly force if need be."

"Thank you for sharing with us, Roger. Crazy things are going on in the world tonight, and you heard it first on City News 2. Back to you, Ken."

Rev. Peters went to the refrigerator and found the last can of beer. He opened the top, which cried of release, "Pshhh . . . ."The Reverend walked back over to the couch and sat down. Lifting the cold beer to his mouth, he took a big sip. The cold, bubbly liquid made its way down his throat. It made him feel a bit more relaxed. He turned the volume down on the news. He watched the large numbers of people, the Others, from all over the country and world pour into churches and other sacred spaces to make their presence known and force relationships.With every scene, people were gathering, hugging, and celebrating their life together. At the same time, there were those standing outside screaming, pointing, and waving their fists, if not guns. It was mass chaos on so many levels. The law enforcement officers were perched in the middle, doing their best to maintain some order without anyone getting hurt. "It's the damn liberal agenda! Socialists are invading the halls of Democracy!" Rev. Peters heard one man scream while the news was sharing a story from Florida. For a moment, it was the first time that the Reverend didn't feel the need to do anything. He had let the Others into the church and defended their presence there. He came home to make things better with Jenny, which didn't work out well but clarified a few things. Mickey actually had a good time, and Rev. Peters thought some time with Dough would be suitable for anyone. He continued to watch the news flash before his eyes until his eyes could no longer stay open.

CHAPTER 23

PRINCIPALITIES & POWERS

S houts and screams raptured the Reverend from his sleep. The noise was coming from outside, and it was the most activity his neighborhood had experienced in quite some time . . . well, other than the police incident he caused just a few days ago. Rising from the couch, Rev. Peters stretched and could feel a pain in his neck after falling asleep, beer still in hand, from an awkward position. The noise outside didn't sound like a few people, but masses. He staggered to the window beside the door and pulled the curtain back to see what was happening outside. *My Lord!*" Many people were walking by, some in groups, families, couples, and individuals, and they all seemed to be progressing in the same direction. Mixed in with this mass of humanity were a wide variety of sounds. Singing, shouting, chanting, and screaming were all interspersed throughout the crowd. Closing the curtain, the Reverend returned to the TV and turned up the volume.

> "City News 2, I'm Cathryn Sidel offering twenty-four-hour coverage of the largest movement of people and communities the world has ever seen. It appears, from our sources, that people are all migrating toward holy and sacred sites. There doesn't appear

to be any real reason behind it, but some claim it might be the end of the world. We will keep you posted as this spectacle unfolds."

Rev. Peters turned off the TV, grabbed his coat, and walked out the door. The procession of people was impressive. People from every background, all together, walking patiently in the direction of First Church.

"Excuse me," Rev. Peters interrupted a lady holding her baby who was walking close by. "Where are you going?"

She stopped for a moment, looked at the Reverend with big eyes, "They are saying amazing miracles are happening and that God is doing something all over the world. I ain't gonna miss out on that. So, I picked up my baby girl, and off we went. It's gotta be better."

Better than what?" Rev. Peters asked.

"Better than the shit we've been working through for years now. I want a better life for my baby girl. I can't take it much longer. So I walk."

Rev. Peters thanked her for her time even though she didn't have any definitive answer as to why? Why so many people? The crowd wasn't in a hurry, and there was plenty of space between people as they walked together. There was an air of hope and excitement. It felt like something was happening and encompassing everyone, and so they walked. As they walked, there was screaming and yelling. The hope and excitement met fear, anger, and tension. It appeared that his street had avoided those who seemed to be in opposition to this movement. The screaming was coming from over on the main streets of the town.

The Reverend kept walking and progressed beyond his neighborhood street out onto the main streets. Along the roadsides, and even standing in the middle of the road, were groups of people. Each group was easily identifiable as they all wore similar outfits identifying their cause and purpose. They were not in favor of the events going on around them. One man standing alone was shouting just as loudly as the groups along the route. He was a tall, older man wearing blue jeans, old sneakers, a plain white T-shirt, and a ragged old camouflage jacket.

"STOP! YOU SINNERS WHO WARNED YOU OF THE WRATH TO COME!"

As he shouted, his finger was pointing and shaking as he rattled off his edict.

"REPENT AND DO NOT FOLLOW THE TEMPTATIONS OF THE DEVIL. THE PATH IS NARROW, NOT WIDE. THOSE YOU ARE GOING TO MEET ARE NOT OF GOD BUT THE DEVIL! REPENT! DO NOT FOLLOW, OR YOU WILL DIE!"

Another group of people, all wearing black leather with multiple patches all over their jackets, were screaming as well.

"DO NOT BE DECEIVED! THIS IS THE LIBERAL AGENDA. SOCIALISM IS TAKING ITS HOLD OF YOU! TURN BACK! THIS IS A LIE! THEY ARE NOT FOR OUR POLICE. THEY ARE NOT FOR OUR WAY OF LIFE! THEY SUPPORT SEXUAL SIN AND THE ABUSE OF CHILDREN! THEY ARE FOR ABORTION! THEY ARE CHILDREN OF THE DEVIL AND HAVE CLAIMED THE USA IS AN EVIL RACIST PLACE!"

Rev. Peters was astonished by the boldness of these claims. He knew there were some extremists out there, but not this many in his town. He recalled an incident many years ago in which a crowd similar to the size and scale of these groups tried to stop an election. Back then, he thought they were all just nuts. Today, he still thinks they are nuts. The Reverend kept walking. Next to him, a large group of young adults was getting ready to pass as they walked at a much quicker pace.

"Hey!" He shouted to catch their attention. "Where are you all going?"

A young woman, probably in her twenties, shared, "We're all joining the effort. It appears that there is a group of people who are standing up against the systems that control them. We want to be a part of that. For years, progress has continually been met with disappointment. This event sounds like progress, and we want to make sure it's not a disappointment."

She gently excused herself to catch up with all of her friends who now were quite a few steps ahead of her.

"Hope to see you there!" she shouted back.

Rev. Peters turned the corner with the group only to be confronted by an extensive line of squad cars. An officer with a loudspeaker was calling,

"Please stop and return to your homes. I repeat! Stop, and return to your homes."

But the crowd kept marching forward. "What are you gonna do shoot us?" A voice proclaimed from amidst the travelers.

On the opposite side of the road, others held pickets signs and banners all denouncing those things they had labeled sin.

"God hates fags!"

"America is a whore!"

"God made Adam and Eve, not Adam and Steve."

"Repent! For all are destined for hell."

"HELL is too good a place for you!"

"Divorced people will burn!"

"Sin lovers suck cock!"

The signs were brutal and held by adults and children alike. There was not a single person walking past them who wasn't being insulted or judged. No one was good enough for their brand of righteousness.

"Hey, you!" one man shouted at Rev. Peters, "You a faggot lover?"

"What?" The Reverend offered in reply.

"I said, are you a whore who loves faggots?"

Rev. Peters was fuming inside and knew that getting into a verbal battle with this asshole wouldn't do any good, so he ignored him and kept walking. The man didn't stop, though; even though Rev. Peters had moved far beyond him, he could still hear him screaming, "Sinner! Whore! God hates you!"

A woman came walking up beside Rev. Peters with concern in her eyes.

"Are you all right?" she asked him politely.

"Yes, thank you for asking."

"I have had people calling me those names my whole life, and they weren't even from some wacky cult."

Her comments surprised the Reverend. "I'm sorry to hear that."

"Yep, I think it's just part of being a woman. They either call out because they like what they see or claim you're a bitch because you stood your ground. Bottom line, you're never good enough to be a man."

"Again, I'm sorry you've experienced that."

"Yeah, I am walking because there has to be something better than all that! I try to be kind and a good neighbor. Still, it just seems like everyone is only interested in their stuff and not interested in others. I hear that whatever god or whoever might be behind this exodus, might bring about something new."

The Reverend looked at her and saw that she was a woman in good health but of quite some age.

"I am sure that's what's going on!" he affirmed. "A new day. It's always a new day."

Rev. Peters scanned the crowd as he walked to see if he could recognize anyone he might know. It was always fascinating to him that you could live in a town for many years and still find yourself, most of the time, in places where you didn't know or recognize anyone. As one street met with the next, the number of people walking peacefully together continued to grow. The protest groups grew as well. Every group in opposition had staked out their space along the roads to promote their message. Driving this movement might have been the media or social networks, but it appeared that all that faded away once people started walking in the streets. Unable to promote their message or conspiracies, "anti" groups had to hit the streets. They were shouting, demanding, and doing their best to keep the platforms running amidst a movement of people who had enough and wanted something more. The Reverend thought about the Others and looked forward to reconnecting.

Something was happening, and it warmed his heart that he was in some small way a part of it. What the Reverend also noticed was that any pretense was gone from within him. He no longer felt the need to control the narrative, protect the institution, or preserve a way of life. He no longer had to perpetuate the lie that everything had to fit. His journey had brought him to a crossroads. A movement away from selfish idolatries to freedom in the Creative. Peeling away the layers is painful and challenging work. Still, it is necessary to know peace. As Rev. Peters walked, he realized that those walking were not bound to themselves or their cause. They could walk because of the freedom, which invited them to move in a new way. Those standing on the street corners screaming their agenda, proclaiming their rhetoric, and seeking to convert the crowd were all prisoners to their idolatries. They made their cause and beliefs their gods, and there was no moving forward. Spending your life defending a system of beliefs, at the expense of everything else, at some point leaves you protecting that system, even if that means hanging the truth on a cross. At that point, there is no longer any conversation or effort to grow. Instead, fear grows and gives birth to altruistic evil and hate. You become one with the "principalities and powers."

"Pop, Pop, Pop, Pop . . ." Shots rang out, and everyone hit the ground. In the distance, there were sirens, and then someone shouted, "Let's keep walking, people!" Rev. Peters slowly picked himself up off the ground and looked around to assess the situation. It appeared that everyone in his immediate area was safe.

He shouted back, "Is everyone OK?"

In response, a unified voice responded, "Yes!"

The shots, thank God, must have been fired into the air—a scare tactic—yet the Reverend knew there were probably people being shot somewhere in the world. He looked at his phone to see if he could catch any news of happenings from other places around the globe. Sure enough, the highlights in the news were all adverse reports of violence, shootings, and blaming radical groups for what appeared to be going on. The Reverend clicked on one message from his phone.

"The local authorities are asking for people to stay at home. Please do not navigate the streets, for many people have posed a threat and could be dangerous. Reports are coming to us that riots, looting, and random shootings are occurring in many communities.

In other parts of the world, national governments are trying to stop people from progressing toward these migration areas. In some countries, soldiers have set up barricades and have fired on the protesters."

"Protesters?" Rev. Peters questioned.

He was perplexed by how the media was shifting what was happening. Those walking were not protesters! Those committing violence and opposition were the very forces who wanted to keep this progress from happening. Amidst the shouts, hate, police barricades, gunshots, and resistance, nothing stopped the movement.

"What are you going to eat? And, where are you going to sleep?" a woman shouted at a young woman who was walking with the group. "You can't leave; I'm your mama!"

The young woman looked at her mother, grabbed her hand, and in a calm voice said, "Come with me, mama."

Her mother ripped her hand from her daughter's, turned her back, and walked away. Rev. Peters watched the young woman as she continued to step forward, never looking back, with a tear running down her face. He wanted to ask the young woman what brought about such conviction that she would keep moving forward at the cries from her mother, but he thought he had better leave her to her thoughts, and he simply said a little prayer that everything would be all right. Through the night, the movement of people all made progress toward an unforeseen hope. For a while, the sound of gunfire and shouting stopped, and they all just walked together. Rev. Peters met and talked with many people from every walk of life, and never once did he mention the Others. He continued to be one with the group outside of any knowledge or more profound understanding surrounding these events. None of that was important anymore. The Reverend didn't feel the need to influence or provide any answers to those walking with him. He wanted them to all experience the journey for themselves and just wanted to be a part of it. So, he smiled as he walked and enjoyed hearing the stories rising around him.

"YO! PETE!" A loud cry came from behind the Reverend.

He turned, and two of the Others he met following the Gathering were standing behind him.

"Hey! How are you both doing? And, why aren't you with the Others?"

Both Roxie and Roo realized that Rev. Peters had forgotten their names.

"In case you forgot, I'm Roxie, and this is Roo. We decided we wanted to get out and see what was going on. We had heard the Breath was doing its thing, and people were responding. We had also heard of the opposition, the 'principalities and powers,' that were causing conflict and tension, and we wanted to see it, name it, and encourage those on the walk."

Rev. Peters was a little embarrassed for not remembering their names, but it had been a busy few days, and they had taken no offense.

"Roo and Roxie, it is great to see you. Are you heading back there now?"

"Back where?" Roo asked.

"Back to First Church?"

"We're not going *back* to First Church, we are moving forward!"

Rev. Peters again was a bit embarrassed that he even asked the question.

"Sure," he said, "we are moving forward."

Both Roo and Roxie began to tell Rev. Peters everything they had experienced after he left. The police continued to maintain their barricade as people tried to access the grounds the Others had inhabited. The authorities made threats that they would remove people if they didn't vacate the property. Those threats never came to be as the movement everywhere had grown too large. Local authorities, drained of resources to protect the city, called on the national guard and military to move in to bring some "peace" to the situation. Tanks, helicopters, and armed soldiers were all established to discourage folks from walking, gathering, and protesting. Their presence didn't help bring peace; it only created further tension with those groups rising in opposition to the company of the Others on holy sites around the world. Unfortunately, some were losing their lives for simply walking. While there was chaos around town, there was peace in those places where people found their way to gather. At the perimeter of those sites, there were incredibly vocal and aggressive groups in opposition. Yet, no one knew what their opposition was actually about. Rev. Peters listened carefully to them and asked,

"Will we be able to get through?"

Roo's eyes lit up, "Pete, that's the amazing part. Yes, you can walk right in."

CHAPTER 24

WELL-SUITED

First Church was only a few miles ahead, and Rev. Peters was enjoying the company of Roo and Roxie. They shared a lot about life, what they had seen around town, and how they got connected with the Others. The more they shared in each other's company, the quieter the screaming voices around them became. As they walked, the Reverend saw what appeared to be three figures walking toward them. Startled for a moment, they all three stopped and focused on seeing who these figures might be.

"Sorry, folks." Rev. Peters stated, "you can never be too cautious."

Roo and Roxie both shouted, "Pico & Dough!" and they took off running toward their friends.

The Reverend took his time, and the closer they came, he noticed Mickey was with them.

"Well, well! If it ain't old Pete making the trek with the people!" Dough said with delight.

"It's good to see you too, Dough. And, a special privilege to see you again, Pico. We have been everywhere, and people are walking, dancing, shouting, arguing, fighting, and debating. They're from everywhere, and everyone is outside!" he concluded.

Dough reached out and grabbed both Roo and Roxie and gave them hugs as well.

"So, Pete, we have come to walk with you," Dough clarified.

"I'm glad, Dough. I am also looking forward to seeing all that's going on. I am concerned about Jenny, though. Mickey, have you seen or heard from mom?"

Mickey looked at his father, and his face dropped slightly. "Nope. Haven't seen her or heard from her. But then again, my cell phone died hours ago."

Pico and Dough came up alongside Rev. Peters, and Mickey tagged along with Roo and Roxie.

Roo tapped Pico on the shoulder, "We're gonna split. See you in a while."

Pico nodded and waved goodbye.

Mickey turned to his father, "Can I go, Dad?"

The Reverend looked to Roo and Roxie, and they waved, motioning Mickey to join them.

"You be careful out there!" Rev. Peters admonished.

The Reverend's mind was spinning in so many directions as he pondered this ordeal. What a crazy adventure with new friends. There was one thing on his mind that wasn't resolved yet, so he asked Dough and Pico, "What's up with Harvard?"

Both of them were shocked that he actually remembered. That's where they had met and left to come to join the Others. Pico lifted her hand in the air as if she was about to enter a ballroom.

"I guess we can share a little bit with you, seeing that we have a few more miles to go before we get to First Church and an eternity after that."

Dough didn't look quite as excited about taking time to share that story.

"Where shall I begin?" Pico pondered.

"How about in line for registration?" Dough suggested.

"Oh, yes, registration. Let's just say, as liberal as Harvard might be, I am not sure they had ever had a trans kid like me."

"You got that right!" Dough exclaimed, "Six foot six, ebony goddess, arising out of the crowd of average-looking teenagers. Everyone was staring at Pico."

Pico interrupted, "It didn't help that I was wearing four-inch pumps, sequin pants, and a halter top!"

"You looked damn good, Pico! Damn good! Caught my attention," Dough affirmed. "With all the commotion Pico was causing, I was having my own issues of drawing too much attention. I guess you shouldn't wear trench coats into a packed hall full of people. Here I was, a young, dark-skinned man dressed in a black trench coat, tennis shoes, and a backpack. Everyone was checking me and thinking I was a terrorist."

"Hell, at first *I* thought you were a terrorist!" Pico joked, and then continued, "Two freaks, at completely different ends of the room looking for someone we could feel normal around, and that's when our eyes met. It was like a force pulling us toward each other."

Dough shook his head, "There goes the romantic! We caught each other's eyes because we were the only six foot six, funky dressing, black people in the room."

"OK," Pico nodded, "it might have been the height. Needless to say, we both fought our way through the lines and crowds of students registering for classes to be together."

"And, we have been together ever since."

The Reverend enjoyed hearing their story, but he was still curious as to why Harvard and why did they leave?

"Got it. Two freaks saw each other across the room of conformity and found each other. But, why were you both at Harvard, and why did you leave?"

"Well," Pico started, "we gave it our best shot. We tried and honestly have nothing negative to say about Harvard, our professors, the students, its administration, or their acceptance of me. It was more about the story behind the story that led us to leave."

The Reverend looked perplexed, "The story behind the story? What the hell is that? Most well-suited students would have jumped on a chance to go to Harvard!"

Dough looked at the Reverend, "You said it very well, Pete. Most well-suited students would jump on that opportunity in a second. I guess that is the question we started asking: What does well-suited mean?

"Oh, and why Harvard?" Pico interrupted, "Because we're fucking geniuses! Creatively gifted geniuses! Dough and I are well-suited, alright, and the perfect candidates for a school established to mold the brightest and best minds for American progress. Even in our freakishness, Harvard was an incubator where we could thrive and succeed. Our success was only ours to waste."

"So, why did you waste it?" Rev. Peters pleaded.

"We didn't. We used our first year at Harvard to consider how our being at Harvard would help usher in a new day. We wondered how being formed by the most brilliant scholars in the world would help us break out of the mold that has sustained brokenness for centuries. We wondered if being in a community with the 'well-suited' was really the change the Breath led us toward. Or, was being in community with those who are not bound by the system, un-suited, and truly free the community that would elicit change?"

Pico paused and Dough spoke gently, "We just couldn't stay. I had been raised with the Others, and something was calling me back. They were actually upset that I didn't stay at Harvard. The Others were proud of me and wanted to see me succeed. We are all so interconnected here that my being at Harvard meant they were all at Harvard. Yet, they knew just as much as I did, my life was conformed to a very different story."

In the distance, the three of them could see the silhouette of First Church rising up out of the earth. The crowds had grown thick, and it seemed like the disruptors were growing thicker as well. The three walked in silence for a few minutes, just reorienting themselves to where they had now traveled. Storytelling and conversation can erase time and distance. What was particularly interesting to Rev. Peters was that his attitude about those screaming and disrupting the events no longer negatively affected him. If anything, he felt sorry for them. He also noticed that as they came closer to the church, the opposition started to change. A few blocks back, away from the church, the groups were positioned around their agendas. Now, it appeared that those gathering in protests were much more personally related. Rev. Peters started to make out parents, family members, friends, and co-workers. Adult children were begging their parents to stop walking and head home. The closer one got to the church, the more intimate the opposition against going became.

Rev. Peters remembered a story in scripture that reminded him of the events unfolding. In the story, Jesus was teaching, and his mother tried to pull him away and explain to the crowd that she didn't know what had gotten into him.

Breaking the silence once again, Rev. Peters asked, "So, why did you leave Harvard Pico? I understand Dough's desire to return home, but you?"

A tear escaped Pico's eye and was quickly wiped away.

"What home would I return to? From everything I'd heard from Dough about the Others and the work they were doing, I was in! The second I arrived, I was included, acknowledged, and encouraged to celebrate my gifts. This has been a far greater education than I would have ever received at Harvard."

Silence came upon them again. The darkness of the night, and the glow of the church, turned the people standing in front of them into silhouettes. The closer to the church, the more intense the energy grew from those trying to stand in the way. It was fear-driven desperation. It was heavy. For a moment, the power and pull were so overwhelming that Rev. Peters started wondering if maybe he was making a mistake. Doubt and fear infiltrated his soul. Anxious, he reached out to touch Dough's shoulder.

"You OK, Pete?" Dough asked compassionately.

"No, I am not. I'm afraid."

Dough reached out and put his arm around him, and Pico grabbed his hand.

"You're here with us. This is real. You are loved, and you will be OK!"

At that moment, Rev. Peters felt someone else tapping on his back. He dropped Pico's hand and turned around out of Dough's arm, and there was Jenny. Rev. Peters turned pale. His heart started racing.

"Where have you been?" he stammered.

Jenny reached out and grabbed the Reverend's hand, pulling him away from Pico and Dough.

Jenny whispered, "We need to talk."

Pico and Dough both stared at the couple.

Dough spoke first, "This is the thing you've gotta do, Pete. You need to talk with her."

Pico nodded, and they turned and walked away, leaving Pete with Jenny.

"I am so glad I found you! After watching the news and the horrible events, I knew I would find you at the church. So, I drove over here. I had to walk blocks because you just can't get through."

"Well, here I am, Jenny, and I want you to come with me."

"No!" Jenny stated, "I am here to bring you back home. We have a son, a church, a career, and future together."

"No!" The Reverend interrupted, "The future is ahead up there."

Jenny threw his hands away from her. "You've gone nuts. They have brainwashed you along with all of the others who are walking into this damned dream world. You can't go! If you loved me, you would not go."

"I love you, Jenny, and that's why I want you to come with me!"

Jenny crossed her arms in front of her, "Are you out of your mind? This isn't right! They are disrupting everything!"

The Reverend listened intently to her and felt sorry for her. She was afraid, and just like all the others standing in opposition to the events unfolding before them, they would rather hold on stubbornly than acknowledge the need to change.

Rev. Peters reached out his hands, "Come with me, Jenny. You don't need to be afraid. We need to walk forward, not back."

Jenny backed a few steps away from the Reverend, wiping her tears, and clutching her fists against her chin.

"I am walking back, Michael, even if you're not coming with me."

As she turned to walk away, Rev. Peters felt the tears come down his face.

"Mom!" Mickey shouted as Jenny was trying to walk away.

"Mickey? Where are you?"

Running up from behind his father, Mickey ran to embrace his mother.

"Where have you been?" Jenny asked.

Mickey smiled at her, which was the first time she had seen that look on his face in a long time.

"Just after you left, Dad and I were able to talk with each other. We actually started laughing and went to get some waffles. That's where I met the coolest people in the world!"

Jenny turned pale, "Oh no, you didn't! You brought him to that cult group you've been hanging out with, haven't you? This is child abuse!"

Her attention turned completely on Rev. Peters, and her angst now turned to rage.

"Mom!" Mickey tried to speak.

"You be quiet! This is between your father and me."

"No!" Mickey shouted. "This is about our life and the new friends I have met that are amazing. I have never been happier, and the stuff they talk about is real. They genuinely care about each other and live that way. I have hung out with them and walked all over town, experiencing the amazing things happening. This is for real. You need to come with us!"

Jenny was so taken back she didn't know what to say. Her emotions were frayed, and her chest was tight. She was grasping at anything to reconnect him to his old life.

"What about your video games?"

Mickey looked at her with disappointment, and something came over her. It was the release confronting the truth created. She fought it internally for a moment but couldn't hold it back. It was the awareness that she would prefer having her son live like a zombie, self-medicating on video games, then move forward with the Others. She wanted him to return to the familiar so she might preserve what? A broken marriage, living with her parents, and growing even farther away from her son? Returning to a way of life where her husband worked all the time and put on airs to pull off the expectations of church members? Return to a life without any real friends? She would instead go back to living the life of false comfort rather than living into a future filled with joy with the two people she had told herself she loved the most. Again, she started to cry and dropped to the ground.

Both Mickey and Rev. Peters dropped down next to her and held her. People walked around them as they huddled together on the ground.

"Come on, honey, let's walk together. You've got a bunch of new friends to meet."

Grabbing her hand, the Reverend helped her up, and Mickey brushed off the dirt clinging to her pants. Jenny looked at both of them and smiled through her tears.

"I am scared. I don't know about this, but I . . ."

"I know." Rev. Peters comforted.

"You're gonna be just fine." Mickey blurted out.

The Reverend mopped the tears from her cheeks, which were red from all of her crying. He grabbed her face with both hands and gently kissed her.

"I love you. You! Just as you are. Now, will you take a walk with us?"

Jenny reached out and grabbed both their hands, and together they started walking.

CHAPTER 25

JESUS! IS THIS THE END?

The Peters continued to walk together toward First Church and the anticipated reunion with the Others. Mickey had dropped his mother's hand and was so excited about introducing her to their new friends that he asked if he could run ahead. Both Jenny and Rev. Peters nodded and then smiled at each other.

"Is that the same kid who used to sit around the house doing nothing?" Jenny asked.

Rev. Peters nodded again in affirmation, "That's him. Our wandering adventurer."

The Reverend and Jenny continued to walk hand in hand, enjoying the moment. There's something powerful about grabbing someone's hand firmly, with intent, and letting that person know you are there for them. It is an intimate act.

Jenny looked up at Rev. Peters, "So, what am I to expect when meeting your new friends?"

The Reverend smiled, "Our friends," he clarified. "They are going to love you!"

He smiled as he mentioned their love and was overjoyed that Jenny was now with him.

"There is one thing you should understand," he interjected, "there are no expectations. You never know what is going to happen. It's always open-ended, and no one has a clue about the outcome. They just know they're to be good news."

Jenny grabbed his hand tighter at that last comment. She was always a bit of a control freak, and stepping out in faith like this was not her typical way of being.

There was a "steadiness" in the air as they walked, and it felt as though they were moving toward something. As Rev. Peters and Jenny walked, the landscape grew darker, and everything in the periphery started to blur. Wisps of fog hovered close to the ground. The mist was comforting and yet unusual. Something bizarre was happening. A light breeze brushed their skin as they walked, and, in the distance, a warm light glowed. It was as if someone was waiting for them. Everything around them began to fade away until Rev. Peters realized he was alone. Jenny was no longer beside him. The glow grew brighter, and the sweet smell of baked bread lofted with the fog in the air. It was beckoning him to move forward. The whole experience was strange and comforting. *This is it!* he thought, believing this might be the moment, the encounter he longed for his entire lifetime. The scene was perfectly cropped, beautiful, magic. As he continued to walk toward the warm light, he heard music. Like everything else around him in the moment, it was gentle. The melody was familiar, and yet he couldn't put his finger on it. He had heard it before. As he grew closer to the light, he could tell it was a campfire. Flames licked at the air and danced about as the logs crackled. There, by the fire, was Jesus.

Chills ran down his spine, realizing Jesus was sitting there. While he talked about how much he looked forward to meeting Jesus, he was

terrified now that it was really happening. This was an encounter with
the one who makes all things right. There, sitting by the fire, just as he
had imagined a million times, was Jesus. He knew it was Jesus because of
the smells, the music, the magic, and the comfort he was experiencing.
Jesus was poking the flames with a stick, waiting for him. Rev. Peters
just stood there for a moment, and Jesus sat quietly, giving some space
at the moment. The Reverend was at a loss for words. He wondered
what he should say. *It's you?, How are you doing?, You're real?, JESUS!*

Instead of making a fool of himself, he decided to remain silent.
The place was so peaceful it was becoming uncomfortable. Jesus looked
up at Rev. Peters and smiled.

"Michael, It's good to be with you." Jesus' words penetrated
his soul.

*This must have been what Mary felt like in the garden after the resur-
rection, and Jesus spoke her name. He knows my frickin' name!*

"Of course I do," Jesus replied.

"Shit!" The Reverend panicked, "He also reads minds."

"Stop worrying about all that, Michael. Pull up a log and have
a seat."

Rev. Peters looked around for a log, and there, next to Jesus, was a
perfectly cut log just for him.

"So, what ya been up to?" The Reverend asked, realizing that was
a ridiculous question.

"Well," Jesus offered, "I'm just trying to help the world and its
people get things right."

"I see," Rev. Peters replied as if curious about this work.

Jesus then looked directly into Rev. Peters' eyes, "What have you
been up to, Michael?"

Rev. Peters was caught up in the gaze of Jesus. *Those eyes!* The Reverend couldn't believe the strength and beauty of Jesus' eyes. His eyes were ice blue, and they had a glow and energy about them as if he was already moving on to the next thing. His hair was long and golden blond, and he was wearing a white T-shirt and blue jeans. He was extremely fit, which Rev. Peters found to be a bit odd, and yet, that is how Rev. Peters had always drawn Jesus as a child. He wore a well-groomed beard and mustache, and his skin was white. *White?* the Reverend questioned.

"I know what you're thinking Michael. I am exactly as you had pictured me in Sunday school."

The Reverend was getting a little annoyed with the mind-reading stuff. Returning to Jesus' question, Rev. Peters repeated,

"What am I up to? Well, I met a group of people that have taken me on the adventure of a lifetime. It has opened my heart and mind to new opportunities and ways of seeing. They tell me we have a lot of work to do and that I'm needed for that work. I have been encouraged to explore new beginnings and be an active participant in living within the equity you desire for your creation. I've been brought out of my tomb, so to speak!"

Jesus laughed, "That's a bit on the nose, don't you think?"

Rev. Peters blushed and Jesus reassured him, "You're funny."

With even more intensity, Jesus reached out and placed his hand on the Reverend's shoulder.

"Michael, I am concerned about these Others you've been hanging out with and the disruptive movements happening around the world. I'm not sure they are on the same page with the great love I desire to share."

Rev. Peters looked stunned. He tried to block everything from his mind, knowing Jesus was a mind reader, as he searched for a response. In an old spy movie, he remembered once that the lead spy told a recruit that no one can read your mind if you think about your favorite food. Favorite food blocks random thoughts.

Continuing to stumble on his words, Rev. Peters asked, "What is your desire?"

"Pizza!" Jesus stated and laughed out loud. "No, actually, Michael, I desire for everyone to know they are loved and that my love is sufficient for them. You don't need anything else. Just me. I am the one who gives life, and I am the one who brings you joy and peace. I am yours Michael, and I am all you need."

Rev. Peters nodded in agreement but still squirmed a bit on his log.

"That's great, Jesus, but what about everyone else?"

Jesus removed his hand and softened his intensity, "I am there for them too, but they have to find their way. You can only offer so much. The main point is that as long as you and I are good, you don't need anyone or need to care about anyone else. I will be there to support your success. You're a good pastor, Michael. You have been doing a fine job leading people to understand what it means to know me personally and live their lives for me comfortably. As long as that is the goal, living for me, nothing else matters."

Rev. Peters was silent.

"I know this whole experience has been overwhelming for you," Jesus continued, "but you need to know that I have been there with you the whole time. I'm the one who brought your son back to you. I'm the one who brought Jenny back. I'm the one with you now to encourage you to return to me and to not be deceived by the false teachings you have heard."

Jesus' beauty was starting to wane for the Reverend. Everything was too perfect, and Jesus was white?

"If you are Jesus—"

Jesus held up his hand, "Let me stop you right there. Doubt has no place here. *If?* I am Jesus, and I need you to get back to work for me. You are so special to me, and I have granted you incredible gifts for ministry. Don't deny the incredible love I have for you and how many people you have brought to me. You're a great advocate, and I love you, Michael"

Rev. Peters stood up from the log and walked to the other side of the campfire flickering in front of them. The flames cast a glow on Jesus' face. The light, it appeared, was changing Jesus' countenance. Rev. Peters squinted to see if he could make out what was happening across the campfire. The fire made Jesus look scary. It made Jesus' face resemble his own.

"Who are you really?" Rev. Peters shouted.

"I am Jesus," he replied.

"If you are Jesus then what's your concern with the Others?"

"Well, they are not helping the systems I have put in place. Some truths must be upheld to preserve prosperity. There are rules and laws which maintain important positions and power. There are orders and hierarchies which maintain proper balances. It is crazy to think that everyone can and should be treated equally! I make all that possible, and I can offer that same power to you. These ideologies about equity, creativity, freedom, inclusion and communal life will tear everything apart. It's up to you, Michael.

No one else but me can help you! You're your own man! You make everything you have possible! Someone has to lead, and I need good and faithful servants like yourself to continue to keep everything and everyone comfortable."

With each statement, Jesus' voice became more direct, pronounced, and bold. Jesus stood up from the log he was sitting on and proceeded to walk around the fire to get closer to Rev. Peters. Each time he moved toward the Reverend, the Reverend walked away toward the other side, ensuring distance.

"What are you afraid of?" Jesus asked.

"I'm afraid of you." Rev. Peters responded.

Fear had taken the place of comfort. It was all a façade.

Jesus dropped his head in frustration. "You don't need to be afraid of me," Jesus proclaimed and, lifting his head, shouted, "You need to be afraid of the torment you will suffer by not following me!"

At that moment, Rev. Peters closed his eyes and prayed. It was a simple prayer but one that came from the depths of his soul. *Lord, Help Me!* As he opened his eyes, the Jesus figure was gone. The Reverend was standing in that place alone. Beams of light streamed down from the sky surrounding Rev. Peters. The light cut through the fog and found rest reflecting off the ground. Rev. Peters stood still and watched the light break through the darkness and encompass him. Then, he saw him. Standing in front of him was the little boy. It was the boy he had seen in the playground and in the lights at the Gathering. He was not alone. All around the little boy were many people, all visible in the light, but not fully present in the space. They were all there, a great cloud of witnesses. Rev. Peters was not alone. At that moment, there was a real presence. While he couldn't see the Human One, he knew that the Human One was present too. There, along with those revealed in the brilliant beams. Those in the light were alive; they were both the present and the future. That future, Rev. Peters realized, was an adventure he would still have to undertake. This journey wasn't over, and the idea that the Human One would come, snap a finger, and everyone and everything would immediately be made right isn't the way the Creative works. It isn't the way love works.

Rev. Peters noticed that the little boy was trying to say something to him, so he walked closer to the beams of light. He bent down on his knees to be at the same level as the little one. The boy's lips were moving, but no sound was coming out. The Reverend paid careful attention to the movement of his lips.

He was saying, "There is no end, only beginning."

Rev. Peters stood up, taking in all those faces and people free and alive within the light. He reached out his hand and offered it to the little boy standing in front of him. The little boy lifted his hand and gently moved to place it on Rev. Peters. At that moment, he was back walking with Jenny, holding her hand.

"Where have you been?" Jenny asked.

"I, well, I got caught up in my thoughts. I'm sorry. I have been doing that a lot lately."

Jenny smiled, "What were ya thinking?"

The Reverend stopped, turned toward Jenny, and grabbed both of her hands.

"There is no end, only beginning."

Jenny laughed, "Wow! I was wondering what we are going to eat."

The Reverend shook his head to clear his thoughts. "Oh, if you're hungry, I believe you're in for a treat!"

They finally made it to First Church. There were no more police cars, screaming people, or blockades on the roads. Tables now stretched across the lawn and down the streets. People brought out chairs and tables from the church and their homes. It was an eclectic collection of furnishings that was colorful, unique. People were talking, laughing, and playing with each other. As Rev. Peters and Jenny walked closer, they saw Dough and Pico talking with an older gentleman. It was Mr. Newcome. Rev. Peters was shocked.

"Hey, how is everyone doing?" he offered with some caution.

"We're great!" Dough replied.

Mr. Newcome turned toward Rev. Peters, "Reverend, it's about time you came to join the party!"

Rev. Peters was floored. "What? How?"

Mr. Newcome noticed his confusion.

"Come on, Reverend!" Mr. Newcome began, "You didn't think we would be able to keep up our hostilities toward such a fine group of people, did you?"

The Reverend was at a complete loss for words. Maybe he had underestimated the leaders of his congregation. Maybe, he underestimated the work and movement of the Breath. In addition to Joel Newcome, other church members joined the most significant neighborhood feats the town had ever seen. Rev. Peters brought his attention back to Mr. Newcome.

"What happened?"

"Well," Mr. Newcome started, "they just kept serving, giving, and loving us. That genuine love forced us to confront our arrogance and pride. That love brought us to a place where we could let down our walls. Most of us, at least. It's miraculous, actually.

Not everyone decided to stick around and get to know these new members of our family, but something spoke to my heart, and I'm glad I stayed."

Rev. Peters grabbed Mr. Newcome and gave him a huge hug.

"Now, don't get too emotional; I'm still a cranky old man after all," Mr. Newcome teased.

People were gathering everywhere, and as they arrived, they filled the tables with bowls of fresh vegetables, fruits, bread, cakes, and drinks. The sun was rising. They had all made it through the night and early morning. It wasn't the culmination of all things, but it was moving in the right direction. Everyone, traveling toward this great event. A sumptuous feast for the whole community, and for the most part, the community was gathering. Families, neighbors, and several people whom Rev. Peters remembered seeing screaming in opposition along the way. Rev. Peters saw Ma Green at a distance and waved. She waved back at the Reverend and blew him a kiss.

She shouted, "This is something, ain't it!"

Rev. Peters called back, "Did you bring your collards?"

Ma Green nodded and pointed to a large bowl on the table.

"I will be right there!" he exclaimed in hopes that Ma Green would save him a scoop.

Jenny was enjoying the energy and excitement everyone was experiencing. People were crossing boundaries. What was it that changed them? What was it that made them come? What was it that changed Mr. Newcome? As Rev. Peters scanned the crowds, there he saw it, "humility." *Humility!* Rev. Peters thought. It was a release, a surrender, and pulling down of walls. During the inhabitation and march that evening, being right, pushing an agenda, or creating division was replaced with a desire to know and be known. It was a willingness to let go of the past and live abundantly into the future. And this was all embodied by those who called themselves the Others. Many misfits found their strength from the depths of love they had for the Creative and each other.

Pico and Dough came up from behind Jenny and the Reverend, grabbing each of their arms like they were at a hoedown and walking them quickly over to a couple of seats by Ma Green. The great feast was spectacular, and people found their places at the table as far as you could see. Everyone had a place at the table. They broke bread, drank wine, told stories, and shared all they had with each other. And most of all, they shared their lives.

"This is one hell of a gathering!" Rev. Peters exclaimed.

"It sure is!" Dough responded.

Ma Green picked up the bowl with their new family and started passing the greens at the table.

Rev. Peters looked at Jenny, "These are some of the best greens you will ever eat."

She smiled and scooped a large amount on the china plate sitting in front of her. Pico, sitting directly next to Jenny, looked intentionally down each side of the long table.

"Who is going to clean all these dishes?" she questioned.

Hearing Pico's comment, Mickey walked up behind his father and placed his hands gently on his shoulders, "I guess we all will, won't we?"

Everyone laughed, and Jenny laughed and cried. Under the table, Rev. Peters felt something rest its head on his lap. He jumped back, startled by the suddenness of the encounter. Out from under the table came that damn dog that had peed on him just a few days before. The dog was wagging its tail and sat down in front of Rev. Peters. Everyone laughed, and Dough shouted, "I guess you've got a new friend." The Reverend reached down to pat the dog on the head. The dog leaned into his hand, and the Reverend knew this friend would be coming home with him.

As they all ate together, Rev. Peters interrupted the meal,

"So, what's next? This is amazing, but it doesn't seem like this is it."

Pico put down her fork, "Nope, this isn't *it*. *It* doesn't happen until we all move into God's future. What's next is we keep moving forward now, embodying good news, and living and imagining life differently as we get along our way."

Ma Green nodded in affirmation, "Yep, we still got a lot of work to do. It is long for new beginnings. Steps, not leaps, Reverend. Steps."

The Reverend was looking a little befuddled.

"So, there's more?"

"Yes, there is more." Ma Green reconfirmed. "It would be boring if we just arrived."

Rev. Peters was so tired that arriving seemed like a good thing. Then again, he had never really been this alive before. Dough leaned on the table, placing his hand under his chin,

"There is no end, only beginning, Pete! Now is the time! Are you ready?"

ACKNOWLEDGEMENTS

I am grateful for all the fantastic people in my life. My life partner Leslie always sees the best in me and encourages me to live into my giftedness. Leslie herself is a gift, and it is my privilege to continue to explore and uncover the mysteries life brings with her. My daughter Emily is our greatest accomplishment, and my love for her is beyond words. She is fantastic in all she does and now has accomplished her most outstanding work in bringing our first granddaughter into the world. I am also grateful for my parents, who have loved and provided for me every step of the way. Their support and belief in me have made me the confident person I am today. They have always been there for me (long hair, metal music, tattoos, and all). To the rest of my family, I love you all! Thank you for loving me.

To my best friends in the world, Dan, and Sylvia Baptista. What a life we have together! I thank God for you and the amazing adventures we have had. Dan, thank you for all the music we have made and played together and for taking the time to be the first reader of this book. Your insight and advice were beneficial. To Jim Lake, who sat me down eighteen months ago and said, "I think you need to write a book!" I followed your advice, and here it is. Thank you for all the work editing, proofing, developing, and critiquing. This book is here today because of your support. To Kelly Scott, who also read the book and provided incredible insight into the content and character development. Thank you for spending hours reading and re-reading to help make this book a work of art. Kelly, you are greatly appreciated, my sister! What a gift you are to everyone who knows you. To Brian D. McLaren, who is a good friend and support. Thank you, Brian, for taking the time to read my book and provide an incredible affirmation. To my covenant brothers, who have been a foundation of support and love for over 30 years! Each of you is a blessing and has poured so much laughter and wisdom into me. While not directly contributing to this book, all of you can be found within the more profound truths expressed in these pages. Thank you for being real!

To my great teachers, mentors, colleagues, and influences. Thank you for giving in ways that help birth better days and new beginnings. A special thank you to The Rev. Dr. Willie Jennings, who provided the framework for the origins of this work. While at Duke, Dr. Jennings taught a class on Eschatology. The final exam was to write the story of the end times (in no more than 30 pages with endnotes). I took on the challenge wholeheartedly, received an "A," and a comment from Dr. Jennings, "Someday you should turn this into a book." (a common theme) Thank you, Dr. Jennings!

ABOUT THE AUTHOR

Roy M Terry IV resides in Naples, Florida, where he has lived most of his life. Roy is a creative enjoying playing guitar, writing music, painting, and other art expressions. He also spends a lot of time around his wife and daughter's horse business and claims to be a professional groom. Daily, he drags the rings with the tractor and takes care of the manure (a spiritual discipline). Roy is an ordained Elder in the United Methodist Church. In 1996, he helped launch Cornerstone United Methodist Church, where he is still serving today. Cornerstone is an eclectic mixture of beautifully messy and amazing people striving to live in this story bigger than themselves. Roy has an undergraduate degree in religion from Florida Southern College and an MDiv from Duke Divinity School. A native Floridian, Roy cares deeply about his community and the great watershed he calls home.